Had Hope just made the biggest mistake of her life?

She'd finally gotten what she wanted—time to spend with Jake McBride.

But what if she made a fool of herself over him again? No, she wouldn't let that happen. She was an expert at hiding her thoughts and feelings. She could hide them from Jake, as well.

He'd made it sound as if she was doing him a favor to let him help her at her new ranch. But was this simply a way for him to get closer to her operation and figure out how to own it himself someday? It wouldn't be the first time someone had lied to her to get something he wanted.

Hope didn't want to doubt Jake's motives for helping her, but wariness was long a part of her nature. A charming, handsome man was always dangerous to an innocent woman like her.

Even if he was the handsome Wyoming cowboy she loved.

Dear Reader,

Make way for spring—as well as some room on your reading table for six new Special Edition novels! Our selection for this month's READERS' RING—Special Edition's very own book club—is *Playing by the Rules* by Beverly Bird. In this innovative, edgy romance, a single mom who is sick and tired of the singles scene makes a deal with a handsome divorced hero—that their relationship will not lead to commitment. But both hero and heroine soon find themselves breaking all those pesky rules and falling head over heels for each other!

Gina Wilkins delights her readers with *The Family Plan*, in which two ambitious lawyers find unexpected love—and a newfound family—with the help of a young orphaned girl. Reader favorite Nikki Benjamin delivers a poignant reunion romance, *Loving Leah*, about a compassionate nanny who restores hope to an embittered single dad and his fragile young daughter.

In *Call of the West*, the last in Myrna Temte's HEARTS OF WYOMING miniseries, a celebrity writer goes to Wyoming and finds the ranch—and the man—with whom she'd like to spend her life. Now she has to convince the cowboy to give up his ranch—and his heart! In her new cross-line miniseries, THE MOM SQUAD, Marie Ferrarella debuts with *A Billionaire and a Baby*. Here, a scoop-hungry—and pregnant—reporter goes after a reclusive corporate raider, only to go into labor just as she's about to get the dirt! Ann Roth tickles our fancy with *Reforming Cole*, a sexy and emotional tale about a willful heroine who starts a "men's etiquette" school so that the macho opposite sex can learn how best to treat a lady. Against her better judgment, the teacher falls for the gorgeous bad boy of the class!

I hope you enjoy this month's lineup and come back for another month of moving stories about life, love and family!

Best,

Karen Taylor Richman
Senior Editor

Please address questions and book requests to:
Silhouette Reader Service
U.S.: 3010 Walden Ave., P.O. Box 1325, Buffalo, NY 14269
Canadian: P.O. Box 609, Fort Erie, Ont. L2A 5X3

Call of the West

MYRNA TEMTE

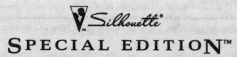

SPECIAL EDITION™

Published by Silhouette Books

America's Publisher of Contemporary Romance

To Cherry Adair, Mary Buckham,
Susan Plunkett and Debra Sims.
You know why, girlfriends.
Many thanks.

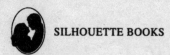 SILHOUETTE BOOKS

ISBN 0-373-24527-0

CALL OF THE WEST

Copyright © 2003 by Myrna Temte

Books by Myrna Temte

Silhouette Special Edition

Wendy Wyoming #483
Powder River Reunion #572
The Last Good Man Alive #643
*For Pete's Sake #739
*Silent Sam's Salvation #745
*Heartbreak Hank #751
The Forever Night #816
Room for Annie #861
A Lawman for Kelly #1075
†Pale Rider #1124
A Father's Vow #1172
†Urban Cowboy #1181
†Wrangler #1238
†The Gal Who Took the West #1257
†Wyoming Wildcat #1287
Seven Months and Counting... #1375
Handprints #1407
†Call of the West #1527

*Cowboy Country
†Hearts of Wyoming

Silhouette Books

Montana Mavericks
Sleeping with the Enemy

MYRNA TEMTE

grew up in Montana and attended college in Wyoming, where she met and married her husband. Marriage didn't necessarily mean settling down for the Temtes—they have lived in six different states, including Washington, where they currently reside. Moving so much is difficult, the author says, but it is also wonderful stimulation for a writer.

Though always a "readaholic," Myrna never dreamed of becoming an author. But while spending time at home to care for her first child, she began to seek an outlet from the never-ending duties of housekeeping and child-rearing. She started reading romances and soon became hooked, both as a reader and a writer. Now Myrna appreciates the best of all possible worlds—a loving family and a challenging career that lets her set her own hours and turn her imagination loose.

McBride Family Tree

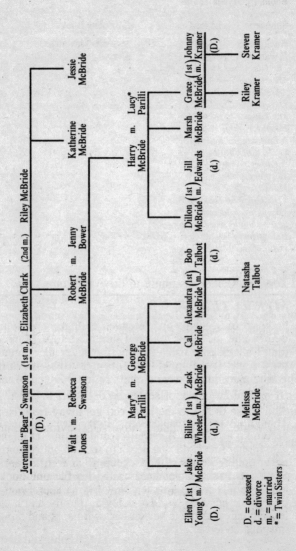

D. = deceased
d. = divorce
m. = married
* = Twin Sisters

Chapter One

Hope DuMaine was going to drive him nuts.

Gulping a stiff whiskey ditch, Jake McBride jerked his gaze away from the dance floor and forced himself to watch the sun dip behind the mountains. The bride and groom had left on their honeymoon. Half of the wedding guests had gone home. Jake's official duties as the best man finally were over.

If he had an ounce of sense, he'd get off his duff, go in the house or out to the barn and get away from Hope for a while. But he didn't move. He obviously didn't have a lick of sense left.

No, he just sat here like an idiot, an elbow braced on one of fifty round tables he'd rented for the outdoor reception. Why? Because it was too late to save himself. Hope DuMaine couldn't drive him nuts.

He'd already arrived.

Jake's younger brothers, Zack and Cal, plunked them-

selves down beside him. Cal hummed along with the
country-and-western band playing in the gazebo. Zack
stretched his legs out and turned toward the dancers. In
a heartbeat his brothers were doing exactly what Jake
had been doing—watching their cousin, Marsh McBride,
waltz Hope around the dance floor.

"I've been lookin' at her all day, but I still don't
believe it," Zack said with a bemused smile.

"No kiddin'." His smile equally bemused, Cal let out
an appreciative sigh, then took a healthy swig from his
drink. "Emma said Hope was beautiful under all that
wild paint and hair dye, but I never dreamed she'd clean
up *that* good."

"Jake didn't either." Zack grinned and elbowed Cal
in the arm. "Hell, Jake, you should've let her catch
you."

Jake shrugged as if their teasing didn't bother him one
bit. A reasonable man might expect that, at thirty-eight
and thirty-four, his brothers would ease up on the sibling
rivalry, but no such luck. In the past two months they—
along with the rest of his big, nosy family—had harassed
him so much about Hope's blatant crush on him, ignoring them had become as automatic as breathing.

Good thing he'd had so much practice at hiding his
reactions.

Truth was, every time Marsh whirled Hope back into
sight, Jake damn near swallowed his tongue. And he
wasn't the only guy doing it. Not by a long shot.

Audacious, flamboyant and unpredictable as a horse
on locoweed, Hope DuMaine was something else.

A member of one of Hollywood's most notable families, she was internationally famous. But not for acting.
Oh, no, not her. Leave it to Hope to be even more un-
conventional than the rest of her relatives.

She'd published her first racy tattletale novel at the age of nineteen. Rocketing straight to the top of the best-seller lists, she'd set the film and publishing industries on their respective ears. Ten years later she was still doing it.

Literary critics despised her. The tabloids and talk-show hosts loved her. The public raced to buy each new book so they could play the which-movie-star-inspired-which-character game. Though Jake wouldn't admit it on a bet, he'd read her last one and found himself sucked right into the game along with everybody else. Hope told an entertaining story, he'd give her that much.

But then, there was her appearance to consider. Her hair color changed on an almost daily basis, and he wasn't talking your usual brown, black or blond. He was talking primary colors—fire-engine red, royal blue, grass green. Her long, talonlike fingernails were always painted to match her hair. And her clothes… He shuddered just thinking about them.

Earlier that afternoon Jake's cousin, Dillon McBride, had married Hope's famous cousin, Blair DuMaine. Hope had arrived at the Flying M Ranch twelve weeks ago. She'd been living in the guesthouse, helping with the wedding plans, working on her latest novel and chasing Jake like a buckle bunny after her favorite rodeo cowboy.

The woman could give lessons in perseverance to a badger.

Jake had no idea what she liked so much about him and didn't care. She wasn't his type. Other than a glance to check out what color her hair was that day and what bizarre outfit she'd chosen, Jake had done his best to ignore her, too.

Until today…

Blair and Dillon's wedding pictures undoubtedly would make every entertainment magazine and TV show in the country. Jake figured Hope must've felt obligated as the maid of honor to pass up her regular "fashion statement" for Blair's sake. The results were nothing short of amazing. Funny thing about it, all she'd done to achieve a near-magical transformation was to look sort of *normal*. For a change.

But it really went beyond normal. Far beyond it.

Aw, man, today Hope was downright gorgeous—a combination of elegant lady and hot sex. Her purple strapless gown faithfully outlined her figure, telling a man with one glance she was one-hundred-and-ten-percent female. Her smooth skin and short, shiny auburn curls made his hands itch to touch them.

Her vitality and the sheer delight she took in her cousin's happiness made Hope's smile sparkle brighter than the glittering baubles she wore around her neck. Her slender, kissable, tempt-a-man-to-nibble neck... Aw, damn, but he had it bad.

Marsh leaned down and said something close to Hope's ear. She tipped back her head and uttered a soft laugh that carried easily on the warm evening breeze. Jake's gut tightened and he found himself fighting an urge to curl his fingers into fists and sock Marsh in that perfect nose he was so proud of.

"Think Marsh is tellin' the truth about just being pals with Hope?" Zack asked.

Cal shrugged. "He'd better be. Poor Sandy's been in love with him forever, and I don't know how much more of this she'll tolerate. Has he even danced with her yet?"

"Nope. And if he keeps on flirtin' with Hope like that, he'll be sorry." Zack turned his chair sideways, crossed one booted ankle over the other and braced his forearm on the table. "Jake, you'd better get out there and cut in. Save that poor fool from himself."

"Marsh's a big boy." Jake gulped half his drink. "Let him figure out his own love life."

"Since when did this family ever let anybody do that?" Cal demanded with a disbelieving snort of laughter. "Think about it, Jake. The rest of us are all married. You're the only one free to get Hope out of the way so Sandy can move in and get her brand on Marsh before he does something real stupid. Again."

"That's right," Zack agreed.

Marsh smoothly twirled Hope as the song ended. The non-dancers applauded. Hope laughed and dropped into a graceful curtsey. Jake had never seen anything quite so appealing, but he forced himself to look away before his brothers caught him staring at her like a starving dog watching his master eat the last bite of a juicy steak.

"Besides," Zack continued, "why don't you admit you kind of like having Hope flirt with you? Hell, she's young, rich and beautiful. If I was single, I'd be flattered as all get-out—"

"Forget it," Jake grumbled.

"Why?" Cal asked. "She's funny, she seems real nice, and she's gotta be darn smart to write all those books."

"Looks like a good breeder, too," Zack said. "Wouldn't hurt the family gene pool to add another pretty gal—"

"Jeez, Zack." Jake tossed back the rest of his drink and banged his glass down on the table. "Stop talking about her like she's a damn heifer."

"Aw, lighten up." Cal chuckled and faked a punch at Jake's shoulder. "He's just having a little fun—"

Jake put a snarl into his voice. "You've all had

enough fun at my expense. I'm not interested in Hope DuMaine, so get off my back and leave me alone.''

The band struck up a sweet country ballad. Claiming he had to make sure the beer and food were holding out, Cal took off. Zack's very pregnant wife Lori crooked her index finger at him and he hurried to escort her onto the dance floor.

Jake sat back, hooked his thumbs into the front pockets of the black slacks of his rented tux and uttered a deep sigh. A waiter delivered a fresh drink, compliments of Cal. Jake thanked him, stretched out his legs and rolled his shoulders, trying to ease the kinks out of his spine.

The dancers shuffled slowly in time to the music, and he soon found his gaze drawn back to Hope and Marsh. Jake had to admit they made a striking couple and danced well together. The urge to hit Marsh returned, stronger this time than the last.

Jake didn't understand the impulse. He had no claim on Hope. He didn't want one, either. No matter how gorgeous she looked today, Hope DuMaine couldn't be more wrong for him. It wasn't rational for him to feel jealous of Marsh or any other man who charmed her.

But he *did* feel jealous, dammit, and the lack of logic to it irritated him no end. Almost as much as did his family's teasing and Hope's dogged pursuit of him. Dang stubborn little woman could drive a strong man to drink.

Heavily.

He ought to know. Lifting his glass, Jake took a healthy swallow, then looked up and choked when he saw Hope standing alone at the edge of the dance floor, looking his way. He took another gulp and felt the whiskey sear a path down his gullet. Confident as any supermodel, she smoothly negotiated the step down to the ground and crossed the grass between them, slim hips swaying gently, the long side slit in the skirt of her gown flashing glimpses of her spectacular legs with each stride.

A sultry smile played at the corners of her sweet full lips, lips painted a rich burgundy shade that reminded him of chokecherries. He'd always loved the taste of chokecherry syrup—the perfect blend of tart and sweet.

A twinge of alarm pinched Jake's gut. Aw, nuts, he had no business noticing her lips. Or her legs. Or that her gown fit her like the peel on an apple.

Damn, but she had lovely shoulders and collarbones and...he didn't dare complete that thought. Or look where his and every other man's gaze had been straying all day. While it covered all the necessary territory, that dress just didn't leave a guy much guesswork when it came to judging a woman's breast endowment. Hope's appeared more than adequate for his tastes.

He had no damn business noticing *that*, either.

"Hey there, Jake," she drawled as she approached, still managing to sound more like Rodeo Drive than Sunshine Gap, Wyoming. Stopping beside his chair, she leaned down and held out her hands in invitation. "Dance with me?"

His tongue stuck to the roof of his mouth and he couldn't have uttered a word if she'd pressed the barrel of a loaded .45 between his eyes. She leaned even closer. Her bosom swelled against that tight bodice, giving him an enticing view of creamy, rounded cleavage.

Damn, but he wanted more whiskey.

The scent of some subtle perfume wafted his way. He couldn't put his finger on exactly what it was, but it sure smelled good. Spicy and a little musky. Made him think of hot, rollicking sex.

His mouth went dust-dry. His heart banged around inside his chest like a cranky old truck engine in dire need of a ring job. His skin felt hot and tight, and his throat contracted on a hard swallow.

Lord, if he could get her alone and peel her out of that dress, he just *knew* she'd look and smell and taste like every one of his most secret sexual fantasies come to life.

He wanted her like he wanted his next breath, his next meal, his most cherished, lifelong goal of... Damned if he could even remember what that was right now. All he could see was Hope.

She smiled directly into his eyes and spoke in a voice gone soft and husky. ''Well? What do you say, cowboy? Want to dance?''

A smart man would ignore this insane but powerful attraction, make a polite excuse and head for the hills. Jake had been a smart man all summer with regard to Hope. But today he was sick and tired of being smart.

With her standing right in front of him, looking so sweet and sexy, and knowing that out of all the guys at this shindig, many younger, more handsome and more charming, she wanted to be with *him*... Well, he had to admit it was flattering as hell. And where was the harm in enjoying that for a little while? After all, it was just a dance.

He wasn't going to sleep with her, fall in love with her, or, God forbid, *marry* her.

So what if this was the fifth family wedding in the past year? He didn't need to get himself all spooked about it. By tomorrow, she'd show up for lunch with green or purple hair. She'd be wearing one of those eye-popping, L.A.-Western getups no self-respecting cowgirl would even try on, much less buy, and he'd remember all the reasons he'd been avoiding her.

Glad to have that figured out, he stood up and offered the lady his arm. "Thanks, Hope. It'll be my pleasure."

Hope blinked in surprise at Jake's laid-back smile and easy acceptance of her invitation. He'd been avoiding her so much lately, she'd expected to have to drag him onto the dance floor, if she managed to get him to dance with her at all. She exhaled the breath she'd been holding while he made up his mind; it probably had taken only a few seconds, but it had felt like an eternity. She didn't even *want* to know what complicated mental gyrations he'd performed in reaching his decision.

Hope's Rule Number One for a Happy Life was never question the Universe when it gives you what you want, and today the Universe was in an extremely generous mood.

The weather had been perfect for the wedding, with only pleasantly warm temperatures for the middle of July. Blair's darling cowboy, Dillon McBride, was now her husband, and the newlyweds were safely on their way to a storybook honeymoon on a tropical island the media would never find.

The reception had turned into a lovely party, with none of the brittle, see-and-be-seen politics so prevalent at Hollywood social gatherings. All in all, it had been a perfect day. Having an opportunity to dance with Jake was a bonus she hadn't dared expect.

Her heart stumbled when he took her into his arms on the dance floor. He was big, strong and solid, and she felt dainty and safe whenever she stood next to him. *Thank you, Universe.*

Honest, decent, deeply devoted to his family and loyal to his friends, Jake McBride was the kind of man other people depended on. The kind of man who never let anyone down if he could help it. He was exactly the kind of man Hope had spent her adult life searching for but never really expected to find. Being with him like this, having him smile at her as if he thought she was fascinating was a fantasy come true.

"Havin' a good time?" he asked, leading her into a competent, dance-class two-step.

"Wonderful." Hope smiled to herself at the respectful distance he kept between their bodies. Jake would never be the smooth and inventive dancer Marsh was, but he got the job done and there was a lot to be said for his predictability. She tipped her head back to smile at him. "And it's all thanks to you. You did a marvelous job of creating this wedding."

His teeth flashed in a surprisingly shy smile. "I can't claim all the credit. Lots of folks helped in putting it on."

"Other people had some ideas for it, but you're the one who made the actual arrangements."

His tanned face flushed. Glancing away, he started to shake his head, but she cut him off before he could speak. "Don't even try to deny it. I know exactly how much you did."

He chuckled and tightened his arm around her waist, turning her toward the middle of the dance floor. "Is that so?"

"Of course it is." To her surprise, Jake didn't loosen his hold when he'd completed the turn the way he usually did. She didn't know why he'd always ignored her previous advances, but she wasn't going to complain if he made an advance of his own toward her now. Never question the Universe. "And believe me when I tell you that false modesty is not an attractive character trait."

"Well, when you put it that way." His decidedly boyish grin softened the strong planes of his face and charmed her completely. "Thank you kindly, ma'am."

"You're welcome."

They two-stepped in a relaxed silence until the song ended. Since he'd never spent any more time with her at a party than absolutely necessary for a "duty" dance, Hope expected Jake to escort her from the dance floor. This time, however, he stood there looking down at her with an unfathomable expression in his dark eyes until the band started another ballad. A slow, decidedly sexy ballad.

Without asking permission, he started moving in time with the music again. While she was mystified by his behavior, Hope willingly moved with him. He gradually pulled her closer until their bodies brushed with each step. Her pulse sped up with each contact, no matter how fleeting, and she wondered if he even realized what he was doing.

She'd dreamed about being this close to Jake since she'd met him a little over a year ago. He'd never given her the slightest encouragement to believe he felt any sort of attraction between them, however, and she'd all but given up hoping he ever would. It was tempting to violate Rule Number One, but Hope firmly resisted the urge.

When he danced right through a third song, she rested the side of her head against his shoulder and inhaled deeply, savoring the faint, spicy scent of his aftershave. She felt, more than heard him release a sigh. His arm tightened one last time, pulling her flush against him.

His body definitely was attracted to hers. She raised

her head. Oh, dear. His gaze met hers and for the first time ever, she glimpsed something hot and excitingly dangerous lurking in the depths of his eyes.

With her breasts firmly pressed against his chest, she felt his heart thumping in tandem with hers. Her lips formed his name, but no sound emerged. He stopped moving and stood there, studying her as if he'd never seen her before.

His gaze latched on to her mouth. Time slowed, slowed, slowed, and she feared it would stop altogether and he never would kiss her the way he so clearly wanted to do. The way she so desperately wanted him to do.

But then, inch by agonizing inch, he lowered his head. One second she was dying of anticipation. The next, she was in heaven, reveling in the firm pressure of his lips against hers, tasting the bite of whiskey when his tongue entered her mouth, hearing a half-stifled groan fighting its way out of his throat.

Giving herself up to the experience, she closed her eyes and wrapped her arms around his neck. Slid her fingers through his thick black hair. Stroked the edges of his teeth with the tip of her tongue.

He nearly inhaled her whole, body and soul.

Kissing him was better than any kiss she'd ever seen on the silver screen. Better than any kiss she'd ever read about in anyone else's book. Better than any kiss she'd ever imagined and written about in her own books. If the reviewers were to be believed, she'd imagined and written some of the best, steamiest kisses in the history of print.

Nothing—real or imagined—compared to Jake Mc-Bride's kiss.

Heat. Hunger. Passion. They were all there in the

movement and pressure of his lips, his tongue and his teeth. In the strength of his arms holding her as if he never intended to let her go. In the unmistakable ridge of his arousal pressing against her through two layers of clothing.

Her pulse raced. Her knees turned mushy. A hot, achy sensation invaded her lower belly.

She felt as if the Universe had read her every fantasy of what a perfect kiss should be and delivered it all in one perfect, dizzying rush of pleasure.

Then he stiffened. As suddenly as he'd started kissing her, Jake yanked his mouth away. Hope opened her eyes and found him staring at her, looking shocked and disoriented, his broad chest heaving as if he were having trouble catching his breath. The sound of laughter and catcalls nearly drowned out the music.

A horrified expression crossed his face. He released her and stepped back so quickly she stumbled and would've fallen if he hadn't grabbed her elbow to steady her. The instant she found her balance, he let go again, muttering something that sounded like, "Sorry, Hope."

Without another word, he turned and strode off. Hope glanced around at the other dancers and the guests seated at the tables, many of them Jake's grinning relatives. Uh-oh. She gave them all a quelling scowl, then picked up her long skirt and hurried after Jake.

A devastating sense of disappointment washed over her to have such a wonderful moment spoiled. If she didn't get to Jake in a hurry, he'd draw so far back into his shell, she'd never be able to coax or pry him out again. She found him leaning against the fence between the corral and the horse pasture, his elbows propped on the top rail, his back and shoulders as stiff as the fence posts.

From the far end of the pasture, a big, buckskin gelding raised his head and nickered, then ambled toward Jake. Hope smoothed down her dress and climbed onto the bottom fence rail, raising herself to his eye level. Three other horses followed the buckskin. Propping her arms beside Jake's, Hope silently watched the animals approach, searching for something to say.

"Jake?" It wasn't much, but it was the best she could come up with at the moment.

"You shouldn't have come out here."

His voice sounded gruff and not the least bit friendly, which wasn't at all like the Jake she knew. He'd always been pleasant, even when she knew she was annoying the devil out of him. "You seemed…upset when you left."

"I'm fine."

She studied him closely. His eyes had become narrow slits. His nostrils flared. A muscle along the side of his jaw ticked madly. She'd heard he had a healthy temper but had never seen it. She suspected, however, she was about to make its acquaintance. How interesting.

"You're not fine," she said, using the same, patient tone she'd use with a pesky reporter. "I just had the most spectacular kiss of my entire life, but you're definitely upset."

His neck and ears turned a dark reddish color. "Leave it alone, Hope. Forget about that kiss, and—"

"Forget about it?" She laughed in astonishment at the very idea. "Oh, I don't believe that's likely to happen. I don't believe you're going to forget it, either."

The horses arrived at the fence. Jake scratched the buckskin's forehead. "That kiss never should've happened."

"You've wanted to kiss me for weeks." She patted a

black mare's glossy neck. "If you weren't such a big coward—"

"Coward! You think I've been *afraid* to kiss you?"

"I've given you every encouragement but an engraved invitation. What other explanation could there be?"

"It never occurred to you that I might not've been interested in kissing you?"

She chuckled. Now she'd nicked his ego, and of course he had to retaliate. "Jake, Jake, Jake, there's been a lovely little sizzle between us since we met last summer. Please, don't even try to pretend you haven't been aware of it."

He gave her a frown hot enough to start a forest fire, but kept his voice low in deference, she assumed, to the horses. "I don't know what the hell you're talkin' about. I'm polite to most everybody and I try to be a gentleman where women are concerned, but—"

"It's more than politeness—"

"Only in your dreams."

Her own temper began to simmer, but she'd never let him see it. Rule Number Two for a Happy Universe— never let them see when words stung. She shot a meaningful glance at the fly of his slacks and grinned. "Funny, it didn't feel like…politeness when you were kissing me."

"Well, don't turn any cartwheels over it. That's never gonna happen again."

"I beg your pardon?" she asked in her sweetest tone. "I believe you enjoyed that kiss as much as I did."

He shooed the gelding and his equine pals away. "Go on now, you big moochers. I've got nothin' for ya." When they'd trotted to the middle of the pasture, he turned back to Hope. "Just because I enjoyed it, doesn't mean it was a good idea."

"Darling," she chided, barely holding in a gurgling laugh. Who would've dreamed he'd be so absolutely adorable when he was in a snit? "Kissing me was the best idea you've had in months. In fact," she paused and leaned closer to him, "I think you should do it again."

"Dammit." He let out an indignant huff. "Would you be serious for one minute?"

She tipped her head slightly to one side, pretending to consider his question, then cheerfully shook her head. "I don't think so. You're more than serious enough for both of us."

Glaring at her, he tightened his big hands on the fence rail, giving her the impression he'd like to have them wrapped around her neck. "You don't understand what we've just gotten ourselves into. My whole family and half of Sunshine Gap saw that kiss. The other half—hell, the whole stinkin' county will know about it before morning."

"The last I checked, we were both single and over twenty-one. What's the big problem?"

"Every matchmaker in a hundred square miles is liable to be after us. If you stay here, the pressure for us to get together will be unbelievable."

"So, why don't we get together a few times?" It was difficult to keep a straight face since she'd only been trying to convince him to do just that for the past three months. "We might actually enjoy it."

He shook his head so vigorously, his hair fell across his forehead, giving him a rumpled look that made him seem ten years younger. "No offense intended, but you're not the kind of gal I'd ever date."

It wasn't easy to hold back a wince at such bluntness, but she managed. "Why not?"

"For one thing, we've got nothing in common."

"That didn't stop Blair and Dillon."

"I'm not Dillon and you're sure as heck not Blair."

Oooh, that one smarted. She'd been unfavorably compared to Blair more than once and, while Hope didn't care about hearing it from some people, she definitely minded hearing it from Jake. "We're not very different from them."

"Hey, at least Blair eats meat," he said.

"That's important?"

He snorted at her. "This is beef country. I'm a rancher. Yeah, it's important."

"Well, I don't care if other people eat meat," Hope protested. "I simply don't like it." In fact, red meat actually gagged her. Jake rolled his eyes as if what *she'd* said was silly. He had some nerve.

"Fine," he said. "How about the age difference? I'm too old for you."

Hope let out an incredulous huff. "You can't be more than forty-five."

"I'm only forty," he grumbled. "But that's still too old for you."

"Oooh, ten whole years. You're ancient, McBride. Shall I find a cane for you?"

"Well, it just wouldn't be right. It's not appropriate." He glanced at her hair, opened his mouth as if he would say something, then clamped it shut again.

"What?" she said. "You don't like my hair?"

"It looks okay now," he admitted, his tone grudging.

"But?" She left the word hanging between them. "Come on, you've obviously got a problem with my hair. Tell me."

"When you make it spiky and turn it all those different colors, it looks mighty strange."

"I suppose it does here." She grinned, enjoying the idea immensely. "But it's just a little thing I do for fun. It washes right out."

"It's not just the hair." He sounded as if his patience was stretching thin in spots. "It's the whole package."

Hope caught a harsher note of criticism in his voice that surprised her. She raised her chin and met his gaze head-on. "Do tell."

"You're too flashy for a guy like me," he said bluntly.

"Flashy?" She raised her eyebrows and patted her collarbones, feigning surprise. *"Moi?"*

"You know what I mean."

She supposed she did, but sincerely hoped she was wrong. "Why don't you explain it to me anyway? Just to be absolutely certain?"

He gave her a long, considering look, as if he were debating whether or not he should answer. "It's the hair. The fingernails. The clothes."

"What's wrong with my clothes?" she asked, carefully maintaining a neutral tone.

"Nothing's *wrong* with 'em. I doubt anybody'd even notice 'em in L.A."

"But they don't work in Sunshine Gap."

Jake nodded. "Yeah. They're not practical or even modest. Everything you wear is missing a strategic hunk or two of material. There're guys all over town nursing sore necks from trying to get a better look at your... assets."

"Oh, really, you're exaggerating." At least she thought he was. It was the middle of July for heaven's sake. Everybody peeled down a bit when the weather was hot.

"The hookers in Cheyenne and Denver wear more on a work day than you do. Your stuff is too damn sexy."

"Women aren't supposed to be sexy in Sunshine Gap?"

"I didn't say that." Muttering a rude word, he jammed his right hand through his hair. "Look, it's not personal. The thing is, if I wanted a woman in my life now, I'd be lookin' for an old-fashioned Wyoming gal with ranching in her blood."

Well, that certainly left her out, didn't it? But it didn't have to.

"Blair learned how to do all that stuff. If she can do it, so can I. You could teach me."

"No way." He held up both hands and stepped back, shaking his head. "I'm workin' on important plans for my future. I don't have time to play with a flaky little California floozy who writes raunchy books, causes scandals and looks like she came out of a can of spray paint half the time."

Time stopped long enough to imprint every humiliating detail of Jake's critical assessment of her into Hope's permanent memory banks. The backs of her eyes stung, her throat closed around a golf-ball-sized lump and her chest ached as if he'd punched her just under her sternum. After three months of seeing her every day and working with her on this wedding how could he still think so little of her?

And how could she have been so wrong about him?

Automatically falling back on Rule Number Two, Hope plastered an amused smile onto her mouth. "My, my my," she drawled. "Been reading the tabloids, Jake?"

His face flushed, but he didn't look away. "You're news, Hope. All the magazines and newspapers have stories about you."

"You believe everything you read?"

"Not *every*thing." His tone told her he believed all but the most outrageous stories. "But you've gotta admit you have one colorful image."

"Of course, I admit it," she said calmly. "I've worked hard to build it."

He frowned as if he'd never entertained the idea a celebrity might deliberately develop a certain kind of image. "I only wanted to point out our differences. I didn't mean to offend—"

"Don't apologize for being honest. There's far too little honesty in this world. And since we're being so honest, I have to say I'm terribly disappointed in you."

"Come on—"

Hope slashed at the air like a conductor halting an orchestra. "Save it, McBride. I've clearly misjudged you."

Frowning, he asked warily, "What do you mean?"

"I thought you were more than just a handsome face. Obviously, I was wrong."

"Wait a minute," he protested.

"You had your turn. Now it's mine," she retorted. "I may be a flaky California floozy, but you're a shallow, narrow-minded idiot who can't see past the end of your own nose."

"Hey—"

Hope continued as if he hadn't spoken. "You don't have the faintest clue what you're passing up, but someday you will. And when you do, you're going to be one sad and sorry cowboy."

Before Jake could even begin to think up a reply,

Hope stepped down from the fence and headed back toward the party. Holding herself straight and tall as a queen, she crossed the barnyard with a smooth, unhurried stride. He watched until she rounded the corner of the house, then returned his attention to the horses, feeling a mixture of relief and regret.

He hadn't meant to hurt her feelings, but she hadn't been listening to him, just brushing aside his arguments as fast as he'd made them. After all of that, any man in his right mind would've gotten desperate, but he'd gone too far and said too much. He was sorry as hell about that. She'd gotten in some good licks of her own, though.

He almost had to smile at the idea of Hope DuMaine calling *him* shallow. Brother. Talk about your pots and kettles.

Still, he'd stop by the guesthouse tomorrow and apologize. He didn't want to cause Dillon any problems with Blair's family. He didn't want to cause himself any problems with his own family, either. They all really liked Hope. When she wasn't pestering the hell out of him, so did he.

But dammit, tonight was all his fault. What had possessed him to kiss her like that? And why had he done it in front of everybody?

He'd love to blame it on the alcohol he'd consumed, but he hadn't had *that* much to drink. And he'd been tired, but not *that* tired. Well, it didn't matter. It wouldn't happen again because he wouldn't let it. Even though he regretted hurting her feelings, he'd meant everything he'd said.

He wondered if Hope had meant what she'd said. That part about him being a sad and sorry cowboy had almost sounded like a threat. Jake laughed and shook his head.

"Yeah, right. I'm shakin' in my boots. What could she possibly do to me?"

Not a blessed thing. And with any luck, by this time next week, she'd go back to L.A. She'd be off the Flying M and out of his life, and he'd finally get a little peace and quiet. After all the craziness of the past twelve weeks, surely that wasn't too much to ask for.

Chapter Two

Still fuming at dawn the next morning, Hope loaded her luggage into the rental car and wedged a thank-you note under the back door of the Flying M's main house. She hated to leave like a thief in the night, but if she ran into Jake, she feared she would hit him. She'd mentally replayed their argument again and again during the night and couldn't believe he'd actually said some of those things to her.

Flaky little California floozy, indeed.

Taking one last look around the ranch yard, she got into her car and drove down the long, winding lane. She turned right onto the graveled county road, intending to say goodbye to her good friend George Pierson at the Double Circle Ranch. Three miles later she rounded a familiar curve.

On impulse, she pulled over and parked the car. She

got out, put her hands on her hips and slowly turned in a complete circle. Yes, this was the right spot.

No matter which way she faced, the scenery was breathtaking. Soaring, snow-capped mountains to the west, and to the north, south and east, the green of irrigated hay meadows, the long, tidy rows of fences and power lines beside the dusty road, the endless blue sky without even a wisp of a cloud in sight.

It was so quiet. So peaceful. So private.

There was room to breathe here. Really breathe. And there was a timelessness to this land that was evident in the rock outcroppings and gullies, in the subtle, shifting colors that stretched out to a horizon that went on forever. Nothing ever changed much in this country.

No wonder Jake and his family worked so hard to keep their piece of it.

What would it be like to belong here? To have a place of her own with some reasonable expectation of permanence? Where people stayed and businesses survived beyond the latest trends in entertainment, fashion and food.

She turned around again, shading her eyes with one hand as she looked her fill of this incredible landscape. Her chest ached with the beauty of it. With the longing somehow to be a part of it. With something close to grief at the prospect of leaving it.

But leave it, she must.

Heaving a deep, regretful sigh, she slid back into her car and drove the rest of the way to George's place. His gangly, rambunctious pup galloped out to greet her when she parked at the back door. A semi-ugly mixture of several large breeds, the dog's name was Doofus. Unfortunately, the name seemed to fit the animal quite well, but at least he was friendly.

Hope scratched his ears for a moment, then climbed the steps and waited for George to answer her knock. If his arthritis was acting up, it could take him a few minutes to get there. Somewhere around ninety and still blessed with an excellent memory, George had been telling her about the history of the area for the next book she wanted to write next.

He was cantankerous, blunt, meddlesome, nosy, opinionated and terribly prone to gossip. The juicier the better. Hope adored him.

George had outlived his friends, chased off most of his neighbors and infuriated his relatives to the point they barely tolerated him. But, to Sunshine Gap's surprise, crusty old George Pierson appeared to adore Hope right back.

Opening the door, he looked out, his rheumy gray eyes alight with pleasure when he recognized her. He wore faded baggy jeans held up with orange suspenders, a yellow Western shirt and a ratty pair of brown leather slippers.

"Well, well, look who's here," he said. "Didn't think you'd be out of bed much before noon after that shindig yesterday. Why's your hair black?"

"Because I'm in a black mood, George." Hope leaned inside and kissed his wrinkled cheek. "May I come in?"

"Well, I reckon I can spare a few minutes, but you'll have to make your own coffee."

Though he had few visitors, George always acted as if spending a few minutes of his valuable time with her was a huge favor. Hiding a smile, Hope followed his thumping cane through the gloomy old house to the kitchen. He also claimed arthritis prevented him from doing much beyond the bare necessities for his survival, but Hope suspected he was malingering in order to get attention. He could be amazingly spry when he chose.

She gladly played along with him, filling his ancient percolator with cold water, adding the coffee and setting it on the stove. Turning around one of the straight-backed wooden chairs at the table, she straddled it, facing George's rocker.

Once they both were seated, he smiled, showing off chewing-tobacco-stained teeth. "What do you want to know this time?"

"Actually, I've come to say goodbye."

"What?" Rocking forward so hard his rocker squeaked in protest, George frowned at her, his bushy white eyebrows jutting out from his face. "You said you were stayin' until you finished your book."

"That's what I'd planned," Hope agreed, touched by how upset he was about her news. Other than Blair, she'd had few people in her life who cared if she stayed or left. "But sometimes plans have to change."

"Why? What the hell's happened?"

Hope tried to smile at him, but found herself surprisingly near tears instead. Jake wasn't the only one she'd grown fond of in Sunshine Gap. She would miss this old man, the other McBrides, her dear friend, Emma, who had married Jake's brother Cal. Hope wasn't ready to leave any of them. But after that scene with Jake...

"Aw, jeez, don't start blubberin'," George grumbled, shifting restlessly in his chair. "Never could stand a blubberin' woman."

"Oh, get over it," Hope grumbled back at him. "I'll blubber if I want to. You won't melt."

Slapping his knee, the old man let out a cackle of laughter. "You're somethin' else, gal. Go ahead and bawl your head off if it makes you feel better."

She uttered a shaky laugh and wiped her eyes with her fingertips. "No, I'm okay now."

He put the chair in motion, filling the room with soft creaking sounds. "Tell me what brought this on."

Hope related an abbreviated version of what had happened at the wedding reception. With a few adroit questions, George dragged the rest of the story out of her. He kept rocking for several moments after she'd finished, his expression thoughtful. "You don't have to go back to California."

"Yes, I do. I can't stay at the Flying M now."

"You want Jake to think he can run you off that easy?"

"No, but there's not even a decent motel in Sunshine Gap."

"So find some other place to stay. Hell, stay here."

"I couldn't impose on you."

"I invited ya, didn't I?"

"Well, yes, but—"

"But nothin'. You wouldn't be imposin'. This old house is so big, I rattle around in it all by myself. We could go for a week and not even see each other."

"It's not *that* big, George," Hope said with a chuckle.

"Long as you don't blubber all the time, I reckon we can get along well enough." George's expression turned shrewd. "Maybe we could even help each other out."

The old man was up to something, but what? In spite of her better judgment, Hope asked, "How?"

"You love livin' here. Around Sunshine Gap, I mean."

She hesitated, then slowly nodded. "Something here calls to me. I don't know quite what it is, but everything's just so...real here. I don't know if it's the land or the people."

"Could be the lack of people," he suggested. "Must be mighty nice to drive down a road that ain't all clogged up with traffic."

"That's true." She smiled at him. "But it's more than that. When I'm in Wyoming, I feel as if...as if I'm home. I can think here. And see life more clearly. I know I've done some of my best writing here."

"Then why don't you buy this place?"

Hope felt her mouth fall open and knew she was gaping at him. "The Double Circle?"

"It's the only ranch I own. I won't even try to rip you off 'cause you're rich. All I want's the fair market value."

"You can't be serious."

"Why the hell not? I'm ninety-one years old, gal. When I croak, somebody's gonna buy it. Might as well be you."

"But I'm a writer. I don't know anything about ranching."

"That's the beauty of my idea. I got a couple of conditions before I agree to this sale."

"Conditions?" She might've known. There were always conditions, and they often were unacceptable.

Scowling, he shook his head at her as if she were trying his patience. "Hear me out before you get your drawers in a knot. First condition is, I can keep my room in this house as long as I want it. I ain't afraid of dyin', but I *am* afraid of bein' helpless. If I get to where I need a nurse to take care of me, I'd like to have somebody I trust here to keep an eye on things. Make sure I'm treated right, ya know?"

Hope blinked at the sudden vulnerability in George's wrinkled face. Having been raised by servants, she knew exactly how it felt to be dependent on people who weren't always kind. But she didn't dare show any emotion he might interpret as pity. "Of course," she said in a businesslike tone. "What are the other conditions?"

"There's just one. If you ever decide to sell this place, I want your word you won't sell it to some developer who'll cut it up into five-acre lots. That's what my idiot nephew'll do if he ever gets his hands on the Double Circle. Kid never was worth the bullet it'd take to shoot him."

"I could live with your conditions, but I still don't know anything about running a ranch. From what I've seen, it involves a great deal of hard work."

"That it does, but I can teach you what you need to know, and you can always hire whatever help you need. Shoot, my hand Scott pretty much runs this place on his own."

"But doesn't Jake want the Double Circle?"

George grinned. "Yup. Jake's wanted this ranch for years. Made me some nice offers and he helps me out when I need somebody to check up on Scott."

"Then why don't you sell it to him?"

"'Cause then I'd have to leave, and where would I go? Some damn nursing home? I'd rather be dead."

"Surely you could make other arrangements—"

"Not in Sunshine Gap, and this is my home. Besides, Jake'd want to take over running everything, and I'm not ready to give it all up just yet. It's a good place. You want it or not?"

Oh, she *did* want it. The Double Circle was smaller than the Flying M but every bit as pretty. And she loved this old house. Redecorating it would be a pleasure. She'd do the kitchen in French provincial, the garden in English casual and completely redo the bathrooms. She'd have to study up on antique furniture and—

The thought of having her very own house that wasn't on anybody's tourist map... But, as Jake had so bluntly pointed out, her sense of style wouldn't exactly be appreciated, much less accepted around Sunshine Gap.

"I don't think I really belong here, George."

"Hell, girl, didn't you get a thing I told you about the settlement of the West? Anybody could belong here if they wanted to bad enough. That's why so many different kinds of people came out here."

"That was the *old* West."

"Horsefeathers. Long as you're honest, halfway decent and a good neighbor, you'll belong just fine. Don't listen to Jake. He's the one who put that fool idea in your head, isn't he?"

Hope nodded stiffly, feeling hurt all over again. But while she was still angry at Jake, she wasn't vindictive enough to take away something he'd wanted—and undoubtedly worked for—for years. And there was a gleam in George's eyes she didn't entirely trust. He was up to something, all right, but he wasn't going to tell her about it. Until he did, she didn't intend to commit herself to anything.

"It's a big decision, George," she said. "I'll have to think about it."

"You do that," he said, grinning again. "I want you to stay here while you're thinkin'. Stay until you finish your book, anyway. What do you say?"

"I'd love to. May I use the room upstairs with the lovely view of the mountains?"

"You bet. By the way, do you cook?"

A week later Jake sat at his desk, studying his personal balance sheet with a critical eye. His cash flow would be awful tight if George Pierson accepted this new offer for the Double Circle, but Jake was getting so desperate for a place of his own, he didn't give a rip. If he didn't get away from the Flying M soon, he was bound to do or say something he might regret for years to come.

But it wouldn't be without just cause.

Of course, being provoked by his big, complicated family was hardly anything new. His mother and Aunt Lucy were identical twins who had grown up in a village in Italy. His dad and Uncle Harry had met them while they were in Europe serving in the military.

After whirlwind courtships, the McBride brothers had married the twin sisters and brought them home to the Flying M. Between them, the two couples had produced seven children and raised them as siblings rather than cousins. As the oldest, Jake had been held responsible for keeping Zack, Dillon, Alexandra, Cal, Marsh and Grace out of trouble.

It hadn't been easy. Since they'd all survived to adulthood, however, Jake figured he'd done a fine job of it. Not that it was doing him one bit of good now.

Though Hope hadn't said a word about him in her goodbye note, Jake's mother and Aunt Lucy were blaming him for Hope's early departure. They'd loved having a famous author living in the guesthouse, and the idea that Hope preferred cranky old George Pierson's company to the McBrides' was, in their eyes, unthinkable. Every time the Mamas, as they were affectionately called, saw Jake, they glared at him, heaved sorrowful sighs and turned away, shoulders slumped, heads bowed as if in shame.

And they hadn't cooked one blessed thing he liked since Hope had left.

It probably shouldn't matter so much, but dammit,

they'd always been proud of him before. It rankled that the two women he loved most would turn on him when he hadn't done anything wrong. And all over some wacko woman from Hollywood.

His dad and Uncle Harry were driving him just as crazy, though for different reasons. They were supposed to be retired and leave the management of the Flying M to Jake. The arrangement had worked well while the four parents had been on an extended world tour for the past two years.

But now that they were home with nothing to divert their attention, neither Gage nor Harry McBride could resist the urge to "help" Jake tend to business. One or the other of them questioned every decision he made and griped over every innovation he'd instituted while they were gone. They were especially disgruntled to discover he'd put the ranch accounts onto a computer rather than using the old ledger system that "had been plenty good enough for three generations of McBrides."

"If they'd just sit down and learn to use the computer, they could still see the books anytime they wanted," Jake grumbled, knowing his dad and uncle weren't going to touch that "dang machine" unless they absolutely had to. "And that'll never happen as long as they've got me around to torture for information all the time."

He loved his job. Loved the Flying M. Loved the Mamas and Papas. But he needed relief from the stress of living so close to them. Somebody was on his back all day, every day.

It wasn't just the parents, either. Whenever he was in the ranch office, his brothers and sister felt entitled to ask him to do all kinds of things for them. It was time for all of them to grow up and handle their own problems.

Dammit, he needed a place where he could have some privacy. A place that was his and his alone to do with as he pleased. A place where he didn't have to consult anyone or be responsible for anyone but himself. But he couldn't be too far away in case of an emergency at the Flying M.

The only ranch close enough that might be for sale in the near future was George Pierson's. Stashing his papers into their file folder, Jake grabbed his straw cowboy hat and hurried out to his pickup. He climbed in and drove off, intending to make that greedy, stubborn old coot an offer he couldn't refuse.

And maybe, if Jake was real lucky, he could convince Hope to come back and stay in the Flying M's guesthouse again. Then the Mamas would smile and cook his favorite meals again, and he could at least try to make up with Hope. Every time he remembered what he'd said to her the day of the wedding, he felt guilty all over again.

He hadn't laid eyes on her since then, and the thought of seeing her now made him smile. He wouldn't say he'd actually missed her. But without the possibility of Hope turning up with some flimsy excuse to see him, his days had seemed a little…flat.

Shaking his head at his own contrariness, Jake turned in at the Double Circle's entrance. He drove around back and parked behind Hope's little red car. Doofus ran across the yard to greet him. Jake leaned down and scratched the pup's ears.

"Hey there, Doofus. You'd better stop growing or George might mistake you for a horse and throw a saddle on your back." The possibility didn't seem to worry Doofus much. He ran off when Jake pretended to throw a stick for him.

Chuckling, Jake climbed the steps to the back door and gave it a good, solid knock. George opened it a moment later, a surprisingly cheerful smile curving up the corners of his mouth. He stepped back out of the way and motioned for Jake to come in.

"Mornin', Jake. What brings you out this way?"

Jake stepped over the threshold and took off his hat. "I want to talk to you if you've got time, George."

"I reckon I can spare a few minutes." Using his cane, George hobbled over to the round oak table and settled onto a straight-backed wooden chair.

Jake took the one adjacent to George's and glanced around the kitchen. He saw new, colorful dishtowels hanging beside the sink in place of the dingy, ragged ones that usually hung there. A canning jar full of fresh flowers sat on top of a microwave oven that hadn't been there the last time Jake visited the old man. Hope must be making herself at home.

"What can I do for ya?" George asked.

"Tell me what it'll take to convince you to sell me the Double Circle," Jake replied.

"Well, now, I've been thinkin' a lot about that since the last time you tried to buy it." George's smile grew wider.

Jake's heart swelled with hope until his chest hurt. This was the first time George had ever admitted he'd even considered selling the Double Circle. Jake had wanted this for so long, the desperation he'd felt earlier returned with a vengeance. Hardly daring to breathe, he said, "Yeah?"

George nodded. "Your offer was damn generous. But back then, I just couldn't stand to let the place go."

"What about now?" Jake asked, his voice tinged with

the desperate agony of hope that had been dashed too many times before.

"I'd like to sell it to ya, Jake. I really would, but…"

His heart already plummeting, Jake read the refusal coming in George's eyes. "But what?"

"But you better look for another place," George said. "I'm gonna be usin' this one myself for the foreseeable future."

His stomach painfully clenching with disappointment, Jake stared at the old man. Then Jake's temper got the best of him. "Dammit, George, what are you thinking?" he demanded. "You're going to have to quit sometime. And you know good and well that even with a hired hand, you can't handle this place anymore."

"I won't have to." George's eyes sparkled with an unholy glee Jake didn't understand.

"What the hell are you talking about?"

"I'm tired of bein' alone." George ran one hand over the top of his head as if he still had hair up there to smooth down. "I'm thinkin' about gettin' married again. Maybe havin' some kids this time."

"Married?" Jake sputtered. "Kids?"

"Yeah. You know, babies. Heirs."

Jake's mouth fell open. Had the old boy finally gone completely senile? Jake doubted there was a woman of child-bearing age in a hundred-mile radius who'd even pretend to consider such a thing.

A soft, whispery sound distracted him. He glanced up in time to see Hope saunter into the kitchen, wearing a shiny purple robe that barely reached the middle of her thighs. Her hair was slicked back as if she'd just stepped out of the shower. He'd never seen it black before.

Hope's gaze met his, her eyes widening as if he was the last person she'd expected—or wanted—to see in

George's house. She hesitated a fraction of a second, then turned toward the counter beside the sink and crossed the room without so much as another glance in Jake's direction. Jake gritted his teeth and found himself watching the sway of her hips beneath that short robe and wondering what, if anything, she had on beneath it.

Her slender legs looked smooth and tanned, and when she went up on her tiptoes to take two coffee mugs from the cupboard, her calf muscles stood out in sharp relief. Jake held his breath while the back of her robe hiked up—but not quite high enough to satisfy his curiosity about her underwear. Or the lack of it.

Lowering her heels to the floor, she moved to her right, filled the mugs with coffee and carried them to the table. She set one mug in front of George, then affectionately patted his bony shoulder, took the chair on his other side and sipped from the second mug.

George glanced over at her, his eyebrows arched in query. "Aren't you gonna offer Jake some coffee?"

"No," she replied with a grin. "He might stay longer if I did."

Jake refused to acknowledge her deliberate rudeness. His sister Alex used to start fights with outrageous remarks and he'd learned not to get suckered in by them. George opened his mouth as if he might protest, but Jake held up a hand to stop him. "Don't worry about it, George. I don't want coffee."

"Don't know what you're missing, boy. Hope brews a mean cup." George exchanged a warm smile with Hope that chilled Jake's blood.

No. It couldn't be. Hope wouldn't take up with an old guy like George. Would she?

Jake gave his head a hard shake in denial, but the shocking idea remained. Hope wasn't from Wyoming.

He didn't have a clue about what she would or wouldn't do. Sure wouldn't be the first time a young, pretty gal married an old man for his money. Happened all the time. Especially in a place like Hollywood.

She scowled at him. "Why are you looking at me that way?"

"What way?" Jake asked.

"As if you think I'm going to steal George's silverware."

George snorted with laughter. "It ain't that, hon. I just told Jake I can't sell him the Double Circle."

"Yeah, he claims he's thinking about getting married and having some kids." Jake's voice sounded harsh in his own ears, but he was too upset to care. "Any truth in what he says?"

Confused, Hope glanced at George, raising her eyebrows in a silent plea for a clue as to what was going on. Tilting his head ever so slightly toward Jake, George gave her a sly wink. Why, the old devil wanted her to play along with him, but what was he up to now?

Deciding to give him the benefit of her considerable doubt, she turned back to Jake with a shrug. "You know George. When he decides to be charming, almost anything's possible."

Jake's tanned complexion flushed a dull red. His eyes glinting dangerously and a vein pulsing in the middle of his forehead, he ground out, "A week ago, you were all over me."

"And you called me 'a flaky little California floozy.'" Reminding herself of Rule Number Two— never let them see when words stung, Hope smiled at him. "I got over you in a hurry."

"Obviously. But I didn't realize you were so desperate. Are book sales that bad?"

''My book sales are just fine. Not that they're any of your business.''

''Give it up, DuMaine. You're not serious about George.''

This conversation was making less and less sense as it went on, but Hope bristled at the derision and the demand in Jake's voice. She really hated it when somebody tried to tell her what she thought or felt. Whatever his problem was, she wasn't going to allow Jake Mc-Bride to take it out on her or on George.

''Well, unlike *some* people, he's always been extremely sweet to me,'' she said.

Jake's face turned an even darker red. His nostrils flared and his hands curled into fists. ''That's no reason to marry a man old enough to be your grandfather.''

''M-marry him?'' Hope sputtered, looking from Jake to George and back to Jake. Good lord, what exactly had George said to him? She'd have to thrash it out with him later. ''My plans are none of your business.''

Shaking his head, Jake grumbled something unintelligible, then stood up so fast his chair scraped the linoleum floor like a fingernail down a chalkboard. ''I've gotta say, the two of you make quite a pair. I hope you'll be damn happy together.''

With that, he left the room, slamming the back door behind him.

Hope turned on George. ''What on earth was that all about?''

George cackled wickedly. ''Aw, I was just havin' a little fun with Jake. Sure gets pompous, don't he?''

Her throat too tight to speak, Hope nodded.

''And imagine him thinkin' you were after my money.'' George chuckled and shook his head. ''I'll bet you could buy me a hundred times and not even feel a pinch in your pocketbook.''

"Why that..." Hope muttered as the truth of what George was saying sank into her brain. "He really thinks I'm a gold digger. Doesn't he?"

"Yeah, that's why he asked about your book sales," George said. "Didn't you get that?"

"No, it all happened so fast and I was too busy trying to figure what you were doing." She smacked her palm against her forehead. "Oh, duh, DuMaine."

"Don't be so hard on yourself. You've got him runnin' scared. Serves him right for thinkin' so poorly of you."

Hope's heart contracted painfully, then filled with a burning, righteous anger she knew only too well. George was right. Only Jake deserved worse than to be running scared. For thinking such awful things about her, he deserved to *lose* the Double Circle.

"As long as I fulfill your conditions are you still willing to sell me the Double Circle for fair market value?" she asked.

"Hell, yes." George stuck out his hand. "Deal?"

She took his hand and shook it. "Deal."

She'd needed a major life change for a long time, and now she was going to make it. She was going to get out of L.A. and move to Sunshine Gap. She was going to take a pen name and write historical novels. She was going to live a simpler, more meaningful life at a slower, saner pace. She was going to make real friends, be a part of a real community and have a real home. Dammit, she was going to *belong* here if she had to give up her fake fingernails and hair dye to do it.

And Jake McBride could take his low opinion of her and sit on it.

Chapter Three

Hot, tired and sweaty after an afternoon of mending fences, Jake packed his tools into his saddlebags, mounted his quarter horse gelding, and turned back toward the house. Spotting a flash of red near the road, Jake reined in, then wheeled Rebel around in a circle for a better look.

A jogger. Coming from the direction of the Double Circle. Only one person crazy enough to be out here running in the middle of August when the heat and the dust were at their worst.

Hope DuMaine.

Wasn't that convenient? During the past month he'd seen her driving on the county road and a couple of times in town, but he hadn't talked to her. Certainly not when she was half-naked and glowing with perspiration. His mouth watered. Hell.

Avoiding her had been so easy since that morning at

George's house, he figured she was avoiding him, as well. Much as he'd like to go right on avoiding her, today he had things he needed to say to her.

If he didn't strangle her with his bare hands first.

Man, she was really moving. She must run on a regular basis in order to go so fast. Even though he thought she was nuts to do it, he had to admire her self-discipline.

When he hadn't heard even a whisper of gossip about an engagement or a wedding in a couple of weeks, Jake had told himself George must've come to his senses. Or maybe Hope had come to hers. Or maybe they'd just been giving him a bad time all along and hadn't ever planned to get married in the first place.

And while Jake had been thinking he had plenty of time to change George's mind about selling, Hope DuMaine had gone and bought the Double Circle right out from under him. Dammit, she'd bought *his* ranch. The sneaky, conniving little witch had even paid cash for it. He didn't know which galled him worse.

According to his source in the real estate office, she'd bought everything—the land, buildings, equipment and animals, which meant she'd had a couple of million dollars handy. Okay, so now he knew she hadn't needed to marry George for his money. She'd still bought the one thing Jake had ever wanted for himself—the Double Circle Ranch. His sanctuary.

He'd never forgive her for that. Or George.

Hell, he'd have bettered any offer she made for the Double Circle. Of course, he couldn't lay out so much cash all at once, but what the heck did George need with that kind of money? Once the taxes were paid, he'd probably lose money doing it Hope's way.

When Jake thought of all the hours he'd spent helping

that cantankerous old man over the years, it hurt to know his friendship meant so little to George. But, business was business. Right?

Dammit, it never would've happened if Hope hadn't butted her nose in where it didn't belong. If she'd just gone back to California...

Insides clenched tight against a hot wave of fury, Jake turned Rebel toward the fence line and kicked him into a ground-eating lope. When she saw him coming, Hope hesitated but kept on running until they met on opposite sides of the barbed wire. She wore skimpy running shorts with a red sports bra and a green baseball cap.

Her skin glistened with perspiration; her body radiated a healthy energy Jake found incredibly sexy in spite of his anger.

Maybe she really *was* a witch. He'd never met another woman who made him mad enough to eat nails and turned him on at the same time. The inconsistency in his own behavior added fuel to his anger.

Chest heaving, she tipped up the brim of her cap and gave him a bland smile. "Hello, Jake. How are you?"

He glared down at her for all he was worth. "How the hell do you think I am?"

Big blue eyes calm as if she were sipping tea with a close friend, Hope raised and lowered one shoulder in an I-really-don't-care shrug. "Taking a wild guess, I'd say you're upset about something."

"Upset?" Cutting loose with an ugly laugh, Jake dismounted. "Honey, *upset* doesn't even start to cover it." He dropped the reins, squeezed himself through the strands of barbed wire and stalked right up to her. "Why did you do it?"

Her chin came up and she held her ground, as if daring him even to try to intimidate her. He had to give her full credit for gutsiness. "Why did I buy the Double Circle?"

"That's right. You knew damn well I wanted it."

"Too bad, McBride," she said, her voice holding no detectable sympathy. "So did I, and I learned a long time ago to go after what I want, not stand around—"

"Why did you want it?" he interrupted. "Just to get back at me for not jumping on your stupid flirting? One of those 'hell hath no fury like a woman scorned' things?"

Her eyes flashed, but her voice remained cool. "Don't flatter yourself. I intend to live at the Double Circle."

He snorted in disbelief. "For how long? Until you get bored with life in the slow lane?"

"Indefinitely."

"Hell, you don't belong in Sunshine Gap and you never will. Once the novelty wears off, the isolation will drive you nuts, and when winter sets in, you won't believe how bleak and unforgiving this place can be. You'll hate it."

She spread her feet wider apart and propped her hands on her hips, her eyes narrowed like a gunfighter's. "I don't think that's any of your concern."

"You're dead wrong," Jake said. "Everything that goes on at the Double Circle concerns me."

"And you believe that because?"

Jake stepped closer, intentionally invading her personal space. "I've been running that place for George for the past ten years. I know every inch of it, every cow, calf, steer and bull on it and where they go whenever a section of fence goes down. I know where to find every irrigation gate, every pump, every piece of equipment and spare part on that ranch. I've *earned* the right to buy it. You haven't."

"Did you have an option to buy it from George?" she demanded. "Or any other sort of legal agreement?"

Jake wanted to lie, but knew if he did, she'd make him produce proof he didn't have. Because he'd been a trusting fool, dammit. Time to change the subject.

"You don't know the first thing about ranching," he said.

Her smile told him she knew exactly what he was trying to do and she wasn't going to fall for it. "George will teach me whatever I need to know."

"It takes years to learn everything you're gonna need to know. I doubt he'll live that long."

"I'll take my chances." Hope's tone was as dry as the dust on her shoes. "George is in terrific shape for a man his age."

"I won't help you the way I've helped him," Jake said.

"I'll hire whatever help I need."

"It's not that easy—"

She cut him off with a huff. "Give me a break. Ranching's a lot of hard work, but it's not rocket science. It's a business, and even us flaky Californians have to conduct business sometimes. I'm not a complete idiot."

"I never said you were," he grumbled.

"Close enough. For your information, I have two full-time employees in California, so I know how to be a boss. I also serve on the boards of directors for several multi-million-dollar charitable foundations."

"It's not the same thing." Hearing his own voice rising to a near-shout, Jake inhaled a deep breath, consciously trying to calm down. He'd never won an argument by losing his temper.

"Of course it's not the same thing," she said with an

exaggerated patience that made Jake grit his teeth. "But I'm a quick study. With George's help and advice, I can learn how to manage one small Wyoming ranch."

"Small? You think the Double Circle is *small?*" In spite of his best efforts, his voice rose again. Rebel whinnied and stamped his feet as if the shouting was disturbing him.

Hope glanced at the horse, then looked back at Jake, a grin tugging at the corners of her mouth. "It's only one business. I can handle that much."

"Don't bet on it." He doggedly ground the words out, desperately wishing she would listen, but not really expecting her to. "You're playing with something you don't understand."

She rolled her eyes toward heaven and her grin widened into a cheesy, Hollywood smile. "Do try to be a good loser, darling. Since you won't have to worry about the Double Circle, think of all the free time you'll have. Maybe you should get a hobby."

That did it. Jake's temper snapped and he found himself shouting. "Dammit, lady, the Double Circle's been a great ranch for over a hundred years, but you'll run it into the ground inside of three months. Then you're gonna come to me, begging for help. You don't belong out here."

"Get over yourself, McBride," she said with an indignant huff. "It's my ranch now. Whatever I do with it is no business of yours, and the devil will play ice hockey before I ask you for anything. You'll have to excuse me."

She turned away and jogged back toward the Double Circle without so much as a glance over her shoulder at him. Jake stood in the middle of the gravel road, watching until she rounded the curve by the big old cottonwood tree marking the boundary between the Flying M and the Double Circle.

His gut churned. His head ached. His chest felt…empty. As if somebody had scooped the heart right out of him and left only an empty carcass behind. He'd lost the Double Circle.

Most likely for good.

And for the first time in years he didn't know what to do next. Hope was right. It really wasn't any of his business what she did with her own ranch.

But he was right, too. She didn't have a clue what a huge bite she'd just gnawed off. If there was any justice in this world, she'd choke on it. And he'd be damned if he'd do one blessed thing to make life any easier for her.

"Wretched man," Hope muttered, dodging around an enormous pothole in the gravel road. "Who does he think he is? I belong here as much as anyone else. George said so."

At the sound of a car coming up behind her, she moved to the side of the road. It wasn't nearly as hot here as it was in L.A., but the elevation and lack of pavement made jogging in Sunshine Gap more of a challenge. She swiped the back of her hand across her forehead, then rubbed the muddy mixture of dust and perspiration down the side of her shorts.

"Hey, baby," a familiar voice called from the vehicle, which had pulled up beside her. "What's shakin'?"

Hope slowed to a walk and turned to find Marsh McBride grinning at her from the driver's side of a black BMW convertible. The top was down, and his black hair was wild and windblown. Though there was a striking family resemblance among all of the McBride men, Marsh was the most classically handsome.

Even in Hollywood, where gorgeous men were as common as street signs, he was considered one of "the beautiful people."

Hope had met him years ago in a screenwriting class at USC. Over endless drafts of screenplays that were never produced they'd become fast friends and writing buddies.

How odd was it that Marsh had never aroused a single spark of sexual attraction in her, but his obnoxious cousin Jake could make her heart pound with a look?

Which only went to prove there really was no accounting for taste. Or, perhaps, she simply was perverse. Or crazy.

Still, after that confrontation with Jake, the sight of a friendly face warmed her heart. "Marsh, darling, where have you been since the wedding?"

Leaning across the gearshift, he opened the passenger door for her. "Get in and I'll tell you."

"I should cool down first." He stared at her deadpan, making her laugh. "Oh, all right. My run's already been ruined anyway." She climbed into the car and pointed straight ahead. "Take me home."

"Yes, ma'am." He drove off toward the Double Circle.

"So tell me. Where have you been?"

"In Reno."

"What have you been doing there? Gambling?"

"More like drinking a lot and sulking at first," he said. "Once I got tired of that, I started thinking."

"About?" Hope prompted, though she didn't need to be psychic to guess the answer. For as long as she'd known him, Marsh had been in love with his high-school and college girlfriend, Sandy Bishop.

"Sandy." Marsh gave Hope a sad smile and shook his head. "What else? I've decided to come back to Sunshine Gap until we get this…whatever it is between us resolved."

"I'm glad, Marsh," Hope said. "It's past time."

"You've got that right. All these family weddings have been messing with my head big-time. One way or another, I'm going to marry her or get over her."

"Do you have a plan?"

"Not yet." He shot her a grim smile. "I'm counting on you to help me come up with something."

"I'll do whatever I can," Hope promised. "How did you know where to find me?"

"I stopped in at the main house and the Mamas said you were staying with George. They weren't very happy about it."

"Jake hasn't told them yet?"

"Told them what?"

"I've bought the Double Circle."

His mouth dropping open, Marsh stared at her while the car swerved toward the other lane. "You're kidding."

"Watch where you're going." Hope grabbed the steering wheel and got them back onto their own side of the road. "And I'm quite serious, Marsh. We closed on it yesterday."

"But Jake's wanted to buy it for years."

"George chose to sell it to me," she said, feeling oddly defensive. "I paid him a fair price. What's the problem?"

"I just said it." Marsh turned into the Double Circle's

drive and parked beside Hope's car. "Jake's wanted the Double Circle for years."

Raising her eyebrows, Hope allowed an acid note to slip into her voice. "And does Jake always get everything he wants?"

Marsh considered that for a moment, then slowly nodded. "Yeah. Usually. Except for when Ellen died."

"You mean his wife."

"That's right," Marsh said, nodding again. "You knew she passed away about eight years ago, didn't you?"

"Yes, but nobody ever mentioned what happened to her. Was it an accident?"

"An accident would've been kinder. It was cancer, but we don't talk about it anymore." A thoughtful frown creasing his forehead, Marsh shifted sideways in his seat, turning to face her more fully. "Are you prepared to face all the ramifications of buying this ranch?"

Ramifications? She didn't like the way that sounded. "What do you mean?"

"Everybody knows how much work Jake's put into the Double Circle over the years. Most folks assume there's been some kind of an understanding between Jake and George."

"I asked Jake if he had an option to buy the Double Circle and he changed the subject to how little I know about ranching."

Marsh's grin returned. "He's got a point about that."

Hope rolled her eyes in exasperation. "Believe me, he already lectured me on that subject. At length. But back up for a second. If Jake and George didn't have any legal agreement, I have as much right to buy it as anyone else—including Jake. Right?"

Smiling wryly, Marsh shook his head. "Sometimes

business is done a little differently around here. Jake's made no secret he wanted to buy George's place. If George didn't plan to sell it to him, he shouldn't have accepted so much help from Jake.''

''Are you saying people will think I've cheated Jake out of something that was promised to him?''

''They might. It's more likely they'll blame George, but you could catch some of the fallout.''

Apprehension washing over her, Hope bit her lower lip. The McBrides didn't always get along with each other, but they were known to close ranks and present a united front in the face of outside opposition. When the rest of the family heard about her purchase, would they all be as angry with her as Jake was? And if the rest of the community sided against her as well, living in Sunshine Gap could become distinctly unpleasant.

Not that she couldn't handle unpleasantness. But she was just starting a new life. All this hostility wasn't what she'd had in mind when she agreed to George's plan.

Marsh gave her shoulder a reassuring squeeze. ''Hey, don't look so worried. It's not *that* big a deal.''

''I really don't think I did anything wrong, but...'' Hope rubbed her temples where a headache was threatening. ''Oh, maybe I should've thought about this more carefully. But I was so blasted angry at Jake.''

''What did he do?'' Marsh asked.

Hope told him what Jake had said to her at the wedding reception and how he'd assumed she would marry George for his money. ''Honestly, he was so judgmental and self-righteous, I wanted to teach him a lesson.''

Marsh tipped back his head and let out a big, booming laugh. ''Well, you did, and he deserved it.''

''He certainly did.''

''The thing is,'' Marsh said, his tone turning sober,

"you've pushed ol' Jake real hard with this. I doubt he'll take it lying down."

Hope looked up at the sky and asked the Universe, "What did I ever see in him?"

"Jake's not so bad," Marsh said. "With a guy like him, at least you always know where you stand. And when your butt's in a sling, there's nobody better to have in your corner."

"I know he's a good man," she murmured. "That's why I kept trying to get his attention."

"Well, you've got it now," Marsh said.

"I think I'd rather go back to having him ignore me. This isn't the kind of attention I had in mind."

"You could always change it."

"How?"

"Stop dressing like a floozy." Marsh snatched her cap and ruffled her hair. "And forget about the hair dye."

"That shouldn't matter so much," Hope protested.

"Maybe not, but Jake's a little conservative. You know, there's such a thing as giving your audience too much to handle at one time." Marsh's face suddenly went blank and his mouth fell open.

"Are you all right?" Hope asked.

After a moment, his eyes came alive and he smacked his forehead with the palm of one hand. "Fine. And that's it!"

"What's it?"

"That's how I'm going to get Sandy's attention." He clasped the sides of her face between his hands and planted a smacking kiss on her forehead. "DuMaine, you're a genius!"

"What are you talking about?"

"The last three times I've been home, Sandy wouldn't even talk to me. But thanks to you, she will this time."

He opened Hope's door and made shooing motions with both hands. "Get out. I've got to go into town."

He fired up the car's engine. Hope scrambled out of the passenger seat and closed the door. "What are you going to do?"

"Buy a house," he called, pulling away. "See you later."

"Yeah, later," Hope said, knowing he'd never hear her.

She watched him drive away until the dust cloud following his car dissipated. The McBrides were crazy. All of them.

Turning toward her own house, she couldn't hold in a sigh of appreciation. It needed paint, landscaping and attention. It needed…her. She already loved the Double Circle, and had no intention of giving it up.

But she didn't want to be at war with Jake McBride. So, she'd give him a few days to calm down. Then she'd go talk to him and maybe they could reach some kind of an understanding.

Jake moved through the next four days on automatic pilot. He ate, slept and did his job. He answered when someone spoke to him. He fended off at least a million well-meaning expressions of sympathy when news of the Double Circle's sale got out, claiming that he was fine.

But he wasn't fine. He was anything *but* fine.

Every time he thought about someone as clueless and flaky as Hope DuMaine owning *his* ranch, he wanted to hit something. He tried not to think about it, but that was like trying not to breathe—it only worked for a little while. The instant he let down his guard it all came rushing back, bringing a fresh wave of anger with it.

The one time he'd ever felt anything close to this before was the day Ellen's doctor had told him she wasn't going to make it. He'd skipped denial, gone straight to anger and stayed there. It had been the only thing that allowed him to be strong for her sake, when what he'd really wanted was to break down and bawl like a little kid.

Of course this wasn't the same situation. Not even close. Nobody was going to die because he couldn't buy the Double Circle.

But the sense of loss and lost dreams was eerily similar.

Knowing he couldn't go on carrying around so much pent-up rage, he decided to take Rebel out for a ride and check the cows on their summer range. Fresh air, a change of scene and some time alone couldn't hurt. Halfway between the house and the barn, he heard an approaching vehicle.

He paused to see who it was and felt his blood pressure surge when Hope's little red car emerged from the cloud of dust it had kicked up. Aw, man, he wasn't ready to see her again. Back teeth clamped together, he marched into the barn, grabbed a bridle from the tack room and went out to the horse pasture.

Just about the time he'd caught Rebel and finished putting on his bridle, Jake heard Hope's voice calling his name. His muscles tensed. Before he could even think about a possible means of escape, she walked around the side of the barn, waving when she spotted him.

Her hair was back to an auburn shade, but today's eye-popping outfit consisted of a low-cut halter top and a pair of indecently short cut-off jeans so tight it was a wonder she could walk in them. The top was made out of a soft suede material nearly the same buckskin color as Rebel. Long strands of fringe decorated with Native American beads and feathers hung across the front and played peek-a-boo with the curves of her breasts every time she moved.

Her high-pitched, slide-on sandals matched the color of her shirt and forced her to take short, bouncy steps that made her hips and breasts sway. Add in those long, gorgeous legs and she was an erotic visual feast in motion. His pulse hiccupped with every stride.

Aw, *damn*. How did she get to him like this every stinkin' time?

"Hello, Jake." She gave him a tentative smile. "Have you got a minute?"

"I'm getting ready to head out," he said, hoping she'd think the raw note in his voice came from gruffness rather than arousal. "This isn't a good time."

"Is there ever going to be a good time for us to talk?"

"Doubt it." He clicked his tongue at Rebel and set off for the barn.

Some people weren't bright enough to get a hint. Jake suspected Hope simply ignored them whenever it suited her purposes, even when they were less than subtle. She followed him right into the barn, waited until he'd started brushing the dirt off Rebel's hide, then leaned back against a stall door and crossed one foot over the other.

She waited a full minute, but when he remained silent, she said, "I don't plan to run the Double Circle into the ground."

"Nobody ever *plans* to do that, but it happens."

"Well, it's not going to happen to my ranch."

"Uh-huh."

"I mean it, Jake. I've been in touch with an Animal Science professor at the University of Wyoming and he's recommended some books for me to read. I've already ordered them. As soon as I finish my manuscript, I'll dive right in and read them.''

"Do you really think you can learn everything you need to know in books?" He set down the brush, picked up a curry comb and went to work on Rebel's tangled mane.

"Probably not everything," she conceded, "but I have to start somewhere, don't I?"

"No. You could always give up this insane idea and sell me the Double Circle."

"You know I'm not going to do that."

"Then there's no point to this conversation."

"We're neighbors, Jake." She straightened away from the stall door and propped her hands on her hips. "My cousin is married to your cousin and my best friend is married to your brother. We're going to run into each other from time to time. Don't you think it would be nice if we could at least be civil?"

"It'd be *nice* to win the lottery, but I doubt that's gonna happen, either."

"If you won't do it for me, do it for Dillon and Bl—"

Oh man, he really hated it when someone used other family members to make him feel guilty. "Leave them out of this."

"How can I?" Hope demanded. "Blair is extremely important to me, and I don't want her to come home from her honeymoon to a big conflict between me and her brother-in-law."

"You should've thought of that before you stole my ranch."

"I didn't steal it. I bought it and I had every legal right to do so."

"Just because something's legal doesn't make it right. What you did wasn't fair—"

"You're whining about what's fair?" She tossed her hands up beside her head. "You already have everything—"

"I wouldn't exactly call you deprived. You're the one who plunked down a couple of million bucks in cash—"

"And I earned every penny of it, but that's not the issue. I wasn't talking about money."

"You're not gonna try to tell me you always wanted to be a cowgirl when you were growing up and now you're just trying to fulfill your lifelong dream."

"Hardly. Until I met your family I never considered leaving L.A."

"What did we do to convince you? Maybe we can undo it."

"It wasn't what you did. It's more like who you *are*. And how you live."

"We live like anybody else. We're not all that special."

"That's not true." Her eyes glowed with a wistfulness he didn't understand. "Your family is wonderful."

"It's a mixed blessing sometimes. Trust me on that one."

"No, you're wrong. You're absolutely wrong about that."

Hell, she could argue the ears off a dead man. "I'm not interested in your opinions about my family or anything else. Until you're ready to sell me the Double Circle, we've got nothing to talk about."

"Oh, Jake, can't you at least try to make peace with the situation?"

Her big, sad eyes and soft, pleading tone tugged at

his conscience, but he shrugged them off. This was no time to weaken, and try as he might, he couldn't see himself ever driving past the Double Circle without feeling betrayed and cheated. "No. I can't. And I'm not going to pretend I can or make nice about it, either. If you're smart, you'll stay the hell away from me."

"Fine. Have it your way." Stepping closer, she crossed her arms over her breasts. "But while you're sitting here brooding, think about your own part in my decision to buy the Double Circle."

"What are you talking about?"

"When George first offered to sell me his ranch, I never intended to buy it because I knew you wanted it. You're the one who changed my mind."

"Right. How did I do that?"

"By assuming I'd marry George to get his land and his money. What did I ever do to make you think so little of me?"

"Nothing. I didn't want to believe you'd do that."

"But you did, Jake. You never even considered giving me the benefit of the doubt, and it cost you the Double Circle."

With that she turned around and marched out of the barn, her head high and her fringe twitching back and forth in time with her hips. He waited until he heard her car start, then muttered a word foul enough to match his mood.

"You're a bigger man than that, Jake."

Startled to hear another voice, Jake whirled around to find his father standing in the doorway behind him.

"How long have you been eavesdropping?" Jake asked.

"Long enough." Gage McBride came farther inside, his jaw muscles bunched tight and his eyes flashing with a rare display of temper Jake had learned to respect at a young age. "It took guts for that little gal to come and talk to you."

"Stay out of it, Dad."

"I would if you two were the only ones who'd be affected, but you're not. This has all the makings of a damn feud and I won't have it. You've got to think of the whole family—"

Furious, Jake flung the curry comb across the barn. "I've done that my whole life, and what's it ever gotten me but more work and more responsibilities? It's always been, 'Think of the younger ones, Jake. Think of the Mamas, Jake. Think of the ranch, Jake.' What about what *I* want? Doesn't that matter?"

"Of course it does, but this isn't the way—"

"She's got no business trying to run a ranch."

"And you've got no business deciding that for her. If you'd ever sat down and visited with Hope instead of running away from her, you'd know she's no gold digger. Maybe you ought to back up and think about why you've worked so hard to avoid her all this time."

"How about she's weird and a pain in the butt?"

"Only to you. The rest of us like her fine. And you know better than to judge somebody by how they look."

"Aw, hell." Jake looked away, then let out a disgruntled sigh. "Can't you see my side of this at all?"

"Sure I can," Gage said. "You've got every right to be disappointed about losing the Double Circle, but what's done is done. Get over it."

"I can't do that."

"Then maybe you need to think about finding another way to approach Hope. There's more than one way to get a ranch."

"What are you suggesting?" Jake let out a disbelieving snort of laughter. "That I marry her to get it?"

Gage shrugged. "All I know is you'll catch more flies with honey than with vinegar."

"That'd be great advice if I wanted flies, but I don't. The Double Circle is *mine,* dammit. And whatever it takes, I'm going to get it back."

Chapter Four

Two weeks later Hope dragged herself out of bed at the crack of noon and headed downstairs in the silk boxer shorts and tank top she'd worn to bed, desperate for an infusion of caffeine. She'd mailed her finished manuscript to New York the previous afternoon, then dragged Marsh and Emma off to Cal's Place, where Cal himself was tending bar. Five minutes into their celebration, he'd received a phone call announcing the birth of Zack and Lori's new baby, Kevin Patrick McBride.

People poured into the bar as the good news spread all over town and a party ensued. Hope remembered dancing to the hot country music playing on the jukebox, buying at least two rounds for the whole bar and singing show tunes at the top of her lungs.

Beyond that, her memory was a colorful blur of images and sounds that would sort themselves out. Eventually. When she finally woke up and got her heart started.

The house seemed awfully quiet, and she couldn't detect any of the usual burned-coffee odor coming from George's pitiful attempt to make it on his own. She stepped into the kitchen, the back of her neck tingling with a sense of foreboding when she saw an envelope propped against the napkin holder in the middle of the table.

She picked up the envelope and studied it. Her name was scrawled across the front in George's spidery handwriting. Her uneasiness growing, she took out the papers and began to read.

Sept. 1

Dear Hope,

You've been working so hard on your book we haven't had a chance to visit lately. Ever since you paid me for this place, I've been thinking about my fool nephew inheriting all that money. It don't sit well with me, so I'm gonna spend every penny I can before I kick off.

By the time you read this, I'll be on my way to San Francisco. From there, I'm going to Hawaii for a couple of months, and then on a cruise that'll keep me out of the cold all winter. Reckon I'll be back in time for branding.

When I told Scott I was leaving for a while, he decided to go back to Riverton and work for his brother. Said he didn't want to take orders from no dang woman. Sorry about that.

I never would've planned this trip if I'd known he'd up and quit, but at my age, it's best not to put these things off. Don't panic. You'll be all right without us.

Jake'll be over his mad by now, and he'll know what needs to be done and how to do it. I know you two ain't been getting along, but take my advice. Swallow your pride and give Jake a call. He'll help you out.

                                        Your friend,
                                        George

"Friend?" Hope wadded the letter into a tight ball and hurled it at the kitchen sink. It fell short, hitting the scuffed linoleum floor instead. "Some friend you are, you old…buzzard!"

Oh, God. He couldn't abandon her like this. Not now. He just *couldn't*. A gaping, aching hole opened up in the center of her chest. The terrifying sensation of being lost she'd felt so often as a child washed over her in arctic waves. Dammit, she'd sworn she would never allow herself to feel this way again.

She wasn't supposed to be solely responsible for hundreds of animals. Not yet. She could handle the horses, dog and cats. But the cows and the calves and the bulls were all up in the national forest on their summer range or pasture, or whatever they called it. What the hell was she supposed to do about them?

"Darn you, George, you promised to teach me ranching. And you know I can't ask Jake McBride for help. Not in this lifetime."

She'd rather shave her head with a dull razor blade. Walk through a field of cactus in her bare feet. Eat raw beef.

Shaking her fists in the air, she groaned. "If you wanted to get rid of the money, why didn't you just donate it to a homeless shelter? Or cancer research? Or the Sunshine Gap schools?''

An engine revved outside, but she wasn't expecting anyone. She hurried to a window facing the ranch yard, praying it was George coming back to tell her he'd changed his mind. The answer to her prayer was a resounding no.

A familiar pickup rolled to a stop beside her car. And speak of the devil, Jake McBride stepped out, clutching an envelope identical to the one she'd found on the table. Looking as pained and unhappy as the star of a heartburn commercial, he bounded up the steps and banged on the door.

Hope looked down at her boxers and tank top, wondered if she should run upstairs for a robe and decided not to bother. She had on more clothes now than when she went out jogging. Besides, from the sound of his pounding, he'd probably beat down the door before she could get back. Muttering, ''Yeah, yeah, keep your shirt on, McBride,'' she crossed the kitchen and yanked open the storm door. ''Is there something I can do for you?''

Jake scowled at her through the screen door. ''You can tell me what the hell's goin' on over here.''

Oh, dear. Even angry and out of sorts, he was a ridiculously attractive man. Not that she was shallow enough to notice his looks anymore. The big jerk. She straightened to her full height and crossed her arms over her breasts. ''Whatever it is, it's none of your business.''

''Wrong answer.'' He held up the envelope and jabbed it toward the screen. ''This makes it my business.''

''I don't see how that's possible,'' Hope said with her best haughty sniff. ''I didn't send it to you.''

"George did," Jake ground out through clenched teeth, a muscle ticking on the side of his jaw.

"This isn't George's property anymore."

"He said you're here all alone and you need help."

"George says a lot of things that aren't true."

"Where's Scott?"

"I have no idea."

Jake's scowl deepened. He tipped back the brim of his Stetson and pinched the bridge of his nose with one hand. "You fired him?"

"That's none of your business, either, Mr. McBride."

"Dammit, Hope, just answer me. Did you fire Scott?"

"No, I did not." That much was the truth.

Jake inhaled a harsh breath and she could almost hear him counting inside his hard head. "Does Scott still work for you?"

"Why do you want to know?"

"If he doesn't, I'm going to help you run this place."

It was all she could do not to gape at him. Of all the nerve. He honestly expected simply to walk in here and take over her ranch without so much as asking for permission? If she allowed him to do that she had no doubt whatsoever he'd move right on to finding a way to take the Double Circle away from her.

Well, it wasn't going to happen. Not while she was still breathing, anyway. How stupid did he think she was?

"No, you're not." She looked him straight in the eye. "The Double Circle is my responsibility. I don't need or want your help."

"For God's sake, don't be an idiot." He pulled open the screen door and raised one foot as if he would step inside without an invitation.

Infuriated at his presumption, she held up one hand

like a cop stopping traffic. "Don't even think about coming in. You're not welcome here."

Jake gaped at her for ten full seconds, then muttered, "You don't mean that."

"I most certainly do," she insisted. "Try coming around here again, and I'll get a restraining order."

"Come on, Hope, that's ridiculous."

"Go home, Jake. This conversation is pointless."

"How do you know that when we haven't even had it yet?"

"The last time we spoke you made it abundantly clear that we have nothing to discuss. I've stayed the hell out of your way. I expect you to return the favor."

He had the grace to flush and look away. "Aw, that was just my temper talking. I got over it."

"Well, goody for you. I didn't. And you're the last person I'd ever trust to help me with anything."

"That's a pretty cynical attitude."

"I prefer to call it being realistic. You've made it perfectly clear you don't respect me. Since I don't want to create problems for Blair, I'll be polite to you in public, but I don't have to put up with you in my own home. Now, get off my land and don't come back."

"Dammit, Hope, you can't do—"

"Watch me, cowboy." She grabbed the edge of the storm door, slammed it shut and locked it. For several seconds they stared at each other through the glass. Then Jake turned and strode down the steps to his truck. Holding her breath, Hope waited, straining to hear the sound of his pickup starting.

When she heard him drive away, she raced upstairs to get dressed. She had animals to feed and arrangements to make. She didn't need Jake's help, but she needed *somebody's* help.

Thank God for telephones and the Internet. With those lovely technologies she could find out anything she wanted to know. She might be scared to death over the enormity of what she'd gotten herself into, but no one would ever see her fear. That was Rule Number Three.

And it was high time Jake McBride discovered that he wasn't the center of the universe. She'd finally found a place that felt like a real home, and nobody was going to take it away from her.

"Damn fool woman," Jake muttered, finding himself battling a confusing array of thoughts and feelings as he drove away from the Double Circle.

He'd never been thrown off anybody's land before, never been told he wasn't welcome, never been threatened with a restraining order. But he believed she'd meant every word of her threat. The thought of anyone disliking him that much angered and upset him.

At the same time, the mental picture of Hope standing there in bright red boxer shorts and a skimpy little tank top, with her hair all rumpled in a just-crawled-out-of-bed tangle had stirred up his libido and made him remember what it had felt like to kiss her and hold her close.

Lord have mercy, the thought of her all riled up and passionate, spitting those words at him and hissing like an enraged kitten tickled his funny bone and made him want to soothe her fury with kisses and caresses…hell, he wanted to take her to bed and keep her there until they both were too exhausted to be angry anymore.

And then he remembered the pain she'd tried but failed to hide when she'd said he didn't respect her or want her there and a nasty little kernel of guilt started nagging at his conscience. He could see how she'd come to the conclusion she couldn't trust him, and he felt lower than a snake's belly in a wagon rut for hurting her feelings.

He hadn't had to deal with a woman's tender emotions in a hell of a long time and he obviously wasn't very good at it. Never really had been, now that he thought about it. He didn't know how to apologize worth a damn, either.

Worst of all, he didn't like to think of Hope being all alone over there. She was in way over her head and still really didn't understand that. When you lived this far from town, you had to be completely self-sufficient in ways she couldn't expect to be.

What if her pump went out and she couldn't get any water for herself or the animals? What if the power went out? Did she have a clue about starting the generator? He doubted it. What if she got hurt working with the horses or just doing the chores?

She could lie there in agony for hours—maybe even days—and nobody'd know there was anything wrong. The people at the Flying M were her closest neighbors. Even if she wasn't Blair's cousin, she had a right to expect them to lend her a hand when she was in trouble.

He'd been raised to take care of women and protect them. Any ranch was a dangerous place. He'd never forgive himself if something bad happened to Hope because she wouldn't ask for help when she needed it.

Shoot, he'd been so dang mean to her, if she accidentally stepped on a metal trap, she'd probably chew off her own foot before she'd ask him for help.

It was hard to believe that the funny, determined little gal who'd chased after him and looked at him with such blatant adoration had written him off. She didn't even consider him a friend—hell, she thought he was some lowlife scum who might actually harm her livestock in order to get his hands on the Double Circle.

But he was a rancher, dammit. One of the good guys. He prized his good name above all else. Realizing anyone could reasonably question his integrity the way Hope had just questioned it struck at the core of who he was now, always had been and ever hoped to be.

And it hurt.

That was when it hit him. Being dismissed stunk to high heaven. This must be exactly how Hope had felt when he'd called her a flaky little California floozy.

Looking back now, he could hardly believe he'd ever said such a rude and thoughtless thing to her or anyone else. What in the world had gotten into him? Fear? Panic? Stupidity? All of the above.

After Ellen had died, he'd buried his emotions in a deep freeze and been more than happy to leave 'em there. Then Hope had come along, poking and prodding at him with her energy, her sunny smiles and weird hair, and her sexy clothes and innuendoes. She'd finally thawed him out enough to feel things again.

He hadn't liked it at first. Reminded him of that fierce, needlelike tingling you got when your foot went to sleep and the blood started flowing into it again. He wasn't too sure he liked it any better now, but he had to admit he felt alive again. And there was no going back.

Now there was a scary thought if he'd ever had one.

He shook his head in an attempt at denial, then reluctantly admitted the truth. There *was* no going back to the deep freeze, and in all honesty, he didn't want to go back. He wanted...

Well, for starters, he wanted Hope's respect back. He wanted her friendship and her trust. He wanted her body, too, but he had too many miles of fence to mend before he could even think about that.

Of course, he still wanted the Double Circle, but not this way. It was stupid to get so worked up about Hope buying it when all he had to do was wait her out. There was no way a sophisticated woman like her would be content to stay in a backwater like Sunshine Gap for long.

When she got sick and tired of all the work and stress of trying to run a ranch, she'd sell out and go back to L.A. where she belonged. How long could it take?

He'd give her a while to cool off, and keep an eye on the Double Circle from a distance to make sure she was all right. And to make sure she wasn't screwing up his ranch too much. Then he'd figure out a way to call a truce.

Stubborn as Hope was, it might take months for her to come to her senses. He didn't want to be at war with her that long. He didn't want to be at war with her at all.

It was a warm, lazy Saturday afternoon two weeks later when Kevin Patrick McBride was baptized at St. Mary's Church in Sunshine Gap with his entire extended family in attendance. To Hope's delight, even Blair and Dillon had come all the way from California for the ceremony.

Sitting beside Blair in the second pew, Hope found the baptism and the atmosphere of love surrounding the child unbearably touching. She could barely breathe for the lump in her throat and the ache in her chest. She felt silly. This was a happy occasion and it was all she could do to blink back the tears that kept trying to fill her eyes.

And Blair, who kept dabbing at her eyes with a soggy-looking tissue, seemed to be suffering the same malady. Hope found it perplexing.

She and Blair were the ones who came from the picture-perfect background. Their family was famous, cultured and blessed with every material advantage money could buy. But Hope couldn't remember any DuMaine family gathering getting to her or to Blair the way this simple christening was.

The McBrides weren't a perfect family; they didn't even try to look like one. According to Blair, the seven McBride cousins had had some horrendous arguments during the past year. What was it about this family that made them seem so special? Unable to answer, Hope focused her attention on the baptism.

Grace McBride Sullivan was the godmother; Jake was the godfather. Hope watched him standing up front, looking so big, strong and handsome in his dark suit, white shirt and bolo tie. His face and voice were solemn as he responded to the priest, his eyes surprisingly gentle whenever he looked at the baby.

With every passing moment, Hope found her anger toward Jake softening. He'd acted like a jerk, but she had no doubt that he was a good man at heart. It was difficult to despise a man who looked at his brother's child with such tenderness.

She'd bought the Double Circle for a lot of reasons, some of which she was still figuring out. But she'd bought it knowing it would provoke Jake. She regretted the enmity between them, but she'd tried to heal the breach once. She didn't have the courage or the energy to try again.

During the past two weeks she'd learned many painful lessons about ranching. She looked down at her hands and grimaced at the scabs and partially healed blisters on her palms. Her long, glamorous fingernails literally had bitten the dust after her first day of chores. The pale natural fingernails underneath them were, in a word, *ugly*.

Muscles in her arms and shoulders she hadn't even known she owned ached from dragging around bales of hay and hauling water. She was so blasted awkward at most of the chores, she was collecting new bruises on top of old ones. She shifted on the wooden pew, easing pressure on the one she'd gotten on her right buttock yesterday when a frisky colt had kicked her.

She'd kill for a hot tub, her old masseuse and a full night's sleep. It was one thing to know intellectually that ranching was hard, dirty work that never ended. The full reality hadn't sunk in until she'd found herself completely responsible for the land and the animals she owned. But somehow, she'd coped.

Goodness, it was warm in here. Her legs felt as if she hadn't sat down in days. Her eyelids weighed a ton, but she was afraid to close them for fear she'd fall asleep and start snoring in front of all these people.

She forced herself to sit up straighter and hid a yawn behind her fingers. No one in Sunshine Gap was going to know how hard she'd been struggling to get through each day. Especially not Jake McBride. She would never give him the satisfaction of admitting the Double Circle was more than she'd bargained for. Not if it took every bit of acting skill she'd inherited and every makeup trick she'd ever learned while hanging around movie sets.

Hope DuMaine might not be as hardy as some of the Wyoming ranch women were, but she was hardly the ninny Jake thought she was. And she was more resourceful than he thought, too. If she could hold on for two more weeks, reinforcements would arrive and she would make it.

Lord, just thinking about her to-do list left Hope feeling exhausted and discouraged. No wonder Jake had tried so hard to warn her. He must be an organizational genius to handle everything that went on at the Flying M, which was three times the size of her spread.

Maybe she was crazy to think she could do this. Maybe she should give up now and save herself and all those animals a lot of grief. She glanced around the little church and felt her heart clench in automatic protest. No. She couldn't quit.

As terrifying as all of this new responsibility was, she loved the Double Circle and the community of Sunshine Gap. It was becoming home to her in ways she'd never had a home before.

The people here had quickly gotten over any undue interest in her celebrity. Nobody followed her around with a camera or asked for her autograph. When she went into town they treated her the same way they treated each other—with a warm, deeply personal courtesy she'd never found anywhere else. She felt like a real person here, not some exotic creature who deserved deference because of an accident of birth. She was absolutely loathe to give any of it up and go back to L.A.

The service ended. Hope's reverie ended as well, and she got up to follow Blair and Dillon out of the pew. Unwilling to intrude on a private family moment, Hope hung back while the others converged on the parents and godparents, everyone oohing and ahhing over the baby.

She jumped at a sudden touch on her arm and found her friend Emma McBride standing there, studying the group at the front of the church, her eyes wide and anxious.

"Emma?" Hope said. "What's wrong?"

"Nothing much." Emma's voice sounded strangely high and breathless. "Let's step outside."

"Whatever you say." Hope accompanied Emma through the doorway and out into the late-afternoon sunshine. The second they were assured of privacy, Hope demanded, "What's up? Why are you so freaked out?"

Emma gulped, then cleared her throat. "I'm uh...oh, jeez, Hope. I'm going to have one."

"One what?" Hope asked, worriedly searching Emma's face for a clue before comprehension dawned. "You mean a *baby?* Emma, that's wonderful!"

"Shhh," Emma hissed, glancing around as if she feared being overheard. "Cal doesn't know about it yet."

"Why not? He'll be thrilled."

"Yeah, but I'm not. Thrilled, I mean," Emma whispered. "I'm scared out of my mind."

"Oh, Emma, no. I'm sure giving birth is difficult, but you'll get through it."

"It's not *that,*" Emma said.

"Then what is it?" Hope asked.

"I don't know how to be a mother," Emma said. "I'll be terrible at it and then Cal will hate me and—"

Understanding at last, Hope wrapped her arms around Emma's waist and hugged her. She knew Emma had grown up in foster care. No wonder she was having doubts about her own ability to become a mother.

"Hush," Hope scolded. "You'll be a great mommy. You'll love that baby and that's the most important thing."

"But didn't you see how tiny and helpless Kevin is? I don't know anything about babies. Or little kids."

"You don't have to know everything today. We'll

research it just like I do when I'm writing a new book. We'll take classes. Practice on dolls. Buy books and look for information on the Internet. Call in experts.''

"That might help." Emma still sounded unconvinced.

"You won't be raising this kid all alone," Hope said. "Cal will help. Lori, Grace and Alex have all been through it. They'll be delighted to help you."

"They'll think I'm an idiot." Emma gulped again and sniffled. "I love being part of this family, but I still don't know all the rules. And sometimes I feel so inadequate. I know more about fixing pickups and tractors than I do about having a baby."

"Em?" At the sound of a deep voice coming from right behind them, Hope and Emma started, then slowly turned to face a wide-eyed Cal McBride.

"Em?" he said again, his voice sounding raw and strained. "Is there something you need to tell me?"

"Oh, Cal." Emma's voice wobbled. "I'm... pregnant."

He gaped at her for a second, looking positively stunned. "Are you sure?"

She nodded. He took a deep breath. Then a silly grin tugged at the corners of his mouth and he opened his arms to his trembling wife. Emma lunged into them, sobbing softly while he gathered her close and rested his forehead against hers.

Kissing her hair, he whispered fervently, "Aw, Emmy, that's the best news in the whole world. God, I love you."

Bleeding inside, Hope turned away from the exquisite intimacy of the moment and hurried to her car. She had never felt more alone. What on earth was wrong with her today, that every emotion felt amplified to the max?

Cal let out a whoop and shouted the news to everyone

within a mile radius. Hope turned back in time to see him whirl Emma around in a circle while the rest of the McBrides converged on them. With her husband's arms securely wrapped around her, Emma's eyes had lost their anxiety and her face literally glowed with happiness.

Hope was happy—no, she was ecstatic—for her friend. Nobody deserved to be happy more than Emma did. After growing up with nothing, she'd found a good man who adored the very ground she walked on. Who accepted her and loved her, warts, insecurities and all. She also had the support of that big, loving family, work she enjoyed and a baby on the way.

It all looked so perfect and wonderful, Hope longed for just some of what Emma had. For a while she'd thought she might find happiness with Jake, but he hadn't wanted her enough to look past the surface to the real Hope DuMaine. She was very much afraid no man ever would.

Some women were meant to have that kind of love. Too bad she wasn't one of them, no matter how hard she tried to find it. Hope turned toward the mountains, which were becoming her symbol of permanence.

Enough of this silly pity party. Rule Number Four was focus on what you *do* have. Not on what you don't.

She was home now. She was going to make a success of running the Double Circle or die trying. And she was going to prove to herself, if not to Jake McBride, that she was more than a flaky little California floozy.

Chapter Five

After the baptism, everyone gathered at Cal's Place for a party. By definition a McBride family party included a sit-down dinner, hours of gabbing and some dancing to top it all off. Mindful of Hope's promise to be civil to him in public, Jake figured this was liable to be his best chance to propose a truce between them.

With so many McBrides around, she couldn't slap his face or stomp off with her drawers in a wad. He'd been trying to pull her aside for a private conversation ever since they'd left the church. So far he'd had no luck whatsoever.

Hope wasn't cooperating.

Not that he'd really expected her to. Nothing was ever easy with that woman. Every time he started to approach her, she skittered off in the opposite direction like a spider on a hot rock. And she was so dang slick about it, nobody else appeared to notice what she was doing.

Dinner had ended over an hour ago. They'd all moved into the bar to take advantage of the dance floor and he was damn tired of chasing after her. He was also starting to feel a tad desperate.

She looked tired, and he felt a twinge of guilt. He should be helping her. According to his sources, she only had his cousin Grace's boys, Riley and Steven, working for her now. At thirteen and eleven, they were good boys and good hands, but she needed somebody with more experience for the long haul.

There was a lot to do at this time of year to get ready for winter. If it didn't get done, defenseless animals would suffer. So would Hope.

If she left this party before he could corner her, he wouldn't have another opportunity this good until Halloween, and he didn't want to live with this kind of tension for that long. For one thing, when he was faced with something unpleasant to do, he'd rather go after it and get it behind him than try to avoid it. For another, the longer it went on, the more likely it became that somebody in the family would pick up on a problem between them and feel compelled to meddle.

Which, undoubtedly, would pull other family members into the conflict. He needed that like he needed an outbreak of mad cow disease. His dad was already watching him with a jaundiced eye as it was.

Aw, shoot, there was no help for it. He was gonna have to ask Hope to dance. It wouldn't be any hardship. Today her hair was that reddish-brown color he liked so much, and she looked mighty pretty in a soft, surprisingly demure blue dress. Demure for Hope, anyway.

He would've asked her before this, but the last time he'd danced with her, he'd lost his mind and kissed her in front of God and everybody. Why risk a repeat? He doubted he was demented enough to do it again, but whenever Hope was around, the damnedest things just sort of…happened.

Still, this dance wouldn't be about any unfortunate attraction he might feel toward Hope. It was business. Yeah. That's all it was. Business.

With that thought firmly planted in his mind, Jake gave up any pretense of subtlety and plowed straight through the crowd toward the table Hope was sharing with Blair and Dillon. Hope immediately raised her head and glanced around, reminding him of a deer catching scent of a predator. The idea she might have the same sensitive radar about his presence he had about hers gave him a grim sense of satisfaction.

After all she'd put him through, she deserved to suffer a little discomfort.

Arriving at the table, he smiled at her. Her eyes widened for a second, then narrowed. Her lips mashed together in a tight line. Her forehead wrinkled up, and he imagined he could see little red puffs of temper shooting out the top of her head. The silly notion made him want to laugh, but he managed to restrain himself.

He held out his hand to her. "Dance with me, Hope?"

Since she'd danced with all of the other guys in the family, there was no polite way for her refuse. He knew it. She knew it. And she knew he knew it, which probably made her feel trapped like a rat. His smile widened.

She let out a quiet sigh that still reeked of resignation and irritation. Then she took his hand and allowed him to help her to her feet. Her hand felt small in his, and touching her skin-to-skin revved his pulse an extra notch as he led her toward the dance floor.

Feeling some unexpected bumps and ridges on her palm, he turned her hand over and blinked at the angry-looking, half-healed blisters, nicks and cuts he discovered. He stopped walking, reached over and took hold of her other hand. It was even more abused than the first one.

"What the…" he muttered, appalled when he remembered how soft and smooth her hands had always been before. "What've you been doing?"

Her fingers curled into her palms. "Working." Expressive eyes shot warning sparks at him. "What else?"

She tried to yank her hands away, but Jake wasn't ready to let them go just yet. "It looks like you've been diggin' ditches. They still hurt?"

She shrugged as if it didn't matter whether they did or not. "If they disgust you, you certainly don't have to dance with me."

"I've seen worse."

"Will you please let go now? People are staring."

"Let 'em." Hanging on tight in case she decided to bolt, he resumed their trek to the dance floor, then took her into his arms and started shuffling his feet in time to the ballad the band was playing. "You've been workin' real hard."

She felt good in his arms. Too damn good. Don't think about that. This was business.

Hope raised her chin to its most haughty angle and gave him a princess-to-peasant look. He didn't know how she could look down her nose at him when she was a good head shorter than he was, but she managed it. Lord, but it tickled him. Made him want to kiss all the starch right out of her. But he wasn't going to think about that, either.

This was business.

"Did you think I couldn't do manual labor?" she demanded.

He gave a low chuckle and shook his head in mock confusion. "Honey, you're just about the most contrary, unpredictable creature I've ever come across. When it comes to you, I never know what to think."

She scowled at him, but he suspected she was secretly pleased at his admission. "Then why did you ask me to dance?"

"I want a truce. I don't like all this hostility."

Her eyebrows shot halfway up her forehead. "You started it."

"That's debatable." He saw angry words trembling on her soft, kissable lips and hurried to cut them off before she could drag him into another argument. "It doesn't matter who started it. Let's end it here and now."

"Why?"

"Because you were right. We're going to run into each other all the time, and feuding's not good. We should at least try to be friends."

"I'm not selling you my ranch, Jake."

"I don't expect you to."

"You don't?" Her expression underlined the skepticism in her voice. Must be all of those acting genes.

"Not any time soon," Jake said. "I'll give you eighteen months at the outside. After nursemaiding a bunch of dumb Herefords that long, you'll probably get this notion of playing cowgirl out of your system and go back where you belong."

She laughed and shook her head. "You wish, Mc-Bride."

He shrugged. "It's a risk I'm willing to take. In the meantime, we don't have to be enemies. You promise me that if and when you want to sell the Double Circle, you'll let me have first crack at it, then there's no reason we can't be friends.''

''You wouldn't sell it to a developer, would you?''

''Hell no.''

''Would you let George keep his room until he dies?''

''What's that all about?'' Jake asked.

''Those were George's conditions for selling me the Double Circle. He doesn't want to end up in a nursing home or at the mercy of someone he doesn't know. I can't sell the Double Circle to someone who won't meet those conditions.''

''All right,'' Jake said after a moment's consideration. ''I could live with that.''

''Then *if*—and that's a very large if—I ever decide I want to sell the Double Circle, I'll offer it to you first.''

''For fair market value.''

''Agreed.''

Jake felt as if a hard, painful knot in the center of his chest had come loose. He spun Hope away from him, then pulled her back. ''Thanks. I appreciate it.''

''You're welcome. But don't get your hopes up. I really do like it here.''

''Find a replacement for Scott yet?''

''I'm not discussing my business with you, Jake.''

''Aw, come on, you don't need to worry about me doing anything to hurt your operation.''

''And I should believe you because…?''

He executed a quick turn that brought her flush against him. Jeez, it felt good. Too good, dammit. He eased her a little away from him and struggled to recapture his train of thought. ''Look at it this way. If I expect to buy your ranch someday, I'll want it to be in good shape when I get it. Doesn't that make sense?''

She pursed her lips, but he saw a grin lurking at the

corners of her mouth. "Strangely enough, it does. And it worries me when you make sense."

"Does that mean you're willing to bury the hatchet somewhere besides the back of my head?"

She rolled her eyes and acted as if she was thinking real hard about it. "Okay, McBride. You've got a deal. We'll call a truce."

"So, have you found a replacement for Scott?"

"I hired one yesterday."

"Anybody I know?"

"You might. She grew up on a ranch near a place called Buffalo. Her name is Bonnie Jorgenson."

Jake turned the name over in his mind, then slowly shook his head. "Nope. Name's not familiar. How'd you find her?"

"She's a graduate student at the University of Wyoming. She comes highly recommended by the head of the Animal Science Department."

"If she's a student, why isn't she in school?"

"She had to take a year off to earn some money. I offered her more than she was making at her old job. And since she's going to be the manager of a working ranch, one of her professors offered her an independent study project. She'll be earning money and college credit at the same time."

"Sounds like a good deal. When does she start?"

"I'm expecting her around the first of October."

"Who's handling everything for you in the meantime?"

"I am. Riley and Steven are helping with chores and Marsh is advising me."

"Marsh barely knows a cow from a bull," Jake said. "Got your cows off those forest service leases yet?"

"Not yet. Riley's going to take me up on the mountain next weekend and show me how to round them up."

Jake missed a step. "You're going to need more help if you wait that long to get started. George was running three hundred pairs and you've gotta get all of those animals out of there before October first."

Hope's big blue eyes widened and a crease appeared in the middle of her forehead. "But that's too soon. Why October first?"

"That's when hunting season starts. Some of those idiots get so excited, they can't tell the difference between a deer and a Hereford or a horse and rider. Believe me, you don't want to be up in those woods when they're all trampin' around with their loaded rifles."

"I see." Hope's voice had grown faint and she looked as if she might be feeling slightly sick. Jake figured she probably didn't like the idea of hunting much.

"And," he went on, "at that elevation, it could snow anytime. You need to move 'em down close to the ranch so you can get feed to 'em when the snow starts stacking up."

"I'll get right on it then."

"You're not going up there by yourself."

Hope's eyes glinted with temper and he realized he could've softened that order into a suggestion. Rather than tearing a strip off his hide, however, she let out a quiet sigh and said, "No, I'll call the employment service in Cody on Monday."

"Don't do that," Jake said. "You won't find any decent hands this time of year, anyway. We'll help you."

"I couldn't impose on you like that. You've all got more than enough of your own work to do."

"It's no big deal. I'll put a crew together and we'll get it all done in plenty of time."

"Oh, but—"

Jake cut her off with a firm shake of his head. "When you get in a bind around here, your neighbors pitch in. And you're more than a neighbor, you're family. You know what that means."

"Not really, but—"

"That's how we've always done things out here. Next time we're short-handed, you'll be first on our list to call."

"I don't know what to say."

"Say yes. And you know something? There's an easy way you could return the favor."

"What's that?"

"Let me be your ranch manager until Bonnie arrives. I know your herd. I know which cows you ought to ship and which ones you'll want to keep. And I can help you get ready for winter so Bonnie'll have an easier transition into the job."

"It sounds great for me, but how would that help you?"

"It'll keep me out of prison," Jake said with a chuckle.

"That sounds a bit desperate."

"That's a good word for it. I'm desperate to get away from Dad and Uncle Harry for a while. They're driving me nuts."

"What's the problem?"

"They're bored," Jake said. "They didn't mind retirement when they were off gallivanting around the world, seeing and doing new things every day, but they're both too young to be retired. They're breathing down my neck all the time. According to them I haven't done one thing right, even though the ranch has shown a nice profit since I took over."

"That hardly seems fair."

"I was expecting it," Jake admitted with a grin. "It'll serve them right to have to do my job for a few weeks."

"Do you really think it'll help?"

It wouldn't solve all of his problems with the Papas, but at least he'd know what was going on at the Double Circle and he wouldn't have to worry about Hope being all alone over there anymore. "Can't hurt."

"Will you teach me about what you're doing? I want to learn how to do everything myself."

"You bet. We'll start Monday morning, and by the time your gal Bonnie arrives, you'll know all kinds of stuff. I'll even fix up the bunkhouse while I'm staying there."

Hope tilted her head a little to one side while she thought about it. Then she nodded and finally, *finally* gave him what he hadn't consciously realized he'd been waiting for—an honest-to-God, sincere, Hope DuMaine smile. Warm, sweet and pretty as a mountain sunrise. His breath backed up in his chest, and his nerve endings practically sizzled.

He saw her lips move. Knew she was speaking, even that she was agreeing with him. But the thinking part of his brain already had given way to a far more primitive section. His heart did a funny little lurch, his skin suddenly heated and that same irresistible urge to kiss her he'd felt at the wedding reception assaulted him again.

Before he could do anything stupid, however, someone tapped on his right shoulder. He turned and found himself eye-to-eye with his dad.

"What're you doing?" Jake asked.

"What does it look like?" Gage McBride retorted. "I'm cuttin' in 'cause I want to dance with this pretty little gal. Ya mind?"

Yeah, Jake realized. He *did* mind. Of all the times for his dad to interrupt him, this was the most annoying Jake could remember. Unfortunately he could hardly refuse. Not without an explanation he wasn't prepared to give. Hoping his reluctance didn't show too much, Jake stepped back and released Hope.

He watched her two-step away in his dad's arms, painfully conscious of the sudden emptiness of his own. He wanted her back, dammit. Wanted to hold her close again. Get her someplace private and… No. No, he didn't. He wasn't going to allow himself to think like that.

This was *business.*

There was no sense in complicating things with a bunch of overactive hormones. It shouldn't be so blasted hard to remember that. But it was.

His dad twirled Hope and her short, full skirt billowed out around her, flashing a tantalizing glimpse of her slender thighs. Jake's mouth went dry. His heart did another one of those funny lurches. His body hardened so fast he felt dizzy.

Business? Yeah, right. He'd never been much good at lying to himself. Damn, but he needed a drink.

Hope had always liked Gage McBride. He was a handsome, silver-haired version of Jake. Though he tended to be quieter than some members of the family, he had a relaxed charm that immediately put her at ease.

"So how do you like bein' a rancher, Miss Hope?" he asked with a smile that reminded her of his eldest son.

"Just fine, Mr. McBride."

"Call me Gage, hon, or I'll think you're talking about my old man. I don't mean to pry, but I know Jake's had his nose out of joint ever since you bought George's place. Was he giving you a hard time just now?''

Touched by his obvious concern, Hope shook her head. "Not at all. Jake was proposing a truce."

"You don't say," Gage said, his tone thoughtful. "Any conditions?"

"Only that I promise to sell him the Double Circle when I decide I don't want to be a rancher anymore."

"How long did he give you?"

"Eighteen months at the outside."

Gage chuckled. "Poor fool doesn't know you very well."

"No, he doesn't," Hope agreed.

"Well, he's pretty green when it comes to handling women."

"How can you say that?" Hope asked, surprised anyone would describe Jake that way. "He was married for a long time, and I've had the impression it was a good marriage."

"It was a great marriage," Gage said, "but it was real unusual. Jake and Ellen clicked way back when they were little kids and never dated anyone else. Those two were just naturally so compatible, they didn't have to work at getting along the way most couples do. I swear they could read each other's minds."

"Oh, my," Hope murmured, her heart aching on Jake's behalf. Such a loss must've been devastating. "That sounds like an impossible act for anyone to follow."

"Hard, but not impossible," Gage said. "It'll take a real patient woman to teach Jake all the stuff most guys learn by trial and error from a whole string of girl-friends."

"Such as?"

"Oh, how to compromise. When to tell a gal how you feel and when to shut the heck up." Gage grinned wickedly. "My son's a good man, but he's a tad short on tact. You may have noticed that about him."

Hope sputtered with laughter. "You make him sound like a bad case of arrested development."

"In some ways, that's exactly what he is. He doesn't know it, of course, and that's why he needs a patient woman. Taking him on would be quite a challenge."

"That's an understatement, Gage."

Gage shrugged. "Well, don't forget the upside of having a guy like Jake."

"What's that?"

"He's no playboy. If he gives you his heart, he'll be as loyal as they come."

"I can get the same thing from a dog with a lot less aggravation," Hope drawled.

Gage choked on a laugh. "Good one. And that's exactly why you'd be perfect for Jake. You'd keep him in line just fine. I guess the question is, are you still interested in trying?"

Hope shook her head. "Actually, I've decided it's time to give up on anything more than a friendship with Jake."

"Aw, don't do that," Gage protested. "I'll admit he's been slow on the uptake lately, but you mark my words, he'll come around. You'd be great together."

"What makes you think so?"

"Well, honey, I don't know about you Californians, but here in Wyoming, we generally don't kiss gals we think of as friends the way Jake kissed you at the wedding." Gage's dark eyes glinted with humor. "I've never seen my boy do anything like that before, and I hope I never do again. It was downright embarrassing to watch.''

''But we don't have much in common,'' Hope pointed out, feeling her face heating at the memory.

''Shoot, you both speak English.'' Gage laughed and his eyes took on a faraway cast, as if he were seeing a scene from his own memory. ''That's more'n Mary and I had goin' for us. If you love each other enough, your differences won't matter.''

Hope looked over toward the bar where she'd last spotted Jake. He was still standing there, holding a drink in one hand and looking right back at her. His eyes dark and compelling, he met and held her gaze. His lips slowly curved into a smile, making her pulse sprint and her breath catch. Carefully masking her reaction, she turned back to Gage.

''Well?'' Gage asked. ''Are you? Interested, I mean?''

''Maybe,'' Hope said, ''but I won't chase after him again.''

''Don't think you'll have to,'' he replied with a chuckle. ''Here he comes now. Thanks for the dance, hon.''

In the next heartbeat Gage handed her off to Jake. After a few steps Jake said, ''What's he up to?''

Hope laughed and shook her head. ''I don't think you really want to know.''

''He was matchmaking, wasn't he?''

''I'm afraid so.''

''Great. Did he mention I've got all my own teeth?''

''He didn't get quite that far, but he did mention a few of your finer points.''

Jake chuckled. ''Oh, yeah? What were they?''

"Never mind. Are you absolutely sure you want to help me with the Double Circle?"

"You having second thoughts about that?"

"And third, fourth and fifth thoughts. I really didn't plan to involve you, Jake. I wanted to do it all myself."

"Nobody runs a ranch alone," Jake said. "And you got help with your chores and a manager hired. That was a decent enough start for the time you've had."

"I still don't like having you bail me out of a problem."

Jake executed a quick turn before Dillon and Blair ran into them. "Don't sweat it. If any one of my brothers or sisters had been in your position, they'd have dumped the whole thing in my lap in a heartbeat. At least you tried to solve your own problems."

Hope returned his smile and felt a fierce tug of attraction in the center of her body. The irony of it didn't escape her notice. She'd been so angry at him when she'd arrived at this party, she could barely stand to speak to him. But in the space of the past hour, they'd not only called a truce, they'd become allies of sorts.

Deep inside her most secret heart, she still wished they could be…close friends. Well, all right, she'd admit it. She still wanted to be more than friends with Jake. A lot more. Silly her.

"It won't be so bad having me around," Jake said. "I promise you won't regret it."

"Uh-huh. Is that anything like the check's in the mail?"

Jake tipped back his head and let out a booming laugh that made her want to provoke another one just like it. When he looked down at her again, his eyes and his smile were warm and inviting. If she didn't know better, she might think he was actually flirting with her. But Jake never flirted with her.

"You'll never know unless you say yes," he said.

"All right, we'll start Monday. Now if you'll excuse me, I need to go home and do the evening chores."

Without saying another word, he escorted her from the dance floor to collect her purse and then on out to her car. The sight of him in her rearview mirror, standing on the sidewalk outside Cal's Place watching her as she drove away, stayed with her all the way back to the Double Circle.

Had she just made the biggest mistake of her life?

She'd finally gotten what she'd once thought she wanted—plenty of time to spend with Jake McBride and a chance to get to know him better. But what if she made a fool of herself over him again? No, she wasn't going to let that happen. She was an expert at hiding her thoughts and feelings from reporters. She could hide them from Jake as well.

He'd made it sound as if she was doing him a favor to let him help her at the Double Circle, but she suspected he was being kind. Or maybe this simply was a way for him to get closer to her operation and figure out how to get the Double Circle. He'd said he wouldn't do that, but…it wouldn't be the first time someone had lied to her in order to get something.

She didn't mean to be paranoid about Jake's motives for helping her, but wariness had long been a part of her nature. When there was business involved, a charming, handsome man was always dangerous. Even if he was a good old Wyoming cowboy.

Jake stood on the sidewalk outside Cal's Place, watching Hope drive away with an uneasy, restless sensation roiling inside him. He didn't want to go back to the party, but he didn't want to go home. He didn't want to think about what he really wanted, either.

"Hey, Jake." Dillon stepped outside and ambled across the sidewalk to join him. "What're you doin' out here?"

Jake shot his cousin a grin. "Getting a little fresh air. What about you?"

Dillon's answering grin distorted the network of scar tissue on the left side of his face, but he looked so happy and relaxed, the old scars barely made an impression. "I'm escapin' all that talk about babies in there. I expect Blair'll be wantin' one before long."

Jake leaned one shoulder against a lamppost. "I suppose you'd rather have Blair all to yourself for a while."

"Maybe for a little while," Dillon agreed with a chuckle. "But that boy of Zack's is a piece of work. It'll be fun to have some little squirts running around the ranch again."

Remembering the more dangerous escapades his other nephews and his niece had gotten into when they were little kids, Jake grimaced. "I don't know if my heart can take that much excitement."

"I hear you." After a companionable moment of silence, Dillon said, "So, what's goin' on with you and Hope?"

"Nothing," Jake answered, the denial as automatic as his next breath. Dillon was a good guy, but there were some things a smart man didn't talk about.

"That's funny. A little bird told me I missed one hell of a hot kiss between you two at our wedding reception." Dillon's grin turned wicked. "You should've done it before we left on our honeymoon. I'd have paid good money to see that."

"Wasn't any big deal." Jake's face felt hot in spite of his efforts to act casual.

"That's not the way I heard it." Hands in his trouser pockets, Dillon gazed at the grocery store across the street. "The little bird also said after that kiss, you two disappeared about the same time and the next day, she left the Flying M."

"It's none of your damn business."

"Hope is real important to my wife." Dillon's tone was mild, but there was a hint of steel in his voice, too. "That makes her real important to me."

"You don't say."

"Yup. Did you know Hope jumped on my case last summer? Told me in no uncertain terms that if I hurt Blair I'd answer to her. And I'm telling you, the woman had blood in her eyes."

Jake chuckled at the mental picture Dillon's words invoked. "Yeah, I can see her doing that. But why are you telling me?"

"Hope needs somebody to stick up for her the way she stuck up for Blair. I'm that somebody."

"Are you warning me off?" Jake asked, incredulous.

"Do I need to?"

"Hell, no. I mean, me and *Hope?* The idea's ridiculous."

"You could do a lot worse than Hope. But if you're not willing to be serious about her, keep your damn hands off her."

"Or else what?"

"Or else you'll answer to me. She's practically my sister-in-law and I won't tolerate you hurting her. Got that?"

"No problem," Jake said. Yeah, right. With Hope, there was always a problem. "We're barely friends."

"Didn't look that way when you were dancing with her a few minutes ago. You looked damn cozy. Blair thought so too."

"I'm going to help her at the Double Circle, but that's all there is to it. We've got nothing in common."

"Blair and I didn't either, but it hasn't mattered a bit." Dillon leered and wiggled his eyebrows. "Tell you the truth, our differences make life sort of interesting."

Jake snorted. "I'm glad it's working out so well for you two, but any fool can see I'm too old for Hope."

Dillon had the gall to laugh at him. "Didn't seem to bother her much when she was chasing you all over the place."

"Be serious. She's ten years younger and she's probably gonna want kids someday."

"So? You always wanted kids."

"I'm too old for that now."

"Zack's only a year younger than you. He hasn't let it stop him."

Jake stared at Dillon. Damned if he didn't have a point. Without waiting for a response, Dillon continued. "You're not too old to have a family. You're too young to give up on having one. And you're making some pretty lame excuses for not getting involved with Hope. Why don't you be honest about what's really hanging you up here?"

Shoving his hands into his back pockets, Jake looked away. "I don't know what you're talking about."

"Liar. It's all about Ellen."

Jake felt the familiar twist in his gut at the mention of Ellen's name. The pain wasn't as intense as it once had been, but he automatically reacted with anger. "Don't bring her into this."

"Hell, somebody's got to. You know damn well she wouldn't have wanted you to stop living."

"Shut up, Dillon."

Dillon ignored the warning. "It's been eight years, Jake. You've got to move on."

Jake swallowed hard. He'd tried to move on, dammit, but his wife had been his soul mate from childhood. He'd given her everything, trying to keep her with him, at first. And later, trying to ease her dying. He didn't have anything left to give another woman. "You don't know—"

"I know all about giving up on happiness and that's what you've done." Dillon jabbed a finger at his scarred face. "If I can find someone to love me with this, you can sure as hell find someone to love you."

Jake held up one hand. "Look, I appreciate what you're trying to do, but I'm not interested in that stuff anymore."

"If you say so, Jake. But do you realize if you go on this way and you live to be as old as George, you'll be spending the next fifty-plus years alone? Is that what you want?"

Chapter Six

Hope spent the rest of the weekend preparing a bedroom for Jake, laying in a hefty supply of groceries and cooking as many meals ahead for the freezer as she could manage. Having witnessed firsthand how much the McBride men ate, she was taking no chances on running short of food. If Jake was going to help her, the least she could do was feed him.

And feed him well. He probably thought she couldn't cook, but she'd show *him*. And enjoy doing it.

A mixture of anticipation and anxiety kept her awake far into the night. She dragged herself out of bed at six o'clock on Monday morning. By the time Jake arrived on her doorstep, she'd made a pot of coffee, put a roast, potatoes and carrots in a slow cooker and taken care of the animals.

Pleased with her efforts, she went to answer his knock. He was petting a gyrating Doofus when she opened the back door. He straightened, took one look at her through the screen door and shook his head. "You can't wear that."

Hope glanced down at her outfit, then back up at him. Raising her eyebrows, she tilted her head to one side and studied him. Dark circles under his eyes told her he hadn't slept any better than she had. His blunt words and a rough edge to his voice suggested he was feeling a significant level of irritation. Oh, *goody*. She just loved the idea of spending the day with a big, cranky man. "Why not?"

He continued to stand on the back steps, scowling at her. After a moment with no answer, she let out an impatient huff and repeated her question. "Why not?"

"We're going to be all over this ranch today doing God knows what. You need work clothes."

She had on jeans, boots and a formfitting, short-sleeved T-shirt. Granted, the jeans had charming little heart-shaped cutouts down the outside leg seams and the T-shirt had a scooped neckline that revealed a hint of cleavage. But a woman could look good when she worked, couldn't she? "These *are* my work clothes."

"I mean *real* work clothes. The heavy-duty kind that'll give you some protection." He waved one hand at her feet, then rolled his eyes in obvious disgust. "And you need some real boots, for God's sake."

If she had any hackles, they'd be up and bristling, but she wasn't going to let him pick a fight with her this morning. Even if he'd forgotten it, they were supposed to be having a truce. Raising her chin, she struggled to keep her own voice calm and reasonable. "What's wrong with my boots?"

"Everything. The toes are too pointed. The heels are too small. You're liable to get that fancy hardware caught on something and hurt yourself. If you get 'em wet or muddy, they'll probably fall apart, and even the cows'll laugh themselves sick at those rhinestones.''

"Whatever.'' She tried to wither him with a glare, but she couldn't see any evidence it had worked. "I'll go shopping when I get a chance.''

Jake gave her another scowling once-over. "No way. You're definitely going to need help. Get in the pickup. We'll go into town and do it now.''

"Don't be ridiculous.''

He stared at her, then laughed and shook his head in patent disbelief. "You're standing there in saggy pink boots with rhinestones and little silver buckles and you're calling *me* ridiculous? Lady, that takes a lot of damn gall if you ask me.''

Her face heated and she wanted to kick him with the very boots he was mocking. "I didn't ask you.''

The wretched man laughed again. "Hey, if you want to be a rancher, you've got to have the right tools to do the job. It's as simple as that. You're wasting time with all this arguing.''

Muttering a string of uncomplimentary adjectives to describe him, she marched back into the kitchen. With her purse tucked under her arm, she filled a mug with coffee, carried it outside and shoved it into his hands.

He held up the mug. "What's this for?''

"I'm hoping it'll improve your disposition.''

"How much poison did you put in it?'' He didn't exactly smile, but his dark eyes glinted with humor.

"Not enough to do any good.''

He blew on it, then took a tentative sip and grinned at her. "You can't dress worth a damn, DuMaine, but George was right when he said you brew a mean cup of coffee.'' He took another swallow, waved her toward the passenger seat and climbed in behind the steering wheel.

She rolled her eyes, then said without any real heat, ''Shut up, McBride.''

Chuckling, he started the engine. Tension hummed between them during the ride into Sunshine Gap. Neither of them spoke, and Hope repeatedly found herself glancing at Jake. More often than not, he was glancing back at her.

The instant they made eye contact, he'd whip his head toward the windshield. She'd turn back to her side window and they'd both pretend they hadn't been looking anywhere else. Oh, brother. This was so junior high she would have laughed if it hadn't been so disconcerting. And irritating. She needed his help, but not this darn attraction. The twelve miles to town had never seemed so long.

At last they arrived at the Sunshine Gap Farmers' and Ranchers' Co-op. It was a squat white building with gas pumps out front and a side lot filled with stock tanks, bundles of fence posts and portable corral panels. By the time Jake pulled into the rutted parking area, it was a relief to get out of the pickup and put some space between them.

He led the way to the entrance, holding the door open for her. Hope sailed past him, determined to get this over with as soon as possible. Darlene Hanson, the gray-haired cashier greeted them. ''Mornin', folks. What can I do for you?''

''Hope needs work clothes,'' Jake said. ''Stuff that'll hold up.''

''You bet.'' Darlene came out from behind the counter and headed for the back of the store. ''Come on, hon. We'll get you fixed up in a jiffy.''

True to her word, within five minutes Darlene had installed Hope in a dressing room. While she tried on stiff, heavy jeans and blue chambray work shirts, Darlene and Jake collected other things they thought she would need. Socks, a sturdy leather belt, a rain slicker, an ugly pair of round-toed black leather boots and an even uglier pair of knee-high black rubber boots all found their way into her dressing room.

Hope hated it all. The fabrics were rough and scratchy, the colors uninspiring. There was not so much as a hint of decoration or style to set one garment apart from a million others exactly like it.

She studied herself in the mirror, turning this way and that, trying to see herself from every angle. Her heart sank. *This* was what Jake expected her to wear every day? She felt boring, drab and plain as a brown sparrow in these clothes.

"Come on out and let's see how you're doing," Jake called from the other side of the dressing room door.

Grimacing at her reflection, Hope took a deep breath, then stepped out into the store, watching Jake's face for a reaction. His eyebrows slammed together. His nostrils flared. His jaw muscles bunched as if he were gritting his teeth. When he didn't say anything, she said, "Well?"

"Looks fine." His voice sounded as rough as her new jeans felt. "Get it."

He shoved a pair of leather gloves and a sheepskin-lined denim jacket into her arms, turned and left her standing there. She must look even worse than she'd thought.

Darlene frowned at his retreating back, shrugged and turned back to Hope. "Is that what *you* want?"

"If you were buying ranch clothes, is this what you'd get?" Hope set down the gloves and tried on the jacket.

"You bet. Everything'll wear like iron for you. Once you wash the starch out, the jeans'll soften up and be more comfortable."

Reluctant but resigned, Hope nodded. "All right. Give me seven shirts, seven pairs of jeans and everything else you two picked out."

Darlene grinned. "Be glad to. You want to wear what you've got on?"

Nodding again, Hope handed over her credit card. She could always jazz this stuff up with fabric paints or sew on some colorful trim. Jake would think it was frivolous, but she wasn't dressing for him. She'd learned at an early age to assert her own identity or disappear into the long shadows cast by her famous relatives. No cranky, overbearing cowboy was going to turn her into a non-entity.

Jake carried the packages out to the pickup while Hope paid for her new wardrobe. The coffee she'd given him churned in his gut and his eyeballs felt seared. He'd thought getting her out of her sexy getups and into some regular work clothes would take away her mystique or whatever it was that made her so blasted fascinating to him.

He should be so lucky.

The instant she'd stepped out of the dressing room he'd known he was in trouble. Big trouble. He hadn't realized it until that moment, but his best defense against Hope's appeal had been her outlandish appearance.

As long as she had blue hair and wore such inappropriate Western wear, he could tell himself she was too weird to take seriously. Looking like that, she'd never fit in in Sunshine Gap. He couldn't even imagine it.

Now he could.

Oh, she'd looked normal enough at Dillon's wedding, but that hadn't really counted. She'd been beautiful, all right, but she'd been too polished. Too glamorous. Too perfect to believe. Real flesh-and-blood women didn't look that good. He'd convinced himself it was all a product of Hollywood magic. Without it, he'd never even notice Hope.

Wrong.

The magic didn't come from Hollywood. It came from inside Hope. It was right there in the stark vulnerability he'd glimpsed in her big blue eyes. In her new work clothes, with her short hair tousled and little if any makeup, she'd looked eminently appropriate. Touchable. Desirable.

This woman could belong in Sunshine Gap. She might even choose to stay here. She was unmistakably real, a flesh-and-blood woman, and he'd wanted to touch her so bad, his hands were still tingling.

Hell. He didn't need this. But after the fuss he'd made about her clothes and her hair, he could hardly complain when she changed them.

She came out of the Co-op and walked across the parking lot, her smooth, sexy stride unchanged by her new boots. He should've known work clothes couldn't hide her curves. He doubted a gunnysack could do that.

The churning in his gut became a sinking sensation. He resisted the urge to play gentleman and let her climb into the passenger seat on her own steam. She didn't say a word, but her glum expression told him she was unhappy about something.

That suited him fine.

As long as they were both out of sorts, there wouldn't be any temptation to step over the line between a business relationship and a personal one. Personal? Yeah, right. Pull the other leg.

The truth was, no amount of coffee was going to improve his disposition. He wasn't suffering from a lack of caffeine or sleep; he was suffering from a lack of sex. That's what all this tension was about. Good, old-fashioned sexual attraction.

He shouldn't be feeling it, but he did. So what? He was a grown man in control of himself. Just because he had an itch didn't mean he had to scratch it.

No matter how she looked right now, there was nothing appropriate about Hope DuMaine and there never would be. Not for him, anyway. She'd never be able to cope with the limitations and the sometimes harsh conditions of living here for any length of time. He kept telling himself that all the way back to the Double Circle, but the tension didn't go away.

And neither did the itch.

By the time he parked beside Hope's little red car again, Jake was desperate to put some distance between them. He climbed out of the pickup, sucked in a deep breath of fresh air to get the scent of Hope's perfume out of his head. Then he gathered up her packages.

Doofus galloped out to greet them, his whole body wagging as if he hadn't seen a soul for weeks. He danced around their feet, woofing and butting his head against their legs in a shameless bid for attention. Hope petted his big, ugly head and cooed at him as if he were a spoiled lap dog.

Jake shifted the packages, making the plastic bags crackle. Hope shot him a quelling glance, then sent Doofus off to lie down and proceeded to enter the house.

Jake followed, careful to avoid brushing against her when she opened the screen door for him.

"Where do you want these?" he asked, raising the bags.

"On the floor in the living room." She set her purse on the countertop. "Would you like some breakfast?"

"I had breakfast at five-thirty."

"Well, I can't face food that early. It's almost ten now and I'm hungry. I'm having a bagel and some yogurt, but I'll fix you whatever you want. Even meat."

He had to smile at that, but shook his head at her offer. "I'm all right. While you're eating, I'll move my stuff into the bunkhouse."

"I've already made up a room for you here."

Right. And how much sleep would he get if he knew she was just down the hall, wearing God knew what— if she wore anything at all? Damn little. "Thanks, but I'd rather stay in the bunkhouse."

"I haven't even looked at it since Scott left." She wrinkled her nose, as if at an unpleasant smell. "I doubt he left it very clean."

Remembering Scott's relaxed attitude toward personal hygiene, Jake doubted it, too. But the cleaning job wouldn't kill him and the extra privacy would be well worth the effort. "I'm not fussy."

Still looking doubtful, she grabbed a key from a rack by the back door, then went outside, calling over her shoulder, "Let's go check it out."

There was nothing to do but follow her. And check out her sweet behind in her tight new jeans. "It'll be fine, Hope."

Ignoring his protest, she patted her leg and called Doofus. "Want to go for a walk, boy?"

That was like asking a trout if he liked to swim. The

pup ran ahead, brought back sticks for her to throw, then chased after them with an unabashed exuberance that reminded Jake of Hope. Smiling at the thought, he hurried to catch up.

Surrounded by a stand of aspen trees, the Double Circle's bunkhouse sat about a hundred yards on the other side of the barn. Long and narrow, it had peeling patches of yellow paint surrounded by expanses of weathered gray wood. The roof and the front porch sagged in places and one of the windows sported a horizontal crack.

Hope unlocked the door and pushed it open, then stepped inside, fanning one hand in front of her face. ''Oh, gross.''

Jake had to agree with her assessment. Scott hadn't bothered to take out his garbage before he left. The flies and the mice had been busy. The smell was putrid.

Doofus put his nose to the floor and ran around the room, sniffing and stirring up dust. Then he shot out the door, barking as if he'd seen a cat. But rather than running off the way Jake would've expected, Doofus dove under the porch and started barking maniacally.

Wanting to see what the dog was after, Jake hurried outside, squatted on his heels and saw Doofus digging at the building's foundation. Aw, jeez, it could be anything under there—a squirrel, a raccoon, a weasel, any of which might be rabid. ''No, Doofus. Come here, before you get hurt.''

Of course, the idiot dog didn't listen; few dogs would in these circumstances. Unfortunately Jake was too big to crawl under the porch after him. Lowering himself to his belly Jake slid through the opening, propelling himself with his forearms and the toes of his boots. The dog's barking reverberated off the walls, creating a deafening barrage of sound.

Jake grabbed Doofus's collar, but the damn dog had gone totally nuts. From this position it was impossible to get enough leverage to drag him out. Jake spotted a little black nose on the other side of the hole Doofus was digging. At that moment, another likely animal intruder occurred to Jake.

He scrambled backward as fast as he could, but he hadn't quite cleared the opening when Doofus jerked back with a yelp and an acrid stench filled the small enclosure. Cursing, Jake slid the rest of the way out and got up on his hands and knees, gasping when he reached fresh air.

"Jake, are you all right?" Hope sniffed, then made a gagging sound. "Oh, good Lord, what is that *smell?*"

Eyes burning and watering to beat hell, Jake could only choke out one word. "Skunk."

A whimpering Doofus crawled out from under the porch, alternately pawing at his eyes and rolling in the dirt. Jake didn't blame the pup. He'd do the same thing if he thought it'd help. As it was, he could only be grateful he hadn't taken a direct hit the way poor Doofus had.

Hope backed away from both of them. Jake didn't blame her for that, either. Man, oh, man, that stink was awful. He peeled off his shirt and ran for the water spigot at the side of the house. Turning it on full blast, he stuck his head under the icy stream and scrubbed at his face.

It didn't touch the stink, but it gradually eased the burning in his eyes. Leaving the water on, he turned to go back for Doofus. Amazement halted him in his tracks when Hope came around the side of the house, half dragging, half carrying the wretched animal. The problem was, Doofus was nearly half her size, and he was struggling to beat hell.

"Come on, sweetie," she coaxed. "Work with me here. I'm trying to help you."

The anxiety in her voice spurred Jake to action. He jogged across the yard and grabbed the dog's collar. Her eyes were streaming now, no doubt from being so close to Doofus. "Here, I'll take him." Jake picked up the dog. "You'll get that stuff all over yourself."

"I already did." She turned her head away from Doofus, inhaled through her mouth, then let out a shaky laugh as Jake carried the dog toward the bunkhouse. "Oh, that's *bad*."

The second his head went under the water, Doofus went fighting-for-his-life berserk. Jake's eyes started streaming again and he found himself wrestling what felt like a demented, seventy-five-pound octopus with scrabbling claws and snapping teeth. With no regard for her own comfort and safety, Hope waded right in and helped Jake hold on, talking in a soft, soothing voice.

"It's okay, Doofus. You'll feel better in a minute. Calm down now."

Doofus obviously wasn't listening, but Jake couldn't help admiring Hope's efforts. She could've just walked away and left him to deal with this by himself. Most sane people would. If he'd thought about it, Jake never would've expected a woman like her to get anywhere near the most powerful stink in the animal kingdom. But Hope hadn't hesitated to do whatever she could to help the crazed pup.

That took character. And guts. With an animal in that much distress, she could've been bitten or badly scratched.

"All right," Jake said when he figured the water had done its job on the dog's eyes. "Turn him loose."

Doofus staggered three steps away, then vigorously

shook himself, spraying Jake and Hope and stirring up the noxious odor still clinging to his fur. Arms raised to protect their faces, they both dodged away, gasping at the cold water and the stink.

"Got any tomato juice at the house?" Jake asked.

"I think so. George drinks it all the time. Why?"

"It helps neutralize skunk spray. If you want Doofus to be socially acceptable any time soon, he'll need a bath in it."

"I don't think he's ever had a bath," Hope said.

"Probably not." Jake raked his fingers through his wet hair. "And I got enough of that stuff in my hair, I'll need one, too."

Her gaze flew to meet his. She bit into her lower lip, but the corners of her mouth twitched as if she really wanted to laugh. "Where, um…" She paused and took a shaky breath. "Where do you want to do this?"

"The barn'll do. There's a small stock tank we can use and hot water for grooming the horses. You go get the juice and I'll round up the beast."

"All right, Jake. I'll meet you there."

She took off at a jog. Jake watched her go, wondering what to make of her until Doofus charged after her. Jake called him back and headed for the barn with the dog running circles around him. He tied Doofus up so he couldn't get away, then found the tank, pulled off his boots and peeled off his wet jeans and socks. He doubted his briefs would preserve much of his modesty once they got wet, but left them on anyway.

Figuring that was the best he could do, he lifted the dog into the empty tank, climbed in after him and sat down with his knees on either side of the stinking animal. Life had one perverse sense of humor. The few times Jake had allowed himself to imagine being naked around Hope, he'd never once considered it might happen when he smelled like a damn polecat.

Chapter Seven

Arms loaded with juice cans and bath gear, Hope hurried to the barn. She heard Jake talking to Doofus when she stepped into the shady interior and smiled at his one-sided conversation.

"You're a screwball, dog. You know that, don't you? Yeah, you do. Bet you've learned your lesson about skunks, though. Whooee, but you reek, Doof. What? I don't smell any better? Well, whose fault is that?"

Hope suspected she smelled almost as bad as they did, but it was impossible to pinpoint any one source of the odor. The stench was so pervasive it seemed to be everywhere. She came around the corner of the last stall, took one look at Jake's broad naked back rising out of the oval metal stock tank and nearly dropped everything.

Some part of her mind had registered him ripping off his shirt, but in the chaos after the skunk's blast, her libido hadn't paid any attention to all that bare skin. But stench or no stench, it was paying attention now.

Oh, dear heaven, he was big. And muscular. And gorgeous—even with his "farmer tan" that would've gotten him laughed off any beach in California. And unless she'd suddenly lost her twenty-twenty vision, that crumpled pile of denim lying beside the stock tank contained his jeans.

Which meant he could be sitting in that shallow, not-even-up-to-his-waist stock tank...naked.

Her mouth went dry. She wasn't fifteen and he wasn't a rock star, but her silly heart actually fluttered at the thought of touching him. Doofus whined and tried to climb out of the tank.

Jake pulled him back in. "Easy there, Doof. Jeez, did she go all the way to China for that damn juice?"

The irritation in his voice got Hope moving again. She had to clear her throat, but tried to sound nonchalant. "Nope. Just Paris."

Jake looked over his shoulder at her. His eyes and nose were streaming and he looked far too uncomfortable to be sexy. But somehow, he still was. "Hurry," he said. "The fumes are about to kill me."

"Tell me what to do."

After one quick peek at Jake's white briefs, she set to work following his instructions. While he held on to Doofus, she opened a can of juice and poured the thick red liquid over the dog's head and back. When the juice dripped into his eyes, Doofus thrashed and fought to escape, sending the stuff splattering in every direction. The dog's toenails scratched angry grooves across Jake's chest and legs, but he managed to hang on.

"No, Doofus," Hope scolded, wiping the dog's eyes

with a towel. "Bad dog. Bad, bad dog. Sit down and behave yourself."

Jake turned his face away from the flying juice.

"Just start scrubbing."

Hope sank her fingernails into the dog's wiry fur and scrubbed. She poured more juice on him and scrubbed some more, repeating the process until her arms and fingers ached. Living up to his name, Doofus continued struggling and carrying on as if they were torturing him. The odors of wet dog and tomatoes blended with the skunk smell in a nauseating mix.

She could see Jake's muscles bunch and strain with the effort it took to control Doofus. There was a lot of dog to wash and a lot of juice splattering around. Though he must have been absolutely miserable with that cold, slimy stuff dribbling all over him, Jake remained admirably patient, talking soothing nonsense to the writhing animal.

Through no fault of her own, Hope's hands occasionally grazed Jake's torso and legs and once, even the front of his briefs. She jerked her hand away as if she'd touched a hot curling iron. He shot her a startled look, then grinned wickedly at her. "Watch the hands, DuMaine."

She was used to fielding sexual banter from men, but not from Jake. Her face heated and she found herself momentarily flustered. "Sorry. It was an accident."

His dark eyes glinted with amusement. "Yeah, yeah. That's what they all say."

"Trust me, cowboy, if I decided to grope you, you'd know you'd been groped."

"Promises, promises."

"You flirting with me *now*, McBride?" She pretended she was going to flick her gunky fingertips at him, then rolled her eyes toward heaven in mock exasperation. "Your timing stinks as much as Doofus."

He laughed. "Nothing stinks as much as Doofus."

Hope sat back on her heels and flexed her fingers. "Except you and me." She glanced down at herself and couldn't help giggling. The front of her new shirt was soaked with juice and covered with dog hair. She could almost see wavy lines coming off of it like cartoonists used to indicate when something smelled bad. Pulling the fabric away from her skin, she wrinkled her nose and said, "Ewwww."

"We're a pair, all right," Jake agreed. "Got any juice left for my hair?"

She picked up the last can and shook it. "Yup. Ready?"

"As I'll ever be. Let me have it."

Hope gleefully upended the can over his head. The juice slimed down his face and neck. He scrunched up his eyes and hunched his shoulders. She wiped his face with a towel, trying to look contrite and sympathetic.

He opened one baleful, bloodshot eye and scowled at her. "You enjoyed that."

"Yes, I did," she admitted with a laugh. "It's not every day a woman can do something like that to a man without expecting retaliation."

"What makes you think I won't retaliate?"

She plunged her hands into his hair and squished the juice through the dark strands. "You told me to let you have it."

Jake snorted with laughter. "You still didn't have to enjoy it that much."

Considerably softer than Doofus's fur, Jake's hair curled around her fingers as she scrubbed at his scalp.

Bizarre as it was, she realized she'd never done anything this personal for anyone before and it felt…nice.

"Rub it on my back and arms, too," he said. "I'd do it myself, but I'm not sure you can hang on to Doofus."

"All right." Hope spread the juice over his warm skin with her palms. She didn't touch other people very often, and when she did touch someone, it usually was just a pat or a quick hug. Now, with Jake, she wanted to linger, to press the pads of her fingertips down and trace the solid muscles in his back, shoulders and arms.

"I think that'll do it." Jake's voice sounded strained.

"All right." Reluctantly, she wiped her hands on the towel. "Now what?"

"We rinse this stuff off, then give Doofus two or three regular baths with soap."

"I brought some shampoo from the house."

"That'll work." Hanging on to the dog, Jake got his feet under him and stood halfway up.

Impossible as it seemed, Doofus hated being sprayed off with the hose more than he'd hated being doused with tomato juice. No amount of soothing words or reassuring pats could make him give up his desperate fight for freedom. Only sheer exhaustion did that.

It took three rounds of scrubbing and rinsing to wear the beast out. An hour and most of a brand-new bottle of her best shampoo later, all three of them were drenched, shivering and utterly miserable. And the odor of skunk still lingered on Doofus's fur.

Hope shook her head at him. "What's it going to take to get you to stop stinking?"

Doofus hung his head in shame and gave the stock tank a couple of weak thumps with his tail. Jake uttered a weary-sounding laugh. "That's as good as it's going to get. The rest'll just have to wear off with time. Let's dry him off and turn him loose.''

Jake lifted the dog out of the tank, then collapsed back in a tired sprawl. Hope let Doofus shake himself before rubbing him all over with a couple of George's old towels. When she let him go, the dog shot her a decidedly suspicious look before slinking out the open double doors to the corral with his tail between his hind legs.

And then, right there in front of them, Doofus lay down and rolled his entire, still-damp body in the dirt. Hope stared at him in appalled, openmouthed amazement, glanced at Jake and caught him doing the same thing. When she looked back at the dog, he stood up, shook himself again and trotted off as if he had other, more important things to do than hang around with the humans who had saved him from his own idiocy.

''Why that lowdown, mangy, flea-bitten….''

''Well, of all the ungrateful….''

They looked at each other and cracked up. Laughing until her sides ached, Hope sank to her knees beside the stock tank. She leaned back, overbalanced and toppled over onto her bottom.

Jake roared with laughter. She raised up, reached across the top of the tank and ruffled his hair. Her hand came away red with tomato juice. She smeared it down the side of his face. She'd never done anything like that before, either, but after bathing a man, simply touching him didn't seem like such a big thing.

He laughed even harder. The sound was so infectious, it fed on itself, growing as it bounced back and forth between them. Before long she was clinging to the side of the tank to keep herself upright. Jake was equally goofy.

Just as one would finally start to regain control, the

other would choke or snort or their gazes would meet and they were hooting all over again.

Finally, too spent to do anything else, Jake sagged against the side of the tank, his arm draped over the rim for balance, his chin resting on the back of his wrist. Lord, he hadn't laughed like this in years. Hope sat facing him on the other side of the tank, her posture a mirror image of his. Her hair stuck out all over her head in wet spikes. Her makeup had washed away, except for a few black streaks under her right eye. Her left cheek sported a reddish scrape and the dark blue shadow of a nasty bruise in the making.

Despite all of that, her eyes literally sparkled with impish delight. Her rueful smile filled the musty, drafty old barn with a soft, inviting warmth. Jake had the oddest sense he was seeing Hope—*really* seeing her—for the first time.

And he liked what he saw.

For once in his life he abandoned logic and went with his gut. Leaning forward, he moved the scant four inches it took to press his mouth against hers. She went absolutely still for a second, then breathed out a sigh and sort of…melted.

It was a fragile moment. He'd enjoyed kissing her before, but there'd been a part of him screaming, "Are you out of your ever-loving mind?" the whole time. But this time, kissing her felt as natural as breathing and more right than anything he'd ever done. He wanted to savor it. To savor *her*.

Refusing to rush, he nibbled at her lips, teasing them with the tip of his tongue. She tilted her head to one side and opened her mouth for him. He'd never associated her with sweetness, but her surrender tasted like wild honey.

Time spun out in an achingly tender, mutual exploration of her mouth and then his. One kiss blended into the next and she stayed right with him, making funny little excited noises in her throat and leaning closer, her fingers gripping the rim of the tank as if she might float away if she dared to let go.

He abandoned her mouth to kiss the sun-kissed freckles on her cheeks and the slender bridge of her nose, her eyelids and forehead. Starving for more of her sweetness, he returned to her lips. So gradually he barely noticed it happening, the tenderness gave way to something deeper, darker, more erotic.

Only their lips touched, but the limited contact generated an incredible amount of heat and excitement. His blood pooled in his groin. His heart raced like a coyote chasing a jackrabbit.

The sound of harsh breathing filled his ears, but he wasn't sure if it was hers or his own. It didn't matter. He delved into her mouth again and again, drinking in her unguarded response, tilting her head back with the driving force of his hunger. A hunger that was rapidly growing insatiable.

He raised his hands to reach for her at the same moment she pulled back and stared at him. Her eyes were wide open, the pupils dilated until the blue of her irises barely showed. Her lips were parted, her chest rapidly rising and falling.

Aw, jeez, he'd been telling himself that first kiss had been a fluke. It couldn't have been as great as he'd remembered. But this one had been even better and he was stunned to realize he'd been lying to himself. In spite of all their differences, he wanted this woman.

"Hope." His voice was little more than croak. He cleared his throat.

She shook her head and held up one palm. "Don't, Jake. Please, just…don't say anything."

His arousal deflated like a slashed tire, leaving him disoriented. "But—"

"No." She shook her head again. Though her lips formed a smile, there was a sadness in her eyes that yanked at his heartstrings. It was gone so fast, he wondered if he'd imagined it. She chuckled, nearly convincing him that he had. "If you say that kiss never should've happened, I'll have to hurt you."

"But—"

"Really." Pushing herself to her feet, she looked down at him. "I know what you think of me. And I know it was meant to be a friendly kiss, so I don't expect anything from you. But don't ever call a kiss like that one a mistake." She handed him the last clean towel. "I'm going to take a shower and then I'll fix lunch. Come up to the house when you're ready. I'll save you some hot water."

Feeling naked in ways that had nothing to do with his lack of clothing, Jake watched her gather up the rest of the stuff she'd brought from the house. Without another word, she left the barn, her head held high with a quiet dignity that belied the smelly, wet towels in her arms.

Jake wanted to call her back. He wasn't sure what would put the impish sparkle back in her eyes, but he knew he was responsible for its disappearance. He wanted to see it there again.

After the way she'd handled herself with the dog and the stink and the mess, he couldn't fool himself any more. He'd been wrong about her. Dead wrong. She'd hung in there like a real trouper. He'd seriously underestimated her, and he'd hurt her because of it. He wanted to make amends, but how?

He could apologize, but what would he say? "Hey, I'm sorry I thought you were such a flake." Or, "You're not nearly as bizarre and wacko as I thought you were." Or how about, "I've decided you're really not a floozy, even though you usually dress like one."

Any one of those overtures was liable to earn him a black eye. Rightfully so. Unfortunately he didn't entirely understand his own behavior when it came to Hope. And he'd done such a good job of convincing her he didn't respect her, he doubted she'd believe any explanations he might make, even if he could think of any that sounded halfway reasonable.

Goose bumps rose on his arms and legs, prompting him to climb out of the stock tank. He shook out one of the towels and discovered it was actually an oversized bath sheet. Judging by its soft thickness and its bright yellow color, he'd say it was new and expensive.

Hope was used to such luxuries and probably wouldn't see loaning him such a nice towel as any big deal. But Jake couldn't help seeing it as an extremely thoughtful gesture, one he doubted his own mother would've made on his behalf. Not when he smelled this bad, and not when he was going to use it in a dirty old barn.

He felt…humbled by Hope's generosity. Aw, dammit. The woman had confused him from day one and undoubtedly would keep right on confusing him. She stirred up all kinds of emotions inside him he didn't want to feel. The only thing he knew for sure at this moment was that he wanted to find a way to make things right between them.

Everything his cousin Dillon had said about her at Cal's Place returned to haunt Jake—as it had done for far too much of the weekend. *Was* there a possibility that he and Hope could have something together? Something beyond sex?

Not that sex with Hope didn't sound terrific, but he couldn't have a one-night stand with her and walk away. Dillon was right about that much; she was part of the family now. Even if she wasn't, he didn't treat women that way. He never had and never would. Besides, he doubted one night with Hope would even come close to satisfying him. He wanted to know how that mind of hers worked. What she wanted out of life. Why she'd really bought the Double Circle.

And after that? What then? Jake didn't know. And maybe he didn't have to. He honestly doubted he had it in him to fall in love again. In the eight years since Ellen had passed on he hadn't even come close.

Still, Hope obviously wanted him as much as he wanted her. She was an experienced woman of the world, not some dewy-eyed virgin who didn't know what she was getting herself into. As long as he didn't make any promises he couldn't keep, where was the harm in exploring this wild attraction that just wouldn't go away? He was sick and tired of fighting it.

He shivered and his stomach rumbled, reminding him to get moving. He cleaned the stock tank and rinsed the tomato juice out of his hair with the hose, then wrapped the bath sheet around his waist, collected his clothes and hobbled barefoot across the ranch yard to get his duffel bag out of his pickup.

The aroma of cooking beef greeted him at the back door. He set his wet clothes in the laundry tub on the porch, hitched the towel more securely around his waist and entered the kitchen. Hope stood at the counter holding the lid to a slow cooker in one hand, a meat fork in the other.

Her hair was still wet from her shower and she wore a tank top and a pair of cutoffs that made her legs look incredibly long and smooth. His mouth went dry. His breath backed up in his chest. And just like that, the itch to have her was back with a vengeance.

She looked up at him but didn't speak. Uh-oh. His marriage had been great, but not without its conflicts. He knew a woman on the prod when he saw one.

Using both hands, he held the duffel bag in front him. "Something sure smells good."

"It'll be ready whenever you are." She replaced the lid. "You can use the room right across from the bathroom. Your towels are on the bed."

"Thanks. Uh, Hope, I want to apologize."

Glaring at him, she tightened her grip on the meat fork as if she'd like to skewer his liver with it. Before she could speak, however, he hurried to cut her off. "Not for the kiss. I'm not apologizing for that."

"What for then?"

"For whatever I did that upset you." Hell, she didn't need the meat fork to skewer him. Her eyes did the job just fine. He squeezed the duffel bag's handle and shrugged one shoulder, barely resisting the urge to shuffle his feet like a little kid.

"You really don't know?"

"I've got some ideas, of course, but...well, no, I don't. Not exactly. But I really appreciated everything you did out there today. I want you to know that."

"I didn't do anything special. Doofus was so freaked out, anyone would've tried to help him."

Jake shook his head. "That's not true. I know plenty of folks who would've felt bad for him, but they wouldn't have put themselves out half as much as you did. It took a lot of heart and guts to get in there and get your hands and everything else dirty.''

''You didn't think I had it in me. Did you?''

Her sad smile returned, causing him considerable pain where his heart ought to be. Dammit, she had him there and she knew it. "Look, Hope...."

He couldn't finish the sentence without making matters worse.

''Go take your shower, McBride.'' She sounded tired and cynical.

Cursing under his breath, Jake went. He wasn't this socially inept around anyone else, but she tied him up in knots without even trying. Maybe after he was dressed and had some food he'd be better able to defend himself.

But he doubted it.

Judging by the way she'd just dismissed him, she didn't even like him much anymore. It didn't help knowing he probably deserved it. He had some major fence-mending to do before he could even hope to kiss her again, much less take her to bed. He'd get there, though. She'd liked him plenty once. Surely he could make her like him again.

Hope waited until she heard the shower running upstairs, then sagged against the counter, covering her face with her hands. The big jerk. She should've drowned him in that stock tank. What *was* she going to do about him?

To her, those moments in the barn when they'd been laughing uproariously together had felt absolutely, delightfully perfect. And that kiss had been so special. No, it had been much more than special. It had been... stupendous. Magic. Sheer heaven. There were no words to adequately describe its effect on her.

Had it meant anything to Jake? Anything at all? No, she didn't think so. When she'd pulled back, he hadn't looked any happier than he had after the first time he'd kissed her at the wedding reception.

How could he kiss her senseless one second and regret it the next? It seemed so unreasonable for him to react that way. But then, she kept forgetting he thought she was a flaky California floozy. For pity's sake, he'd been surprised when she'd tried to help a suffering animal. She wanted to hit him for that. Really hard.

She took an onion from the wire basket in the pantry and hacked it to pieces. Realizing she'd cut way more than she needed for the omelet she intended to cook for herself, she banged down the knife, washed her hands and smacked the omelet pan onto the burner.

Honestly, she didn't know which of them was dumber. Jake for not loving her. Or herself for loving him anyway. And still secretly hoping he *might* learn to love her someday.

Where the hell was her pride?

And what kind of a fairyland was she living in? Yes, Blair and Emma had found love with McBride men. But, as Jake had so succinctly put it, he wasn't Dillon, and she wasn't Blair. She wasn't Emma, either.

No, she was Hope DuMaine, eccentric writer. Hell-raiser. Darling of the tabloid press. The kind of woman mothers warned their sons to stay away from.

She'd waited her whole life for someone to love her. Someone who would look behind the image she projected to the woman she really was inside. No one but Blair, Emma and Marsh had ever come close. Not even Hope's own parents.

So what if she'd foolishly fallen in love with Jake? Why had she thought he might be different? Simply because she wanted him to be? Life didn't work that way. Even she had figured out that much.

Grabbing a green pepper, Hope diced it into perfect cubes. She scraped the vegetables into the skillet with her knife, wishing she could clear her unproductive thoughts as easily as she'd just cleared the cutting board.

"There *is* no Mr. Right." She slammed the board onto the counter. "Get over it and move on."

Discouragement crashed on top of her like a dump-truck-load of rocks. Maybe Jake was right and she really didn't belong here. Living so close to him would be difficult at best. After the way George had abandoned her, she certainly didn't owe *him* a thing. Should she simply pack her things and go back to L.A.?

Every part of her rebelled at the idea. She'd so wanted to start a new life. One that was far away from the media and out of sight of the relentless public eye. One that would allow her to be a real woman, not a celebrity. She could have that here in Sunshine Gap if she wanted it enough to fight for it.

The question was, did she want it that much?

Yes. Yes, she did. Nobody had ever said starting a new life would be easy. Anywhere she went there would be problems and obstacles, and she would have to learn how to solve them or work around them. Jake was only one of many problems she'd have to deal with if she stayed here.

But she could handle it, dammit.

It would be a long and difficult two weeks until her new manager arrived, but she would use that time to her best advantage. She'd be pleasant and friendly to Jake. She'd learn everything about ranching she possibly could from him. Then she'd send him home, relegate him to casual-pal status and get on with her new life.

Rule Number Five was she didn't need a man to be happy. She certainly didn't need Jake McBride. And if he could act as though that stupendous kiss was a mistake, so could she. In fact, she'd go one better. She'd pretend it had never happened.

Chapter Eight

Jake spent the next three days in a perpetual state of confusion. It was all Hope's fault, of course, but blaming her wasn't going to get him any closer to a solution. He was beginning to wonder if anything would.

Dammit, it was already Thursday. Tomorrow they'd go up and start pushing her cows down out of the high country, and on Saturday the rest of the work crew would be up there with them. It would be obvious to the more astute members of his family that there was something going on between him and Hope, and there were going to be questions asked he didn't want to answer.

He wasn't even sure he could answer them, because he wasn't exactly sure what was going on. He only knew he had a problem with Hope, and he didn't have a clue what to do about it. Lifting a bundle of fence posts onto his shoulder, he carried it out to his pickup and went back to the storage shed for more.

As near as he could figure, the real trouble had started back on Monday, sometime after he'd gone upstairs to shower away the rest of the skunk smell. Leaving Hope alone to cool off from her snit had seemed like a reasonable thing to do at the time.

He should've remembered Hope and his definition of *reasonable* weren't even on speaking terms. The woman didn't play by the same rules he did. Hell, he wasn't sure she played by any rules at all.

The only predictable thing about Hope DuMaine was her complete and total unpredictability.

After his shower he'd come back downstairs prepared to gag down a terrible dinner and pretend he liked it. No way could a vegetarian do a decent job of cooking beef. Right? Hah!

It turned out that Hope had once written a book about a master chef. She'd gone to a cooking school in Europe for research purposes and enjoyed herself so much, she'd finished the course and graduated with honors. Jake couldn't even guess what she'd used to flavor the roast—wine maybe—but he knew folks who'd drive a hundred miles for food like that.

Hope had knocked him off balance with that first fantastic meal and he hadn't recovered yet.

He'd also been prepared to let her tell him what he'd done to upset her. The instant he heard, "Jake, we need to talk," he'd planned to be patient as a saint. All he had to do was wait for her to bring up that mind-blowing kiss out in the barn, and he'd listen until his ears fell off, nod in all the right places and say whatever it took to get back in her good graces.

Only the subject never came up. Not once. Not even when he'd tossed out hints so easy even Doofus would've gotten them. She wasn't the least bit cranky about it, either.

While the memory of that kiss lingered in the back of Jake's mind as stubbornly as the skunk odor clung to the dog's fur, Hope acted as if they'd never shared anything more intimate than a polite handshake.

It was as if sometime during his ten-minute shower, the Hope who'd relentlessly chased him for weeks and kissed the daylights out of him twice had vanished. In her place was a pleasant, businesslike Hope who couldn't learn about ranching fast enough to suit her. All she wanted from him now was information.

She took no more notice of him as a man than a mare in heat would take of his gelding. Jake had developed a lot of sympathy for poor ol' Rebel; being treated like that was enough to give a guy one nasty complex. If Jake hadn't suspected Hope had inherited a fair share of the family acting talent, he might've bought her performance. But he knew better.

He'd admit it'd been damn scary until he'd figured out what she was trying to pull. Oh, she was a smart one, all right. A guy could usually find a way to mollify a woman's anger. But what did you do with a woman's indifference?

That was a new one on him. He was still looking for a way to shake her out of her act. If he could just get her to talk about that kiss...but this woman was a professional writer. When it came to turning words to her own advantage, she was slicker than the greased pigs the kids chased at the county fair.

Dammit, any other woman on the planet would've brought up that kiss at the first opportunity. But Hope? Hell, no.

Why do anything a guy might want or expect her to

do? Especially if it meant she could torture him and drive him crazy in the process. The woman was diabolical.

He was dang near desperate enough to violate every rule in the book of manhood and bring up the subject of that kiss himself. The only thing stopping him was the fear of what he might do if she laughed when *he* said, "Hope, we have to talk."

How the hell had he sunk so low?

More important, how could he solve the problem? Jake loaded the last of the fence posts into the pickup and went back for a roll of barbed wire. If he couldn't win a war of words with Hope, then he had to shift the battle to a different arena. She had the edge verbally, but he believed she was far from immune to him physically.

In fact, thinking back to the wedding reception, he distinctly remembered her calling the first kiss they'd shared, "The most spectacular kiss of my entire life."

He'd felt so guilty about hurting her feelings, he hadn't wanted to push her, but it was time for this nonsense to end.

He was a McBride, dammit. When a McBride wanted something, he didn't sit on his duff and wait for someone else to hand it to him. He went after it and kept going after it until he won.

He wanted Hope. If he kept waiting for her to make the next move, he'd be collecting Social Security checks before he kissed her again, much less got her into bed. And now that *that* idea had taken root in his mind, he couldn't get it back out.

One way or another, the woman was at least going to talk to him about something more personal than the price of fence posts before the day was over, or his name wasn't Jake McBride.

He'd never really had to woo a woman before. He was surprised to realize the prospect of being the hunter rather than the huntee wasn't entirely unpleasant. He wasn't entirely sure how to go about it, but if his idiot brothers and his cousin Dillon had managed to do it, how hard could it be?

"Okay now, hit it again," Jake said. "Harder, Hope. Really whale away on it."

Though her arm and shoulder muscles were screaming for mercy, Hope tightened her grip on the pounder's handles and rammed it down on top of the fence post again and again and again. Lord, what a fool she'd been to insist on learning every blessed job there was to do on a ranch. She'd been lifting weights three times a week for the past four years, but it didn't seem to be helping her much now.

It simply took tremendous brute strength to beat a steel fence post into the ground. This must be one of those few things men were inherently better at than women. As far as Hope was concerned, they were more than welcome to it.

"Atta girl," Jake said. "Get some momentum going there."

Scowling at him, Hope kept pounding. Jake McBride was up to something. She didn't know exactly what it was yet, but he'd ditched his somewhat taciturn personality and become an encouraging Mr. Nice Guy. In fact, he was starting to sound like an overgrown cheerleader, and it was getting on her nerves.

"Hang on a second. Let's check it." Stepping close beside her, Jake reached out a big hand and wiggled the post. To Hope's dismay, it listed to the right and would've fallen over if he hadn't held on to it. He pulled it free and moved it over a few inches. "It was on a rock. Try again."

Barely stifling a groan, she settled the heavy metal cylinder over the top of the post and whanged away on it again. This time it sank steadily into the dirt, and when Jake gave it the wiggle test, the post stood firm.

"Great job." Jake gave her shoulder an approving squeeze.

Oh, she wished he wouldn't touch her. She could ignore a smile, deflect a personal remark, pretend she hadn't heard a compliment. But even the briefest physical contact with him made her entire body hum. Trying to be subtle about it, she stepped back, dislodging his hand. "How many more?"

"That's it. All we've got to do now is restring the wires and tighten 'em up. Remember how to do it?"

"If I don't by now, I never will." Hope picked up the clips and the wire stretcher, stepped around him and went to work, painfully aware he was watching everything she did.

Jake was a great one for taking a task and breaking it down into simple, numbered steps anyone with an IQ higher than a turnip's could follow. The only drawback was, he expected his student to follow his steps in his exact order.

If the student dared to get creative with the process, however, she was in for a lecture about doing a job "right the first time," and a detailed explanation as to why Jake's way was the only "right" way to get the job done. Since Hope rarely did anything exactly the same way twice, she'd heard the lecture and the explanation often enough to know them both by heart. And this was only their third day of working together.

She didn't know how much longer she could resist the temptation to start messing with his head for the sheer fun of seeing how long it would take him to catch on. Someone really needed to work with the man on his rigidity issues. But it wasn't going to be her.

That was a wife's or at least a serious girlfriend's job. She didn't qualify for either position. And Rule Number Five was still in force. She didn't need a man to be happy.

Especially not one who was so darn big and so in her way. She couldn't remember him crowding her personal space this much before. What was with him today, anyway? Every time she took a step, he was right there underfoot, brushing against her or looming over her, surrounding her with his body heat and the scent of his skin. Reminding her foolish libido how much she'd once wanted him.

Hope fastened the barbed wire to the steel post, then attached the fence stretcher and ratcheted the clamps closer together, moving from top to bottom until all four of the wires were as tight as a lady's corset strings when tiny waists were in fashion. Jake tweaked each wire, then turned and gazed down the fence line.

He turned back to her and smiled. "That's a real pretty piece of work you did there."

His smile made her uneasy. It was too warm, too approving, and she liked the way it made her feel too much. "It's a barbed-wire fence. I wouldn't call it pretty."

"Depends on how you look at it." He walked along beside her, carrying the pounder back to the pickup. "It's straight and it's strong. Barring some disaster, it'll last a long time and it's not very complicated. There are lots of things in life that don't have any clear-cut answers, but a fence'll either hold cows or it won't.''

"That's how you like things, isn't it?'' Hope asked. "Right or wrong. Black or white. Nothing in between.''

"It does make life simpler.''

"Sometimes people aren't that simple,'' she said.

He paused in mid-stride. "Are we talking about us?''

"No, we're talking about fences.'' She tossed her tools into the pickup, then climbed into the passenger seat.

A moment later Jake climbed in behind the steering wheel and drove off across the pasture. The silence in the cab was as thick and palpable as the rooster tail of dust billowing behind the pickup. Unwilling to acknowledge it, Hope stared out her side window until Jake stopped for a gate.

Biting back a groan, Hope clambered out of the truck. Whoever rode "shotgun'' was responsible for opening and closing all gates. Unlike normal gates one might find in a civilized world, ranch gates often were obnoxious, jury-rigged affairs built with barbed wire and wooden poles, intentionally designed to be as difficult as possible to open and shut.

She'd already fought with this one once today and lost, which had done nothing to improve her mood. Knowing Jake was watching her with every expectation of being entertained and amused didn't help, either. Promising herself that when her new ranch manager Bonnie arrived, she was going to replace every damn gate on the Double Circle with a steel one—no matter what it cost—Hope slid the wire loops off both ends of the gate's pole and dragged it across the grass far enough to let the pickup pass through.

So much for the easy part of the operation. When the truck's rear bumper cleared the opening, Hope dragged the gate back across the grass, sucked in a deep breath and inserted the top of the pole through the upper wire loop attached to the fence post. Pushing and shoving, she wrestled the bottom end of the pole through the lower wire loop.

"Come on, you miserable, rotten, son-of-a-gun."

Jake walked up to her with a big grin. "Well, you're getting the talking to it part down fine."

"Do shut up, McBride."

"Now, now, no need to get owly. All you've gotta do is think it through. What's your first step?"

"Why don't you just tell me?"

"Which side of the gate are you on?"

She would *not* look into those big cow eyes of his. Or return his damn grin. Or let him tease her out of a perfectly good sulk. Laughing with him was dangerous.

Without a word, she pulled back the gate and stepped through to the other side. The right side. Switching hands on the pole, she pushed it toward the gate post.

"Come on, let's see some muscle." He moved in close behind her and leaned down until his mouth was beside her ear. His warm breath caressed her neck. "All you've gotta do is squeeze that big ol' stick into that sweet little round hole there."

Hope responded with a blank stare, then turned and shoved the pole again. And failed to secure it again.

"Bottom loop always goes first, honey," Jake said.

Hope jammed the pole into the bottom loop and pushed with every bit of her strength, but she simply couldn't get the pole to stand straight enough to catch the top loop. Jake reached around her and pulled it into place with one quick yank. Infuriated by how easy it was for him, she whipped her head around to glare at him.

And came face-to-face with his smiling lips. His knowing, gorgeous eyes gazed right into her soul. Two inches. All she needed was two lousy inches and she would taste the wild excitement of his kiss again.

He was tempting her. Tantalizing her. Daring her. In exactly the same way she once had tempted, tantalized and dared him. The clever, wretched man was turning her own tactics against her. Even though she recognized what he was doing, she found it incredibly seductive.

She couldn't move. Couldn't blink. Couldn't breathe without inhaling the musky, sun-warmed scent of his skin, the faintest trace of his aftershave.

His gaze fastened on her mouth. His pupils dilated. His nostrils flared and his eyelids lowered halfway. Ever so slowly he began closing the distance between his lips and hers.

While she'd never wanted anything so much in her entire life, an unreasoning sense of panic erupted inside her. She'd been pretending he was completely unattractive, mentally dressing him in ridiculous clothes and imagining him with long, greasy hair and the world's most awful whiskers. If she worked at it hard enough, she could kill the tender feelings she still harbored for him. But she wasn't there yet. If he kissed her now, she wouldn't be able to hide her real response to him.

When he realized who he was kissing and pulled away in horror again, it would be more humiliating than she could endure.

At the first brush of his lips against hers she jerked back, overbalanced and grabbed at the gate to keep from falling, impaling her palm on one of the barbs. She yanked her hand away, ripping a gash in her skin. Instinctively cradling her arm close to her side, she folded her fingers over the cut. "Jeez, McBride, what on earth were you doing?"

"Well, I sure as hell wasn't gonna bite you." Jake sounded almost as upset as she felt. "How bad is it?"

There was blood oozing under her fingertips, but she shook her head in dismissal. "It's no big deal. Let's go."

"Let me see it, Hope." She turned away and would have headed back to the pickup, but he stopped her, holding out his own hand, palm up. "Let me see it."

Reluctantly, she rested her hand against his palm and allowed him to peel her fingers back enough to expose the wound.

"Youch," he said. "That's gonna need stitches. When's the last time you had a tetanus shot?"

"I don't know, but I'm sure I don't need one." Tugging her hand free, she stepped back. "And I don't need stitches."

"It's not smart to fool around with injuries on a ranch." He propped his hands on his hips and gave her the stubborn stare her friend Emma called "the mule-headed McBride look."

"Oh, all right," Hope said. "I'll go to the clinic."

"Good. Hold that thought." Jake strode to the driver's side of the pickup, poked around behind the seat and came up with a bottle of water and a first-aid kit. Working quickly, but carefully, he washed away the worst of the blood, then sprayed on antiseptic and taped a gauze pad over the cut. "There. That'll do until we get to town."

"I can drive myself," Hope said as he helped her into the passenger seat.

"Yeah, you could." He fastened her seat belt. "But isn't it nice you don't have to? If it hasn't already started, that sucker's gonna hurt like the devil any second now.''

By the time Jake climbed in behind the steering wheel and turned on the engine, his prediction about imminent pain had come true. Hope went back to staring out the side window. Jake turned on the radio, and for the next half hour Hope listened to the announcer from Cody giving them an agriculture report she thought had something to do with livestock and grain prices. Beyond that, she didn't understand a word of what the man said.

What the heck was a ''hundredweight,'' anyway?

Jake took the first right after they passed the Sunshine Gap city limits sign and drove another block before pulling into the graveled parking area in front of the log building that housed the clinic. Hope climbed out of the pickup and followed Jake inside. A woman with shoulder-length auburn hair sat at a desk in the reception area, talking on a telephone. The nameplate on the desk read, ''Sandy Bishop, Nurse Practitioner.''

Hope's heart sank. Uh-oh. She'd forgotten Marsh's former girlfriend provided most of Sunshine Gap's medical care. Hope had met Sandy the previous summer and seen her on several other occasions. Hope didn't like the other woman much, and the feeling obviously was mutual. If Jake hadn't been there, Hope would've left and driven on to Cody.

''Are you sure about that, Mavis?'' Sandy looked up at Jake and raised an index finger, as if telling him she'd only be a minute. ''I see. Well, thanks for the call.''

Sandy hung up the phone, shut her eyes and raised a trembling hand to her mouth. Tears leaked out from under her lashes and she exhaled a ragged-sounding sigh.

''Sandy?'' Jake said, approaching the desk. ''What's wrong?''

"Oh, Jake." Sandy's voice broke on a sob. "It's Marsh."

Hope stepped out from behind Jake. "What happened to him?"

Sandy's eyelids flew open and she stared at Hope in pure shock for a second. Then her cheeks turned red, her green eyes narrowed and her face contorted with what looked like rage. She rose to her feet and spat out one word. "You."

"What's going on, Sandy?" Jake demanded.

She barely glanced at him. Glaring at Hope, she raised one arm and pointed at the door. "Get out of my clinic."

Chapter Nine

Jake shook his head in disbelief. "Sandy, what the hell is going on here?"

"That was Mavis at the real estate office on the phone." Sandy's eyes again filled with tears. She dashed them away with the backs of her fingers and spoke in a venomous tone he'd never heard come out of her mouth before. "She wanted me to know that Marsh bought 'our' house. They closed on it this morning."

"What house are you talking about?" Jake asked.

"The old Bermann place. Marsh and I wanted to live there and fix it up and raise our family there. Someday. And now he's gone and bought it and he told Mavis that *she,*" Sandy pointed at Hope, then looked back at Jake, "gave him the idea. He bought our house and now he's gonna move that...witch into it."

Jake turned to Hope, his mind whirling with confusion. He hadn't seen any evidence to support Sandy's accusation, but what if it was true? "You know anything about this?"

Hope nodded, but didn't speak. Her big blue eyes spoke volumes, however. The woman was getting seriously ticked off.

"Of course she does," Sandy said. "She's probably been playing house with Marsh ever since he went to California. And what are *you* doing here with her, Jake?"

"I'm helping her out at the Double Circle until her new manager gets here."

"And I suppose you're staying at the Double Circle with her until then?"

Enough acid dripped from her voice to make Jake's temper start to simmer. "As a matter of fact I am. What business is it of yours?"

"I just wondered if Marsh knows he's sharing her with you."

Jake had long had a lot of sympathy for Sandy and her problems with Marsh, but she'd gone too far with that one. "Wait a minute. You're not thinking straight, Sandy. You can't honestly believe Marsh would do that. Or me either."

"Why not? I've seen her dancing with him often enough with her hands all over him. And I saw you kiss her at Dillon's wedding. She looked willing to take both of you on that day. And Marsh has been in California so long, he's probably just like her."

"Come on, you're not serious."

"Oh, yes, I am. And I've finally had it, Jake. You can tell Marsh for me that I hope he's real happy living there."

Hope stepped forward and stuck her chin out as if

daring Sandy to take a swing at her. "I'll tell him that for you."

"I wasn't talking to you," Sandy said.

"Too bad. I'm talking to you. Insult me all you want, but don't you dare talk about Marsh McBride with such disrespect. If he's so awful, why don't you cut him loose?"

Sandy leaned across the desk until she was right in Hope's face. "I cut him loose a long time ago."

Hope didn't even blink. "No, you didn't. You've been sitting here in Sunshine Gap, playing the poor little victim and making him feel guilty for things he didn't do, and making everyone else feel sorry for you. Well, I don't feel sorry for you. As far as I'm concerned, you're a jealous, spiteful, insecure hag, and you don't deserve a man as special as Marsh."

Sandy stripped off her lab coat and jerked her stethoscope off her neck. Jake wondered if he was going to witness one hell of a cat fight. Too bad Marsh wasn't here to see the mess he'd made of things. It'd be nice to have a camcorder along, too. Jake could make good money off a video of this confrontation.

"You can't talk to me that way," Sandy snarled.

"I just did," Hope said. "And now I'm going to tell you something else. You don't have enough heart to understand Marsh and you certainly aren't woman enough for him."

"And I suppose you are?"

"I love Marsh dearly, but not that way," Hope said.

"But you're having an affair with him."

Hope looked at Jake, rolled her eyes and let out an exasperated huff before turning back to Sandy. "You know, for someone with such a great reputation as a medical professional, you are one stupid woman. You may not be the dumbest bimbo I've ever met, but you're right up there in the top two.''

Eyes wild, Sandy turned to Jake. ''Can you believe *she's* calling *me* a bimbo?''

Jake would rather go one-on-one with a rabid cougar than get between these two gals. If he was a betting man, however, he'd pick Hope to come out on top. Sandy'd gotten in a couple of good jabs, but he figured she'd already shot off most of her verbal arsenal. Hope was hardly even warmed up yet.

''I'd call you a lot worse, but I don't want to embarrass Jake,'' Hope said. ''Now shut up for one minute and listen to what I'm saying because you might learn something valuable.''

''Why, you—''

''Read my lips, Sandy,'' Hope said, enunciating each word as if she were addressing a very young and not particularly bright child. ''Marsh did *not* buy that house for me.''

Sandy stared at her for a few seconds, then spoke in a doubtful, but quieter voice. ''He didn't?''

''No, he didn't. He got the idea when I bought the Double Circle, but my involvement in his house buying ended there. He bought that house because he was hoping you'd get so upset, you might forget you weren't talking to him.''

''How do you know that?''

''He told me so,'' Hope said. ''Oh, and by the way, not talking to him is a *great* way to solve problems.''

''Well, he always twists everything I say and takes it the wrong way and he just drives me crazy.''

''It's quite mutual,'' Hope said dryly. ''Trust me on that one. And here's another news flash. I consider my friendship with Marsh McBride to be a sacred thing, but

I am not now having, nor have I ever had an affair with him. Furthermore, I have no desire whatsoever to have an affair with him in the near or distant future. I don't think of him that way."

"Oh, right," Sandy scoffed, though she didn't sound as sure of herself as she had earlier. "I'm supposed to believe that?"

Hope shrugged. "Feel free to believe whatever you choose. But if you were smarter than a toadstool, you'd *ask* Marsh about it rather than assuming the worst of him. Which you do with disturbing regularity."

"Oh, yeah? I talked to him about you last summer and he didn't deny he was involved with you then."

"Why should he? He knew you wouldn't believe him anyway. I can tell you from firsthand experience that defending yourself against stupid assumptions gets very tiresome very quickly. After a while you simply stop trying to defend yourself, and you stop caring what someone like you thinks."

"Someone like me?"

"Someone who's already made up her mind and really doesn't want to hear anything contrary to what she believes. Not even the facts. I don't know why Marsh has tolerated your ridiculous immaturity for this long. You claim to love him, but I wouldn't treat a rabid flea-bitten dog as shabbily as you've treated Marsh. I'll be glad to see it end for his sake."

Since Sandy looked too thunderstruck to respond, Jake got in a question. "What do you mean, end?"

"What do you think I mean?" Hope asked and turned back to Sandy. "This is your last chance with Marsh. He told me he came back here to marry you or get over you. If you keep acting like an idiot, he'll find someone who'll see what a great guy he is. Once the word gets out in L.A. that he's looking, it ought to take him all of thirty seconds to replace you.''

''He really said that?'' For the first time, Sandy's voice carried a strong note of vulnerability. ''About marrying me?''

''If you want to know, stop listening to gossip and innuendo and go ask Marsh,'' Hope said. ''Not that I expect you to believe him any more than you'll believe me. After all, we're just a couple of…flaky California floozies. Everybody knows how bizarre we are. And you are *so* not worth his time.''

With that, Hope turned around and stalked out the door, her head high, her backbone straighter than a yardstick and her boot heels clomping against the tile with every step. Sandy looked up at Jake and in her troubled eyes, he saw a miserable sort of guilt he recognized all too well.

Hope had nailed Sandy, all right, but she'd nailed him, too. Now he knew why she'd withdrawn. Why she'd jumped like a scalded cat when he'd tried to kiss her this morning. Why it was going to take a lot more than listening and nodding in the right places to get back into her good graces.

He'd done every single thing to Hope that Sandy had done to Marsh. He hadn't been able to see it before, but he sure could see it now. He owed her an apology for making assumptions about her. For never asking her about things he didn't understand—like her hair colors, for instance. For listening to gossip about her and for saddling her with that awful California floozy phrase she wasn't going to forget anytime soon.

Damn, he'd really hurt her with that one.

''Do you believe her, Jake?'' Sandy asked. ''About not fooling around with Marsh, I mean?''

"Yeah," Jake said, nodding. "I've seen 'em laughing and carrying on together same as you have, but they seem more like pals than lovers. If she was really after him, I don't think she would've told you any of that stuff."

Sandy nodded, then said, "Why did you come in here today?"

"Hope tangled with some barbed wire this morning," Jake said. "She needs a few stitches and a tetanus shot, but maybe I'd better take her to the emergency room in Cody."

"Don't be silly." Sandy pulled on her lab coat and picked up the stethoscope. "I know I didn't act like it just now, but I'm a professional. Unless she needs a plastic surgeon, I can fix her up."

"You're sure?"

"Yeah, but you'd better stick around as a witness so she can't claim I hurt her. And did I hear her right? Did she actually call Marsh a...floozy? What was that about?"

"Never mind," Jake said.

It took a lot of talking, but he finally convinced Hope to go back inside. In a silence so thick it would've taken a chain saw to cut it, Sandy stitched up Hope's hand, then gave her a shot and some pain pills. After a quick stop to see Marsh at his new house, Hope climbed into the pickup for the ride home looking pale and exhausted.

"You all right?" Jake asked.

"Peachy."

"Need anything else while we're in town?"

"No." Closing her eyes, she rested her head against the seat back.

Jake drove to the county road, casting worried glances at Hope. It spooked him to see her sitting still and quiet.

"I've got a bottle of water here. Maybe you should take a pain pill."

Her eyes remained shut and her lips barely moved. "No."

"Hey, you don't have to act tough for my benefit."

"I'm not."

He subsided, but the longer her silence continued the worse he felt. "So, uh, did you tell Marsh about Sandy?"

"Yes."

"What'd he say?"

"Not much."

Jake bit back a snort of disgusted laughter. He'd had other conversations like this one, where one person wanted to talk and the other one didn't. Lots of 'em. But this was the first time he'd ever been the one who couldn't shut up. It was damn frustrating. No wonder Ellen used to get so angry at him whenever he'd pulled this kind of thing on her.

He managed to keep his lips zipped the rest of the way to the Double Circle, and then he found himself fussing around Hope like a mother hen. It would've been funny if he'd seen another guy acting this way, but it wasn't another guy. It was *him*. Strangely, instead of feeling like a fool, he kind of liked it.

Even back at the ranch Hope kept reacting to him with the same strained, irritable patience she'd shown in the pickup. This seemed to be her day for showing him his own worst behavior. Talk about a humbling experience.

With a combination of begging and bullying, he got her into the house, fed her some soup and convinced her to take a couple of pain pills and a little nap. Once she was settled, he forced himself to leave her alone. While he drove to the Flying M to pick up Rebel and the horse trailer they'd use the next day, he kept seeing her angry blue eyes and hearing her painful but heartfelt words to Sandy. And to himself.

Well, he'd find a way to make it up to her. He didn't know how for sure, but he'd think of something. Otherwise, his guilty conscience was going to eat a hole in his gut.

Hope lay on her bed listening to the sound of Jake's pickup growing fainter and fainter until she couldn't hear it at all. Convinced she finally was alone, she rolled onto her side, released a deep, shuddering sigh and allowed the tears stinging the backs of her eyes to trickle down her face.

Goodness, she'd put her foot in her mouth all the way up to her kneecap this time. Poor Marsh. He'd been so understanding when she told him what she'd done, but God only knew what price he'd have to pay for her loss of temper. Not that she hadn't meant what she'd said to Sandy.

Every single word of her diatribe had been the absolute truth. Unfortunately it hadn't been her place to deliver it. Marsh should've had that privilege. He should've been allowed to choose the time of delivery, as well.

And Jake. Why in heaven's name had she said all of that in front of him? He wasn't the sort of man who understood or appreciated emotional outbursts. He must think she was insane.

"Yeah, well, so what else is new?" she muttered, swiping under her eyes with her fingertips.

The poor guy had treated her like the most fragile creature imaginable from the moment they'd left the clinic. She could hardly fault him for it. She certainly felt fragile.

And exposed. Her tirade had been the emotional equivalent of a striptease. All the way down to the skin.

Maybe Jake hadn't realized that, though. He was a guy, after all. A guy who rarely talked about feelings, especially his own. Maybe he hadn't noticed she'd been talking about anyone other than Marsh and Sandy.

Groaning, Hope grabbed the extra pillow and put it over her head. Like hell, Jake hadn't noticed. Of all the times for him to become astute. She knocked the pillow aside and flopped onto her back.

There must be something she could do to salvage her dignity, but she was too tired to figure out what that might be. She'd never be able to sleep, of course. She never took naps, but maybe if she just closed her eyes for a few minutes, her mind would clear and she'd be able to think straight again.

"Hope?"

Hope heard the man's voice. Felt a hand nudge her shoulder. She pushed at it, wanting it to leave her alone. She was having a nice dream about Jake, and she wanted to finish it.

"Hope, honey, wake up."

"No," she mumbled, pushing at the hand again. The insistent fellow kept nudging her. He sounded a bit like Jake, or was that a part of her dream? "Tired."

"Yeah, I can see that." The mattress dipped beneath his weight when he sat down beside her. He caressed her hair, her forehead, her cheekbones. His fingertips felt rough against her skin, but they stroked her with such exquisite gentleness, she turned toward his touch rather than away from it.

"That's a mighty sweet smile, Miss Hope."

She knew that deep voice. Knew the earthy scents of horses and leather and the soap he used. Knew those firm lips teasing hers with butterfly kisses that didn't even come close to satisfying her. Jake wouldn't kiss her like that, though. This was just her dream, right? No matter. It was a great dream.

With a Herculean effort, she raised her hands to the back of her dream Jake's head and sank her fingers into his hair. It was thick and springy, as if it might have a tendency to curl if allowed to grow out. She felt his lips curve into a smile, then he pulled away from her.

"All right, princess. Wake up now." A fingertip stroked her cheek again. His voice sounded…odd. Thicker. "Let me see those pretty blue eyes."

She tucked her hands beneath her cheek and snuggled deeper into the pillow. "But I still have more sleep in me."

His chuckle warmed her. She opened her eyes and blinked a few times, trying to orient herself. Jake gazed down at her with an endearing, lopsided grin on his face.

"Are you real?" she asked.

"Yeah. I was last time I checked, anyway." His smile slowly faded. His eyes filled with concern. "How do you feel?"

The last remnants of her dream evaporated. Memories of what had happened at the clinic flooded into her mind. Why was there never a handy rock to crawl under when a person really needed one? Mortified, she turned her head away. "I'm fine."

"Hand's not hurting?"

After tentatively flexing the fingers on her bandaged hand, she shook her head. "Not much. What time is it?"

"Almost six."

She started to sit up, but he didn't move out of her way. "If you'll excuse me," she said, "I'll fix dinner."

"Don't worry about it. I've got it covered."

She shot him a doubtful glance. "You cook?"

"Not half as well as you do, but I can scramble eggs and nuke leftovers like a champ."

She forced a smile onto her mouth. "Great. Well, um, how about letting me get up?"

"In a minute. I want to talk to you first."

"Not right now, Jake. Maybe later." Yeah, that sounded reasonable. Later. Like in about a thousand years.

He didn't budge. "Look at me, Hope."

She shook her head. He reached out and cupped the side of her face with his big hand. She resisted his gentle pressure. He sighed and stopped trying to turn her head around, but he left his hand where it was, his palm curved around her jaw, his fingertips reaching to the tender spot behind her ear.

"Okay, just listen then." His voice was even deeper than usual. "You said some things today that made me take a hard look at myself and I didn't much like what I saw. I let my small-town comfort zone drown out my common sense, and I hurt you. I'm real sorry for that."

"It's all right, Jake," she murmured.

"No, it's not. I was raised to respect people of other races and religious beliefs, but I haven't been giving you even that basic respect. It's not right. Lots of folks around here poke fun at Californians because some of the stuff we see on TV that goes on down there seems alien to us and we don't understand it. There's probably even some fear of the unknown involved, but that's no excuse for being rude or cruel."

He paused for a moment, as if he expected her to say

something. Unfortunately her throat had constricted painfully when she'd realized he was apologizing, and she doubted she could speak. Finally, he continued. "I'm really not as ignorant as I've been acting, Hope. Deep down, I've known I was wrong about you for a long time, but I didn't want to admit it."

Jake paused again. "Don't you want to know why not?"

She cleared her throat, but her voice still sounded scratchy. "Why not?"

"Because, honey, you scare the bejesus out of me."

Choking on a surprised laugh, Hope rolled onto her back and looked up at him. His sheepish smile made her smile in return. "Little ol' me? Scares Big Jake McBride?"

"Yeah. Go figure."

"But how?" She stacked the pillows against the headboard and struggled into a sitting position, her eyes suddenly alight with a childlike curiosity. "Why? I'm not scary."

Jake shook his head in amazement at her instant mood shift. Hope's moods were like Wyoming's weather. If you didn't like it, all you had to do was wait five minutes and it'd change to something else. You might not like it any better, but it'd be different. And right now, the woman wanted an answer, and he felt like he was walking through a geyser field over in Yellowstone Park. One wrong step and he could wind up over his head in real hot water.

"It's complicated," he hedged. "Don't know if I could explain it."

"Try, Jake."

He rubbed the back of his neck with one hand, then leaned forward, bracing his elbows on his thighs. "At first, I couldn't figure out what to make of you at all. I'd never met anyone quite like you before, and I don't mean that as a criticism. You're just sort of...."

"Unique?"

Her impish smile tickled him. "There you go. That's the perfect word. Must be why you're a writer."

"Must be." She pulled her knees up and wrapped her arms around them. "Do go on. This is fascinating."

"Well, it seemed like you took one look at me and decided I was Mr. Wonderful. And that set me on my ear."

"I'm sure other women have found you attractive."

"Yeah, they have," he admitted, "but nobody else was ever quite so...honest about it. It confused me."

"I thought I was making myself perfectly clear."

"I didn't know if you meant it or if you were making fun of me, Hope."

"I'd never do that. You know I wouldn't."

"Now, I do, but I didn't back then. And everybody else thought you having a crush on me was so damn funny—"

"Who did?"

"Everybody. My whole family. The folks in town. I don't think anybody figured we'd make a good match."

"And you just let *them* decide we couldn't be a couple?"

When she put it that way, it sounded pretty stupid, but at the time it had seemed reasonable enough. He shrugged. "I didn't want to look like a fool, but it was more than that. I couldn't figure out what you liked so much about me. There was the age difference, too, and I never dreamed you'd want to live here. I figured I'd see you once in a blue moon because of Blair and Dillon, but it didn't make sense to start anything romantic with you.''

''But weren't you ever tempted to start something? I mean, I knew you had doubts, but there were times when I really thought you were attracted to me. Did I just imagine that?''

''You didn't imagine anything. Surprised the hell out of me to realize I had the hots for a gal with blue hair.''

''The hots?'' She laughed and faked a punch at his arm. ''Oh, McBride, you sweet talker.''

''Hey, you asked.''

''Did you ever actually *like* me?''

''Yeah. I liked a lot of things about you. I just didn't know what to do with you.''

''What did you want to do?''

Whoa. Talk about a loaded question. And there was a naughty glint in her eyes and a husky rasp in her voice that went straight to his groin. All of a sudden the room felt real cozy and private, the bed seemed awful handy and his jeans were way too tight. ''You want polite or the truth?''

''The truth.'' Her eyes were big as dinner plates, but her gaze stayed rock-steady on his. ''I always want the truth, Jake. What did you want to do with me?''

Turning toward her, Jake reached across her hips and braced his hand on the bed. ''Everything. I wanted to strip you naked and love you every which way, over and over again until we were both too tired to squeak.''

Chapter Ten

Flustered by the sudden fire in Jake's gaze, Hope leaned back against the pillows and suppressed a nearly overpowering urge to gulp, murmuring, "Oh my."

"You wanted the truth."

"I know. I just didn't expect you to be quite so, um, blunt about it." Or to look at her with such blatant...hunger. But there it was in all its thrilling, lusty reality.

One side of his mouth quirked up in a smile. "Sometimes blunt is the only way to go."

"Mmmm. I suppose you're right." She wasn't going to try to deny that she'd led this man to believe she was ready, willing and eager to fulfill all of his sexual desires. Whatever they might be.

Taking a wild guess, she imagined there might be a large number of them.

Unfortunately for all her brazen flirtation, clever repartee and scandalous reputation, most of her knowledge in this area was theoretical rather than practical. She knew the mechanics, and what her book characters would do, but they were much more adventurous than she was. She needn't panic, however.

For every situation there was always a Rule for Happiness to follow. Sometimes more than one applied. Hope suspected this might well be one of those times.

Rule Number Three, never let them see your fear, certainly fit. Or perhaps Number Six, be extremely careful what you wish for, would work. Yes, that was a good one. But there was always good old reliable Number One: never question the Universe when it gave you what you wanted.

And she *did* want Jake. She'd never wanted another man the way she wanted him, or she'd have more hands-on experience, so to speak. It was just that when she'd imagined making love with him, she'd always imagined Jake actually, well…*loving* her.

He hadn't said anything about love yet. Nor did she expect him to. Granted, it would've been nice to hear the words, but was it really necessary to have a declaration of love first? Until this moment, she'd always thought so, but what about Rule Number Four, focus on what you *do* have, not on what you don't?

Jake was right here. They were alone. He'd admitted he wanted her. He'd even admitted that he liked a lot of things about her. Perhaps love would come later.

And if not?

Well, if not, she would have found a few answers to one of life's greatest mysteries and Hope DuMaine would no longer be the biggest fraud in all of Hollywood and the publishing industry combined. Those were good things.

Besides, if she passed up this opportunity to make love with Jake, she might never get another one. If that happened, she'd never forgive herself for being such a coward. The only question was, should she tell him the truth?

Jake leaned down and kissed her, and already it was too late for confessions. The pleasure immediately took her to that place where rational thought ceased and physical sensations ruled. Oh, yes, kissing him was exactly as she remembered it, an amazing, bone-melting, mind-blowing rush of excitement she'd never expected to find in real life.

She clasped his face between her hands, wanting to keep him there until he satisfied all the aches and yearnings his mouth engendered. He made a low, rough sound in his throat and deepened the kiss, driving her head deeper into the pillow. He followed her down, resting his elbows on the bed on either side of her, rubbing his chest against her breasts.

A tantalizing heat radiated from his body. Crossing her wrists behind his neck, she completed the contact from shoulder to waist. She felt a fierce sense of satisfaction when he slid his arms under the small of her back and held her so tightly against him she could count his heartbeats.

He dragged his mouth from hers and kissed his way down the side of her neck. A day's worth of whiskers on his chin scraped her skin, raising gooseflesh along the way. She drew her shoulder up to her ear, instinctively protecting the ultra-sensitive spot where her neck and shoulder came together.

Undeterred, he simply moved to the other side of her neck, nipping with his teeth, and then soothing with the tip of his tongue while her toes curled and she shivered in delight.

"You are one tasty, delectable woman." He fingered the third snap on the front of her work shirt, then raised his gaze to meet hers. His pupils were dilated so wide his eyes looked black and the intensity in their depths made her shiver again.

His voice sounded raw and strained. "If you're gonna stop me, better do it now."

She slowly shook her head. He raised his eyebrows. "What? You don't want me to stop? Or you don't want me to go on?"

"Don't stop. But what about birth control? Safe sex?"

A slow, sexy smile turned up the corners of his mouth as he pulled his wallet out of his back pocket, retrieved a pair of foil-wrapped packets and set them within easy reach on the nightstand. Deftly dispensing with the rest of the snaps on her shirt, he slid his fingertips across her shoulders and stroked the straps of her red satin bra. Following the upper curves of the cups to the center, he flicked open the clasp and peeled the material away from her breasts. She held her breath, feeling beautiful, bashful and a million other emotions in between.

His voice was husky and fervent. "Sweet, merciful heaven."

Curving his fingertips under her rounded flesh as if testing the weight and firmness of her breasts, he let out a soft, ragged sigh. He drew his thumbs across her nipples, hardening them into tight little peaks.

Grasping his shirt, she separated the top four snaps with one yank and slid her hands into the opening. Her palms encountered warm, hard flesh dusted with crisp black whorls of hair. He froze for an instant, then swooped down and captured her mouth in a searing kiss that had her digging her fingertips into his skin in search of something stable to cling to.

She gave him back kiss for kiss, caress for caress, mirroring his movements. His skin heated, his breathing roughened. His clever hands quickly dispatched every article of clothing between them to the far corners of the room.

He pulled back and swept his gaze over her, from the top of her head to the soles of her feet. Heart pounding at the base of her throat, she smiled and silently prayed her inexperience didn't show. She'd never been completely naked with a man before, never been with a completely naked man, either.

But she didn't want Jake to know. He might get noble on her and stop no matter what she said. If he pulled away from her now, she'd simply have to kill him. Then she'd go to prison and she was positive there must be a Rule for a Happy Life about avoiding prison at all costs.

Allowing her own gaze to take him in, she felt her breath catch. He was big everywhere and beautifully formed, with long, muscular limbs, broad shoulders and a deep, well-padded chest tapering to a tight waist and a flat belly. And at his groin…sweet, merciful heaven, indeed.

"Oh, my," she murmured again, reaching out a shaky hand in case her eyes were deceiving her. "You never felt inadequate in the locker room, did you?"

He let out a ragged chuckle. "Not as I recall."

Circling his shaft with her fingers, she traced its length, down and then up again. He jerked at her touch, then sucked in a harsh breath, clenching his teeth so tight the tendons in his neck stood out. He was smooth and hot, and the thought of trying to fit him inside her made her mouth go dry. Was it possible there could be too much of a good thing? So to speak.

"Look at me." He tucked a finger under her chin and tipped it up. Her doubt must've shown in her eyes. "It'll work."

"You're absolutely certain of that?"

"Trust me." His grin was the wickedest, most appealing one she'd ever seen.

"Any woman who believes a man in your condition—"

"Will be damn glad she did."

His eyes never leaving hers, he stretched out beside her on the bed, resting his head on her pillow. She turned to face him, and then he was stroking her again, kissing her again, murmuring earthy suggestions that thrilled, amused and amazed her all at the same time. How wonderful to discover he wasn't even close to being conservative in this particular area of his life. It was even more wonderful to have their height differential vanish, allowing them to kiss without straining to reach each other.

His big hands gently moved over her, tracing the curves of her bottom, her hips, her breasts. He nuzzled her neck, then moved lower, licking and suckling at her nipples. With each caress he communicated a growing sense of urgency, igniting in her a restless craving to get closer, to touch and be touched even more intimately.

She pressed herself against him, draping her leg over his hair-roughened thigh. He returned to her mouth, kissing her repeatedly, reaching down and touching her as no one else ever had. Pleasure streaked through her body, the sensations so powerful she forgot to feel nervous.

He rolled her onto her back and rose above her, settling between her raised knees. Lost in the heady excitement he'd created and the mesmerizing desire in his eyes, she held her arms up to coax him closer, barely aware of what he was doing with the foil packet. She ran her hands up his sides and across his shoulders.

Leaning down, he kissed her once more and surged into her with a powerful thrust.

The tearing pain shocked her speechless.

He started to withdraw and just about the time she found the breath to yell at him, he surged forward again.

Teetering on the edge of a testosterone haze, Jake sucked in a harsh breath and fought for control. Man, was she ever tight. Her fingernails were biting into his shoulders hard enough to draw blood. Her body was rigid. Her face was scrunched up like a dried-out apple.

He froze—half in, half out.

Something was wrong with this picture. "What?"

"Nothing."

Her voice sounded so strained he didn't believe her. "Am I hurting you?"

She wrapped her legs around his waist. "It's all right."

"It's not all right if I'm hurting you." He tried to pull out, but she clamped down with her thighs.

"It's better now." Her face smoothed out and she smiled at him. Her smile looked a little forced, but he knew he wasn't in any shape to judge such things. "Please. Just…finish it."

She raised her hips, forcing him deep inside her and he was a goner. He thrust himself into her again and again and then lost it. Completely and totally lost it, and dammit, she wasn't even close to being with him. It had been quite a while since he'd been with a woman, but he'd never left his partner unsatisfied. He wouldn't leave Hope unsatisfied, either.

The instant he withdrew, however, she scrambled out from under him and fled the room. He flopped onto his back until he caught his breath, looked down at himself, saw blood on the condom and muttered a string of curse words that would've sent his mother running for a bar of soap.

Oh, *dammit*. Hope DuMaine was a *virgin?* Dammit, was *anything* about that woman what it seemed to be?

Rushing into the hallway, he looked both ways, saw a light shining under the bathroom door. He tried the knob, found it locked, then pounded on the door, shouting, "Hope? Are you all right?"

"Just ducky, but I can't believe I waited thirty years for *that.*"

"Hell, woman, you could've warned me."

"Don't you yell at me, Jake McBride."

Oh, damn, if she wasn't crying, she was close to it. With an effort, he lowered his voice. "Sweetheart, I'm not yelling at you. Come on out and let me make it better."

"Forget it. I'm never having sex again. Ever."

Guilt settled onto his shoulders like a two-ton Hereford bull. "Aw, honey, it's not supposed to hurt. It's supposed to feel great. It'll be lots better next time. I promise."

"Gee, where have I heard *that* before?"

"Sarcasm won't help anything. If I'd known you were a—"

"What would you have done differently?"

"Everything. I'd have gone slower. Been more careful. I thought you were pretty aroused, but..." He paused and dragged his right hand through his hair. "Well, it just never occurred to me that you hadn't done it before. You know?"

"No, I don't know. Why didn't it occur to you?"

"For one thing, you're thirty. Even around here it's a little unusual for someone to wait that long."

"So, I happen to be picky. And that's not really the reason. Is it?"

"Not the only one," he admitted. "I mean, you flirt a lot and the way you usually dress might lead a guy to think you had some…experience."

"Don't forget California. Hollywood. Everybody *knows* they're all floozies and nymphomaniacs down there."

He silently counted to ten. "I already got that message today, and I already apologized for acting stupid. And it's not just the way you dress or where you're from that made me think you weren't a virgin. It's the way you write."

Jake paused, but she didn't answer him. He propped his shoulder against the door casing, crossed his arms over his chest and lowered his voice. "I mean, how can you say things like, 'He pumped into her hard and fast, stretching her and building a delicious friction that pushed her to the edge of sanity,' if you've never done it?"

The doorknob turned. The door swung open and there stood Hope, hair wildly tousled, a whisker burn on her chin and a hickey on the side of her neck. Wrapped in a bath sheet that covered her from her armpits to her knees, she regarded him from damp, disbelieving eyes. "You've read one of my books?"

"Yeah." If he'd had pants on, he'd have stuck his hands into his pockets. *"What a Day for a Funeral."*

"What did you think of it?"

"I liked it."

"Oh yeah?" Eyes narrowing, she tipped her head slightly to one side. "What did you like about it?"

"Just about everything."

She didn't roll her eyes, but he suspected she wanted to. "Uh-huh."

"I *did,* Hope. That little actress character, Alyssa, was a real pistol, and I got so caught up in figuring out who was trying to kill her, I read the whole dang book in two evenings. And then at the end, I had it all wrong, but the real villain made perfect sense. I think it'd make a great movie."

"You do?"

"Yup. And I can see why you've made all those best-seller lists. I ordered the rest of your books off the Internet when I was over at Flying M today."

"You did?"

"Yes, ma'am. I want you to autograph all of 'em for me, too. Will you do that?" This was the strangest after-sex conversation he'd ever had, but if it calmed her down and took her mind off the disaster on the bed for a bit, he'd talk about anything.

"Of course."

"Good. But you never answered my question."

"What question?"

"How do you describe sex so well if you've never done it?"

Now she *did* roll her eyes. "Do you think mystery writers have to kill someone in order to write about murder?"

"Well, no, I suppose they don't." He scratched the bridge of his nose. "It's all in your imagination, huh?"

"Yes. And I happen to have an active one."

"You certainly do," he agreed fervently. A couple of the love scenes in her book had darn near fried his eyeballs. "So why don't you imagine trying it again? Only this time, it's great."

"Even my imagination has limits."

He wouldn't smile, dammit. Not at her crabby tone or her doubtful frown. "Aw, c'mon, it won't hurt like that again. If it did, there wouldn't be so many women who make love with their husbands all the time. You ever heard Blair or Emma complain?"

Hope shook her head. "They seem to enjoy it."

"There you go." He straightened away from the door casing. "If it was always awful, don't you think one or both of them would've told you?"

"Probably."

"Do you believe I'd hurt you intentionally?"

She shook her head again. "No, Jake."

"Well then, come back to bed."

Her eyes widened, then flickered with something close to panic. "Now?"

"Right now. The bad part's over, honey. From here on out, you'll love it."

"Oh, but—"

He cut her off before she could lay down an argument she'd have to defend. "Ever fall off a horse when you took riding lessons?"

"Once."

"And did your teacher make you get right back on?"

Scowling, she tightened her grip on the towel. "That was different."

"No, it wasn't. The same exact principle applies here. The longer you wait to make love again, the scarier it's going to get. You wouldn't saddle me with the guilt of knowing I ruined one of life's greatest pleasures for you?"

Her skin was pale, her eyes enormous. Extending his

hand, he held his breath while he waited for her answer. She hesitated so long he finally had to breathe again. "Please, Hope. If I do anything you don't like, all you have to do is say so and I'll stop. Let me at least try to make amends."

Hope looked up into Jake's eyes and felt her resolve crumble like a sand castle in a rain storm. Only a bone-deep cynic would doubt his sincerity, and she couldn't deny her own share of responsibility for this fiasco. She probably should have told him the truth. Besides, right up until that shocking moment of pain, she'd been enjoying herself immensely.

When he'd sensed her distress, Jake *had* tried to stop. She'd been the one who'd insisted on continuing. And what if he was right? She would've suffered for no reason, no reward. And he looked so hopeful, standing there with his hand held out to her, seemingly oblivious to his own nudity. She doubted she would ever be that evolved. He was too gorgeous.

"All right, Jake." When she gave him her hand, he raised it to his lips and kissed each knuckle with an old-fashioned gallantry she found incredibly touching. And arousing.

"Thank you," he said.

"For what?"

"For trusting me. I won't let you down." Scooping her into his arms, he carried her back to the bedroom and gently deposited her in the middle of the bed. He lay down beside her, rolled onto his side facing her and propped his head up on the heel of his hand. He gazed down at her without speaking, raised his free hand as if he would touch her, hesitated, then lowered it again.

"What is it?" she asked.

"I'm just wondering what else I don't know about you."

"Does it matter?"

"Yeah. This is really important and I don't want to foul it up. Is there anything you want to tell me?"

Why, he was nervous. Big Jake McBride was as nervous about making love to her as she was about allowing him to do it. He hadn't said the actual word, but she could see it in his eyes, hear it in his voice.

Her heart melted and the last of her reservations melted with it. She cupped her hand around the side of his face and caressed his cheek with her thumb. "Kiss me, Jake. Just shut up and kiss me."

His solemn expression gave way to a rueful smile. Then he leaned down and did as he was told. His kiss was warm and sweet, with a tenderness that nearly brought tears to her eyes.

Lifting her other hand, she buried her fingers in his hair and kissed him back, teasing the tip of his tongue with her own. She felt him smile against her mouth. Then he went back to kissing her as if there was no hurry, no urgency, no need to move on to anything else.

He lightly stroked her neck and shoulders, sensitizing her nerve endings to every nuance of his touch. His kisses gradually deepened into slow, drugging ones that gave her a wonderful floating sensation. Her towel fell away and he explored her body with his hands and his mouth as if he hoped to discover some small detail he'd missed the first time.

As he strayed into more intimate territory, her heart rate zoomed. Her temperature soared. The aching yearnings settled low in her belly again. She reached for him, but he captured her hands and pushed them back to the bed.

"This one's all for you, sweetheart," he said. "Relax and let me make love to you."

He returned to her lips, kissing her until her bones and muscles became pliant. His mouth nibbled the length of her neck, across her collarbones and down to her breasts. He took her right nipple between his lips, sending a jolt of pure pleasure through her. He transferred his attention to her left breast, licking the underside and tracing teasing circles around the areola, driving her crazy until she arched her back, practically demanding relief.

"Easy, easy," he murmured, his warm breath striking her nipple just before his lips closed around it. He bathed it with his tongue, then suckled it. The pleasure was immediate and intense. He made a low, rough sound that reminded her of a purring tiger.

While he continued to nuzzle at her breasts, he caressed between her thighs and carefully slid a finger deep inside her. She tightened around him, wanting to hold him there. Wanting something more. Wanting…him.

She was burning up from the inside out. Every nerve ending felt aroused and exposed. She couldn't keep her legs together or hold them still. He slid a second finger inside her and she lifted her hips to drive them deeper.

"That's it," he said, stroking her with a slow, steady rhythm. "Show me what you want. Tell me what feels good."

She was beyond speech, but what he was doing right now was just fine. Oh, really, really fine. She felt the oddest gathering sensation in her private parts, drawing her tighter and tighter. Theoretically she knew it was supposed to be something like this, but the reality far exceeded anything she'd imagined. She dug her heels into the mattress and thrashed her head back and forth, while the sensations swelled and grew. She could hardly breathe, but it didn't matter. She was reaching for something exquisite and elusive, something a millimeter beyond her grasp. She whimpered in frustration.

"It's all right," he said. "Let go and I'll catch you."

He gave her no choice. When he touched her with his thumb, the world contracted to that one small point of contact and then flew apart in powerful waves of pleasure. It *was* like flying. Or speeding across the Nevada desert in a convertible with the top down and the music blasting. Or seeing all the lights and colors of the Las Vegas strip all at once.

There simply weren't any accurate words to describe it, but it was…fabulous. Totally fabulous was the closest she could come. Before she could catch her breath he was kissing her, praising her, carefully pushing inside her again.

At the first sign of resistance he backed up a fraction of an inch, paused, then slowly surged forward. Backed up, paused, surged forward. Backed up, paused, surged forward, gradually shortening the pauses and establishing a smooth, driving rhythm that pitched her headlong into a churning ocean of delight.

Clutching his shoulders with both hands, she rose to meet each down stroke, gasping and whooping at the excitement, the searing intimacy of the contact. The gathering sensation returned, tossing her from one wave to another, each one higher than the last until she reached the top of the world, balancing on the crest for a heartbeat. He surged into her one more time and sent her flying through a bright, color-drenched universe.

As if from a distance, she heard him shout, felt him frantically pounding into her, pushing her right back up to the crest and flinging her over the edge again. This time, he flew with her, collapsing into her embrace and rolling them onto their sides. Breathing hard, they faced each other, grinning like a pair of naughty little kids.

And now she knew why people made such a fuss about sex.

"Better?" he asked.

"Oh, yeah." Gazing directly into his eyes, she cupped the side of his face with her palm. "I love you, Jake McBride."

Chapter Eleven

By ten o'clock the next morning, Hope found herself two-thirds of the way up a mountain, feeling as if she'd been dropped in the middle of a Western movie. Her horse was a chestnut mare named Susie, and for some bizarre reason, Susie thought *she* was the boss. If a cow or calf strayed one step away from the others, the horse lowered her head and charged at it, forcing it back into line with no prompting from Hope. She didn't bother to give Hope any prior warning, either.

Between the rough terrain and Susie's bone-jarring starts and stops, Hope found staying in the saddle a major challenge. Her thighs quivered with fatigue from gripping the horse's sides. Her bottom felt like raw hamburger. And certain private parts of her body, which had been sore when she'd dragged herself out of bed at four o'clock this morning, were going to catch fire any moment and burn down the national forest.

This was not the glamorous, romantic world of John Wayne, where the good guy works hard, shoots straight and ends up getting to keep the horse, the ranch and the rancher's pretty daughter, and everyone lives happily ever after. This was more surreal and nightmarish, like an old Clint Eastwood Western, where most of the characters wind up dead, maimed or otherwise miserable. The set even came complete with a brain-baking sun, dust flying everywhere and smelly, recalcitrant Herefords who never stopped bawling in protest—as if they knew their final destination was going to be a meat-packing plant.

Of course, Hope would bite off her own tongue before she'd utter one complaint. Not within Jake's hearing, anyway. Besides, whatever physical pain she now suffered was nothing compared to the ache that had started in her heart the instant she'd made the colossal blunder of saying the L-word to Jake.

It had seemed so natural, so right at the time, but his reaction was going to haunt her for the rest of her life. Her long, agonizing, humiliating life. And she absolutely was not being a drama queen.

The image of his stunned face at that appalling moment had been permanently etched into the insides of her eyelids where it could lacerate her feminine ego every time she blinked.

"What's wrong, Hope?"

Hope started at the sound of her name, then turned to face her cousin Blair, who was riding up to her on a black mare named Molly. As usual, Blair looked disgustingly beautiful, and two months of marriage to Dillon McBride had added a soft glow of contentment no cosmetic could ever hope to duplicate. The very last thing Hope wanted to do was mar her cousin's hard-won happiness. She forced herself to smile. "Nothing."

Blair leveled a doubtful, yet expectant stare at Hope. It was an old, extremely effective technique their paternal grandmother had often used to drag information out of reluctant family members. The technique worked well for Blair, but Hope had never mastered the art of staying silent and keeping a straight face long enough for it to do her any good.

"Stop it. You know how much I hate when you do that." Uttering an exasperated laugh, Hope glanced away. "I'm simply overwhelmed with all of this cow business."

"If Hollywood didn't overwhelm you, I doubt cows will. Now stop fibbing and tell me what's wrong. It's not like you to be so quiet. Especially during your first roundup."

Hope looked toward the mountain's summit, wanting to know where Jake was before she replied. Blair reined Molly around in a half circle, turning the mare toward a stand of ponderosa pines. "Come on. The horses need a rest as much as we do."

Nudging Susie with her heels, Hope followed Blair into the limited privacy offered by the trees. They dismounted and led the horses to a small stream.

"It's about Jake, isn't it?" Blair asked.

"Did he say something to Dillon?" Hope demanded.

"He didn't have to. It's written all over your face every time you look at him, and he doesn't look any happier. I thought you two had called a truce."

"We did."

"So what happened?"

"It's no big deal. Men are just…bizarre, you know?"

"Yes," Blair agreed with a smile. "And some are more bizarre than others. What's up with Jake?"

Hope shrugged. "Nothing, really. Things are a bit awkward between us at the moment. That's all."

"What things?"

"Just…things." Hope waved one hand in a dismissive gesture. "It'll all work out with time."

"You know you're going to tell me eventually." Blair ground-tied the horses and turned to face Hope. "Why don't you do it now instead of making me drag it out of you? You didn't sleep with him, did you?"

"When did you take up mind reading?" Hope grumbled.

Blair's eyes widened. "You made love with him?"

Hope's eyes burned; her throat threatened to close around a lump the size of a tennis ball. Fearing she might weep if she tried to answer, she drew in a ragged breath and nodded.

"Oh, honey." Blair's voice and her expression softened. "Your first time is a very big deal. Especially when you've waited so long."

In spite of Hope's best efforts to hold back her tears, Blair's understanding opened the floodgates. Hope scrubbed her cheeks with the backs of her fists, but it didn't help. Blair pulled her into a hug, patting her back and offering silent comfort, which only made Hope cry even harder.

"Don't." Shaking her head, Hope finally pulled away. "Don't be nice to me, or I'll never stop. Please."

"All right. I'll be really mean," Blair promised. "Just as soon as you tell me what happened."

Knowing her cousin wouldn't relent, Hope filled Blair in on the latest developments with Jake. Sharing the burden with a sympathetic listener provided Hope enormous relief, enough to get her past the urge to sob uncontrollably, anyway. "You should've seen him, Blair. It was awful. All I said was, 'I love you,' but you'd think I'd asked him for his liver."

"From his perspective, maybe you did." When Hope frowned at her, Blair held up one hand and continued. "I've been trying to figure out the McBrides for a long time. They're such strong people individually and as a family, they're fascinating."

"I agree, but what's that got to do with me and Jake?"

"Bear with me a second. My theory is that sometimes their greatest strength is also their greatest weakness."

"Which is?" Hope asked.

"An extremely well-developed sense of loyalty to the people they love. That's what makes them so strong. They always know they've got backup, from the family if nowhere else."

"Granted," Hope said. "But how is that a weakness?"

"It's not always. But sometimes it blinds them or gets in the way of them knowing what they feel as individuals."

"I'm not following you."

Blair sat on a big rock and motioned for Hope to join her. "Dillon and his sister Grace are both prime examples. Remember when I told you how Dillon was involved in the accident that killed her first husband?"

Hope nodded. "Dillon tried to stop Johnny from driving drunk, and when they crashed, Johnny died and Dillon's face got all torn up on a barbed-wire fence. Right?"

"Right. And even though Dillon was trying to do the right thing, he felt responsible for the accident. He felt so guilty about depriving Grace of her husband and a father for her boys, he gave up his rodeo career and refused to have reconstructive surgery on his face so he could be there to take care of them.''

''I always wondered why he never got his scars removed.''

Blair gave her a sad smile. ''It was as if he had to do penance, even though Cal, Zack and Jake were all there, too, and probably would've done exactly the same thing if they'd been able to get into the pickup before Dillon did.''

''You're right. Any of them would've tried to stop a drunk from driving. Poor Dillon.''

''Exactly. I don't think he ever would've married me or anyone else if I hadn't been able to convince him Grace needed to grow up and face the truth.''

''Which was?''

''Johnny was cheating on her the night he died. Everyone felt so bad for her and the boys, the whole family tried to protect her by keeping the secret. But all it did was make Grace remain stuck in a loyalty to Johnny he didn't deserve long after his death. Do you see what I mean?''

Hope nodded. ''But how does your theory apply to Jake?''

''Well, if ever a man was born to be married and have a family, Jake McBride was. From everything I've heard, he and Ellen had a wonderful relationship. But you know, when someone who really enjoyed being married is widowed, they usually remarry within a couple of years. Doesn't it strike you as odd that Jake's waited this long? It's been eight years, Hope.''

''You think that's because of excess loyalty to his wife?''

"I think it's possible."

"I suppose it could be," Hope said. "In fact, if you add in a little survivor guilt, it makes sense. Maybe he loves me, but he thinks he can't admit it without betraying Ellen."

Blair frowned. "I didn't mean that, exactly."

"What did you mean then?"

"According to Dillon, Jake's had a couple of other relationships since he was widowed."

Hope felt as if the bottom of her stomach had just dropped out. She hadn't heard anything about other women in Jake's life. Nor did she want to know about them. "So what?"

"So, nothing ever came from those relationships."

"Well, there's no way a man like him was going to stay celibate for the rest of his life."

"Granted, but Jake's no tomcat, either, Hope. I'm concerned that maybe he *can't* love anyone else."

Hope emphatically shook her head. "No. I don't believe that. I won't."

"But, Hope—"

"No. Unless you're some sort of psychopath, you don't lose your capacity to love. And it's not as if Jake doesn't love anyone. Look how protective he is with his family."

"But loving family and loving a wife are two different things. Two very different types of commitments."

Hope didn't know much about family love, but Blair didn't either. "It doesn't matter. Maybe Jake simply wasn't ready to fall in love again. Or didn't meet the right woman. There could be hundreds of reasons why those relationships didn't last."

"What makes you think yours will?"

"It just will, that's all. He'll come around, you'll see."

Blair sadly shook her head. "You know better than to start a relationship with a man expecting to change him."

"He doesn't need to change," Hope said.

"Oh, yes, he does. You're not listening to me, Hope, and I don't want to see you get hurt."

"It's too late to worry about that. I'm already in love with Jake and he loves me. He just doesn't know it yet."

"Hope, please. You've got to be reasonable."

"I'm being perfectly reasonable. Jake and I have come a very long way in the past few weeks. I'd be crazy to give up on him now." Hope gazed toward the mountains on the other side of the valley. Jake could be as hard and stubborn as those granite peaks, but she'd wear him down. Just see if she didn't.

"What are you going to do?" Blair asked.

"I'm going to keep loving him and give him time to get used to the idea of loving me."

"How much time?"

"Whatever it takes."

Jake had never felt like such a louse in his life. Or so resentful. He'd hurt Hope again, but he sure hadn't meant to.

"Come on, girls, time to go." He waved his coiled rope at a pair of cows and their calves standing in a patch of brush. The cows looked back at him, obviously unimpressed and with no inclination to obey. Rebel's ears twitched and his hide shivered with eagerness to show those Herefords who was boss. Jake nudged Rebel with his knees. "Get 'em, boy."

Rebel lowered his head and charged. The cows and

calves ran out of the brush. They'd barely gone three yards before the quarter horse wheeled around and harried them down the mountain. Jake usually enjoyed working cattle with Rebel, but today all he could think about was Hope.

Making love to her the second time had been great. Hell, better than great. It'd been…mind-boggling.

For the first time in a very long time, he'd had sex without feeling empty and lonely afterward.

He wanted to do it again darn near as much as he wanted his next heartbeat. His next meal. His next breath.

But when Hope had looked up at him and told him she loved him, she might as well've doused him with a bucket of ice water. His muscles and joints had locked up on him. A paralyzing sense of dread had stolen the air from his lungs. His brain had gone blank and he couldn't think of a single thing to say to her.

Of course, he knew what she'd wanted him to say, but he couldn't do it. He didn't love her. He couldn't love her. He *wouldn't* love her. Not the way she had in mind, anyway.

She wanted hearts, flowers and forever, and he couldn't give that to anyone now. He didn't have it to give. That part of him had died with Ellen.

He had no intention of even trying to resurrect it, but he still wanted to make love with Hope again. Unfortunately he doubted he'd ever get another chance. Since that awful moment in her bed, Hope had barely looked at him, much less spoken to him. Why couldn't anything with her be easy?

"Hey, Jake!"

Jake turned to his right and saw Dillon riding behind him. From the number of cows he'd gathered, Jake fig-

ured Dillon's palomino loved working cows as much as
Rebel did. Reining in Rebel, Jake waited for his cousin
to catch up.

"I'm ready for a break and some food," Dillon said.

"Sounds good." Jake rolled his shoulders to loosen
the kinks in his spine, then nodded toward the top of the
mountain. "That the rest of 'em?"

"Far as I could tell," Dillon answered. "I'll take another look after dinner, though."

Five minutes later, Jake saw Blair and Hope ride out
of a stand of pine trees ten yards ahead. Dillon stuck
two fingers in his mouth and let out an ear-splitting whis-
tle. Both women looked up. Blair's immediate, radiant
smile when she saw Dillon twisted Jake's guts into a
knot.

He glanced toward Hope, half-expecting her to bolt
back into the woods at the sight of him. True to form,
however, she did the unexpected and waved, then rode
uphill to meet him while Dillon rode downhill to meet
Blair.

"Hey there, handsome." Her sassy grin and dancing
eyes warmed the crisp mountain air and made him want
to kiss her so bad his lips itched. "Mind if I join you?"

"They're your cows." The brusque words were out
of his mouth before he could think about how unwel-
coming they might sound. He tended to misplace his
social skills when he felt uncomfortable. And Hope
brought out the uncomfortable in him faster than any
woman he'd ever met.

"That's right, they *are* mine," she said, her grin widening.

What the hell was she up to now? Four hours ago
she'd been looking at him as if he'd murdered her puppy
and now—without a word of apology or explanation

passing between them—she was acting as if everything was fine? If he believed that, he'd better rethink Santa, the Easter Bunny and the tooth fairy.

Much as he'd love to avoid a discussion of their ''relationship,'' he knew it was inevitable. Pretending it would go away if he ignored it was like ignoring a weakened cinch. Sooner or later the damn thing was gonna snap and he'd wind up flying ass over teakettle before he landed in the dirt. ''Hope, about last night—''

''Don't worry about it, Jake.'' She wrinkled her nose at him and shrugged one shoulder, looking adorably chagrined. ''It takes me a while to process things sometimes and now that I've had a chance to think about it, I realize I was just caught up in the excitement of the moment. I'm sorry if I made you uncomfortable.''

Jake had no idea what to say to that. She looked sincere enough. She sounded reasonable. Too reasonable for Hope? Hell, who knew? Did even God know what went on in her head?

She stood in the stirrups, leaned across the horses, slid one hand around the back of his neck, pulled him close and kissed him full on the mouth. Her lips were cool but soft, so soft. She teased him with her tongue, and in the space of a heartbeat, half his blood headed south. Settling back into her saddle, she reined her mare a couple of steps away from Rebel. ''No hard feelings, all right?''

''Uh, well, sure,'' Jake stammered.

''I'm glad.'' Her eyes took on a wicked glint and a decidedly husky note entered her voice. ''By the way, what do you want to do tonight?''

''I don't know,'' he lied, still not convinced he could trust his ears. ''What do you want to do?''

''Oh, I'm sure we'll think of something.'' She gave him a sexy little wink, sending the rest of his blood supply to his groin. Then, chuckling, she rode off after a calf that had broken away from its mother.

Jake stared after Hope, wondering if he really *was* losing his mind. She'd just offered him everything he'd wanted—more sex without declarations of love and commitment. Logically, he should feel relieved, even happy about her attitude.

But he didn't feel either of those things. He felt disappointed, somehow. Maybe even a little…angry. Hope shouldn't be willing to settle for no-strings-attached sex. She deserved better. And if that wasn't the most contrary, idiotic thought he'd ever had, it was right up there in the top three.

"Damn," Jake muttered. He was in trouble here. Big trouble. The only questions were how big and why.

Chapter Twelve

As October passed, Hope dared to believe she was making real progress with Jake. When her new ranch manager, Bonnie Jorgenson, had to delay her arrival at the Double Circle for an additional month, he stayed on to help. Hope had a lot to learn and she couldn't have asked for a better teacher.

During the daytime, he taught her about weaning calves, vaccinating and shipping cows to market and getting a ranch ready for winter. In the evenings he taught her about keeping ranch accounts on her computer. At night, he taught her about the joys of having an intimate physical relationship with a strong, sexy and virile man.

Whether they were working together, playing together, making love or arguing, she loved being with him and he gave every impression of feeling equally happy to be with her. He challenged her in ways no one ever had. Each day sparkled with the excitement of discovering some new facet of his personality, and for the first time in her life the chronic ache of loneliness lifted from her heart. She found herself starting to think in terms of ''we'' instead of ''me.''

Even after Bonnie arrived early in November, Jake remained at the Double Circle, ostensibly to make sure the graduate student knew what she was doing. Hope suspected he simply didn't want to leave her. The thought absolutely thrilled her.

She longed to hear him say he loved her but told herself not to be greedy. Rule Number Seven was actions speak louder than words. Jake treated her with tenderness and acted as if he loved her. That was enough. She'd live without the words for now, but when he said them, she'd be the happiest woman alive.

She couldn't imagine her life without him. While she never brought up the future, she refused to consider the slightest possibility he didn't love her. His family had even started treating her and Jake as if they were a couple, and to her knowledge, Jake wasn't saying anything to discourage them.

When the McBrides gathered at the Flying M for their Thanksgiving celebration, Hope felt as if she'd magically walked into her most secret, cherished dreams of having a home and belonging to a real family.

The whole clan was there. The Mamas and the Papas. All seven cousins and their spouses. Five teenagers, including Grace's boys, Riley and Steven, Alex and Nolan's kids, Natasha and Rick, and Lori's son, Brandon. And, of course, baby Kevin. Even Marsh's old girlfriend, Sandy Bishop, had been invited.

The entire day was rich in home-baked pies, roast turkey and dressing, cranberries and candied yams, women's gossip in the kitchen, men shouting and laughing at the football games on TV, and hungry kids trying to sneak goodies before dinner.

Hope soaked up every nuance of positive karmic energy floating through the house. Everything she'd ever wanted was so close she could see it, hear it, smell it, taste it and touch it. But she couldn't claim it. Not just yet.

Baby Kevin traveled from one eager set of arms to the next, charming everyone with his smiles and coos. Now six months into her pregnancy, a glowing Emma received almost as much attention as the baby. When Grace and Blair declined to drink wine with dinner, the rest of the family teased and tormented them into admitting that they, too, were expecting babies.

Joy erupted around the massive table in a flurry of hugs, back slaps and happy tears. After so much excitement, dinner was almost an anticlimax. Not that it stopped anyone from enjoying the meal, Hope noted with a grin.

Contentedly sitting beside Jake, she watched Marsh and Sandy laughing and making eyes at each other on the other side of the table. They seemed lost in a private world of their own, blissfully oblivious to the commotion going on around them. Before falling in love with Jake, Hope had never understood why Marsh had always carried a slight aura of sadness with him. Now she understood it perfectly, and she fervently hoped Sandy wouldn't hurt him again.

When the pie and coffee had been served and Hope had decided that life simply didn't get much nicer than this, Marsh stood. Tapping his water glass with a spoon to get everyone's attention, he said, "Sandy and I have another surprise for you."

He reached down and helped Sandy to her feet. Sliding a blatantly possessive arm around her waist, he pulled her close against his side. "We went to Idaho yesterday and got married."

A stunned silence followed his announcement. Then the Mamas simultaneously burst into tears and started scolding him in a combination of rapid-fire English and Italian for not waiting to have a proper wedding. The rest of the family converged on the couple, and the hugging and backslapping began all over again.

Jealousy slammed into Hope. Awful, small-minded, green-eyed-monster jealousy at Sandy's good fortune. Why did every other woman on the planet get what Hope so desperately wanted? Why did everyone else find love and belonging? She deserved those things, too.

"Mama and Aunt Mary," Marsh continued, "I know you'd have loved to have another big wedding but we've already wasted so many years, we didn't want to lose another day we could've had together." Marsh winked at them, then flashed a grin in Jake's direction. "Don't forget, you still have one more chance."

Jake inhaled sharply. Hope's stomach clenched as all eyes focused on him. Oh, damn and double damn. She'd been around the McBrides enough to know they'd all start ribbing Jake now. Sometimes it was all in good fun, but couldn't they see this wasn't one of those times? Evidently not.

"You're doomed, Jake," Zack said, starting it off.

"Yeah," Cal agreed. "Might as well give in and marry Hope now."

Hope cringed inside. Those fools might as well get out a shotgun and force Jake to the altar. As if she'd ever want him or any other man on *those* terms?

"Want to borrow my tux?" Dillon's voice held a

sharper edge than Cal's or Zack's had, and his smile didn't come close to reaching his eyes.

Not now, Dillon. Hope wanted to scream those words at the top of her lungs, but, of course, she couldn't. No, she just had to sit here and be polite while all of her hopes and dreams went up in smoke because these fools couldn't resist taking their adolescent jabs at Jake. Families were supposed to be supportive, but if this was supportive, she'd hate to see what non-supportive behavior looked like. Maybe having a big family was a mixed blessing, after all.

"No thanks," Jake said without missing a beat. "I've already had a big wedding."

Hope nearly groaned out loud. There it was, the inevitable reminder of the sainted Ellen—the woman who'd been able to read Jake's mind and had died so tragically young. The woman he'd loved, cherished and lost, and who'd ruined him for anyone else. The woman Hope had come to resent, even though she felt petty and unreasonable for doing so. Her lips trembling with the effort to hold a smile, Hope lowered her clenched hands to her lap so the others wouldn't see her fists.

Dillon braced one elbow on the table. "You have, but Hope hasn't, and she might like to have a big wedding. Wouldn't hurt you to think about it."

"I'll do that," Jake said.

If she could've reached Dillon under the table, Hope would've kicked him. Hard. She knew he meant well, but it had taken her weeks to get Jake this comfortable with their relationship.

They'd come a long way since last summer, but he wasn't ready for a permanent commitment. Not yet. All she needed was a little more time and he'd see they were meant to be together, but it wouldn't happen if his family pushed him now.

Dammit, she could still lose him.

Making her tone of voice sweet enough to rot teeth, Hope mimicked Dillon's posture and made a show of smiling at him. "Tut, tut. It's not polite to squabble after a lovely dinner. And you know, darling, I'm fairly certain that if you search hard enough, you'll discover some business of your own to mind."

As she'd hoped he would, Dillon laughed and sat back in his chair. Blair pointedly asked Marsh and Sandy about the renovations on their house. The family's attention shifted to the new topic of conversation, and Jake's stiff shoulders gradually relaxed.

Leaning over, he murmured close to her ear, "Nice save, DuMaine. Thanks."

"One does what one can," she replied softly.

He squeezed her hand. The discussion around the table continued amid second helpings of pie and refilled coffee cups until the family's teenagers volunteered to go out and feed the animals before it got dark. The Mamas excused them, then bustled off to the kitchen, their departure somehow signaling the official end of the dinner.

The men made a beeline for the TV room to watch football. Jake gave Hope a quick hug and a kiss before he hurried off to join the other guys. Feeling sick with relief, she picked up a load of dessert plates.

Blair sidled up to Hope. "That looked awfully affectionate. Perhaps I was wrong about Jake."

Hope smiled at her cousin. "Yes, you were."

Lori brought the baby over and offered him to Hope. "You did so much cooking this morning, why don't you go play with Kevin and let me take a turn in the kitchen?''

Grateful for a chance to regroup in relative privacy, Hope handed Blair the dirty plates and gathered little Kevin into her arms. He studied her intently and then smiled at her, making her yet another one of his willing slaves. ''I'd love to,'' she said, ''but I don't know much about babies.''

''Jake does,'' Grace said with a wicked grin. ''Take the little guy into the living room and see how long it takes Jake to find you. I'm betting ten minutes.''

''Five minutes, tops. I've never seen a man who loves babies more than Jake.'' Alex leaned over and rubbed the tip of her nose against Kevin's. ''But you'd better hurry before somebody else comes along and demands a turn holding him.''

Knowing Alex was right, Hope headed for the living room. She paused at the doorway, however, and turned back to the other women. ''Please, pass the word in the family not to tease Jake about me anymore.''

Grace frowned. ''It's obvious he cares about you, Hope. A little teasing won't put him off.''

''I suppose not,'' Hope said. ''It's just…''

''It's just what, Hope?'' Lori asked.

''If Jake ever wants something more permanent with me, I want it to be because he loves me.''

''I'm sure he will,'' Lori said.

''He already does,'' Grace said. ''He just hasn't figured it out yet.''

''Yeah, sometimes Jake's a little slow on the uptake, but sooner or later, he'll come around,'' Alex added.

Wondering if they were trying to convince her or themselves, Hope carried little Kevin into the seldom-used formal living room. She kicked off her shoes and curled up on the sofa, sitting with the baby on her lap, facing her. She played with his fuzzy hair, kissed his tiny fingers and tickled his tummy, promising herself that Jake *would* figure out he loved her.

She'd see to it.

She *wouldn't* lose him. Not now. Someday she'd marry him and become a member of this big, complicated, nosy and delightful family. She'd have a baby of her own to love and cuddle. Perhaps two or three babies. And they'd live happily ever after, dammit. She'd see to that, too.

If Jake's family hadn't already scared him off forever.

Jake preferred baseball to football to begin with, and he didn't particularly like either of the football teams playing that afternoon. The game degenerated into a rout for the home team and when the other guys started talking about the joys of married life—they were about as subtle as a bugling bull elk hunting for a mate—Jake got up and left the family room.

As soon as he shut the door on the TV noise, he heard a woman's soft laugh and a baby's gurgle. Somebody had his nephew nearby and it sounded as if little Kevin was in a mighty good mood. Jake followed his ears through the old parlor and on into the living room, halting abruptly in the doorway.

Hope sat on the sofa with her back braced against the arm rest, her stocking feet propped on the middle cushion. Kevin's back was braced against her upraised thighs; his face lifted toward Hope's. He thrashed his chubby little arms and legs, practically vibrating with a need to communicate while she talked to him.

"Yeah, you're one cool little dude." Hope stroked the tip of her index finger across his dandelion-fluff hair, grinning when it bounced right back up after her finger moved on. ''And I do believe you're going to be every bit as handsome as your daddy and your Uncle Jake. My goodness, you have those gorgeous McBride eyes, don't you?''

Kevin gurgled and thrashed some more. Jake couldn't blame the kid for getting so excited. He'd never seen anything more beautiful than Hope was at that moment. She looked soft and utterly maternal, her body sort of curled protectively around the baby, her eyes alight with a special glow that came from inside her. She might not have much experience with children, but she obviously enjoyed them and had all the right instincts for nurturing them.

Sliding her hands under Kevin's rump and the back of his head, she lifted him up and cuddled him to her breasts. Closing her eyes, she rubbed her cheek against the top of his head and inhaled a deep breath as if she were breathing in the baby's essence, sort of like a cow memorizing her calf's unique smell. If he lived to be an old man, Jake knew he'd never forget the naked longing on her face.

Something inside him melted. At the same time his body hardened and he desperately wanted to give her what she so clearly wanted—a child of her own. And why shouldn't he?

He didn't love Hope the way he'd loved Ellen, but where was it written that he had to? They had other things going for them—a love of children for one. They'd been getting along surprisingly well lately. They were fantastic in bed. And while some gals might've found his extended family overwhelming, Hope seemed to enjoy being with them.

Sharing the Double Circle with her would be a bonus.

He hadn't realized just how frustrated and stagnant he'd been feeling until he'd gotten away from the Flying M, his dad and Uncle Harry. Teaching Hope about ranching had given him a fresh perspective on a thousand-and-one things he'd been taking for granted. It was almost like seeing the world through a child's eyes; the woman asked more questions than a five-year-old. Her boundless curiosity and enthusiasm still amazed and amused him.

Of course, he didn't really expect her to be a full-time rancher. She was already making noises about getting back to her writing—just as he'd figured she would. She was too gifted a writer to do otherwise.

But at least she wasn't going to be some clueless, absentee landlord. If she never did another chore in her life, he'd always respect her efforts to learn about how to do them. Should her manager get sick or injured, Hope now knew what needed to be done for the well-being of her stock and her land. She could handle things on her own long enough to get help.

Somehow Kevin managed to connect his grasping fingers with Hope's hoop earring. She captured his hand before he could really yank on it and hurt her, but the little stinker wasn't planning to let go of the shiny gold object.

"Whoops, sweetie." She winced. "I'm attached to that."

Jake hurried across the room to help her. "Hey, there, Kevin. Aren't you a little young to be pickin' on girls?"

Kevin turned his head toward Jake and gave him a drooly smile. Jake went down on one knee beside the sofa and gently peeled the tiny fingers off the earring. The baby clouded up to bawl. Jake grabbed him under the arms. Supporting the back of Kevin's head with his fingers, Jake held the baby up and blew a raspberry on his tummy.

"Oh, thank you," Hope said, grinning when Kevin chortled.

"My pleasure." Jake blew another raspberry, then sat on the sofa beside Hope, settling Kevin on his knees facing them. "He's getting pretty good control of his head now, isn't he?"

"He certainly is." Hope reached out and chucked Kevin under his chin. "He's so adorable."

"Just wait until he's two, into everything and the only word he says is *no*."

"You'll still adore him."

Jake snorted. "Maybe."

Hope laughed at Jake's doubtful tone. "McBride, you are such a faker. Everybody knows you're a big, gooey marshmallow when it comes to kids."

"Oh, yeah? Well, at least I don't give my cows names like Cowthryn Hepburn and Tallulah Beefhead."

"When cows have that much attitude, they need good names."

"It only makes it harder to ship 'em to market."

"Right. As if you're so heartless and unattached. You can look at a cow and recite her whole sexual and obstetrical history."

"That's just business."

Hope snickered at his aggrieved expression. "Uh-huh."

They continued to wrangle and entertain the baby. One by one, the rest of the family drifted into the living room. When little Kevin finally got fussy from too much attention, Lori took him upstairs for a feeding and a nap. Jake rested his arm along the sofa back behind Hope's head, absently caressing her hair and shoulder.

Hope leaned against his side, soaking up more of the cozy, relaxed atmosphere this family generated without even trying. She thought it must be a product of the love and respect the McBrides had for each other. If they only knew how rare and special that was, they would guard it far more closely.

Glancing around the room, Hope spotted Emma and Blair happily snuggled up with their husbands, much as she was snuggled up with Jake. Conversation ebbed and flowed as people came and went; food and drink appeared and disappeared as the hours passed. Through it all, Jake remained at Hope's side, acting as if there was nowhere else he'd rather be.

By the time he quietly asked if she was ready to go home, Hope couldn't wait to be alone with him. In spite of the earlier glitch at the dinner table, the day had been so perfect, surely the night to come would be fantastic.

While Jake went to get their coats, she hurried to the kitchen to collect the dishes she'd brought for her contribution to the dinner. When she stepped through the doorway, she found Sandy taking a container of cranberry salad out of the refrigerator. Hope abruptly halted.

Uh-oh. She'd forgotten about the newest member of the McBride family. Marsh was in love with the woman, but Hope remembered how consistently Sandy had hurt him over the years. Still, Hope promised herself she would try to get along with Sandy for Marsh's sake.

Looking every bit as ill at ease as Hope felt, Sandy shut the refrigerator and set the salad on the work island. "Hi."

"Hi." Hope detoured around the opposite side of the work island and took her pie plates from the dish drainer beside the sink. "That was a great salad you brought."

"Thanks." Sandy turned around, resting the small of

her back against the counter. There were faint lines of
strain around her nose and mouth. "Your pies were
good, too."

"Thanks." Hope met Sandy's gaze and tried hard to
be sincere. Or at least *act* sincere. "Congratulations
again. I hope you and Marsh will be very happy together."

"Do you mean that?"

So, the nurse wanted to tango, did she? Slowly walking back to the work island, Hope set her pie plates down
beside Sandy's salad container. "Marsh is my friend. Of
course I want him to be happy."

"But you don't really think that'll happen. With me,"
Sandy said. "Do you?"

Hope shrugged as if she had no vested interest in the
matter. Which was a big, fat lie. Marsh wasn't simply
her friend; he was her very best writing buddy. Losing
access to him would be as devastating as losing her
sight. "It's *your* marriage. What I think really doesn't
matter, does it?"

"Probably not in the long run," Sandy agreed, "but
your friendship means a lot to Marsh."

"Marsh's friendship means a lot to me," Hope said
softly.

"He says you two help each other a lot with your
writing."

"That's right. We've been trading suggestions ever
since he came to California. It's worked well for both
of us."

Sandy turned more fully toward Hope and looked her
straight in the eye. "Then I hope you'll continue to help
each other."

"Are you sure of that? I don't want to cause him any
problems."

"I want him to be happy, too, Hope. I certainly don't intend to try to choose his friends for him." Sandy glanced away and spent a moment fiddling with the plastic wrap covering her salad. "Do you suppose maybe we could be...friends? You and me?"

"I suppose we can at least be civil when we see each other," Hope said cautiously.

One side of Sandy's mouth twitched. "I was hoping for a little better than civil."

"Why?"

"You're awfully important to Marsh."

"And that still bothers you, doesn't it?" Hope asked.

Shaking her head, Sandy smiled. "Not anymore. Not the way you mean, anyway. I've finally learned to trust him."

Intrigued by the other woman's honesty, Hope asked, "Why didn't you before?"

"It's complicated, but he always seemed so...perfect, somehow, I couldn't believe he really wanted to be with me. When he insisted on going to Los Angeles, I didn't think I could compete with all of those gorgeous Hollywood women."

"You never had to. No matter who he dated, Marsh never forgot you. You could've had him back any time you wanted."

"I know that now. Believe it or not, I'll always be grateful to you for letting me have it the day I stitched up your hand." Sandy's smile turned rueful. "No one but my mother's ever talked to me quite that way before."

Hope smiled back at her. "No one's ever ordered me out of a clinic, either."

"And I've never done that to anyone else." Sandy laughed and shook her head again. "Lord, I was so embarrassed when I thought about that. I can't believe how unprofessional I was.''

"I'm sure you felt provoked.''

"I'm still sorry about it. Can we start over? At least try to get to know each other and be friends?''

"I will if you will.'' Hope offered her hand to seal the bargain.

"Gladly.'' Sandy shook Hope's hand, raising her eyebrows in query when Hope refused to release her.

"So, if you come home late from work some night and find me and your husband holed up in his den, drinking wine and thrashing out plot points for a book or a screenplay, you'll be all right with that?''

"How often should I expect this to happen?''

"No more than once or twice a month.''

Sandy grinned. "I can handle it if Jake can.''

"Jake's got nothing to say about it,'' Hope said.

"Not yet, but after watching him with you today, I suspect he will before very long. For whatever it's worth, I'm glad to see you two together.''

"Really? Why?''

"I think you're good for him. He seems younger when he's with you. Happier.''

"If you want to be my friend you could point that out to him.''

"Gladly. We'd all love to see Jake settle down and get his ranch.''

"*His* ranch?'' Hope's insides froze in an instant and it hurt to draw a full breath. Dammit, she'd finally started to feel okay about her relationship with Jake again, and here it came, her old pal, insecurity. She wanted to ignore it, but she couldn't; Rule Number Eight was trust your gut. She'd been doing that too long to stop now. "You're talking about the Double Circle?''

"Yeah." As if she'd read Hope's thoughts, Sandy hurriedly added, "Not that he'd marry you to get it or anything. He'd never do that. But everybody knows he's always wanted it."

"Of course not," Hope agreed, even while her mind screamed, *what if he would?* Heavens, didn't she have enough issues to sort through when it came to Jake?

Jake entered the kitchen with Hope's purple parka folded over his arm. "You two look mighty serious. Something wrong?"

"Not at all." Hope turned her back and allowed him to help her with her coat, then picked up her pie plates and forced a smile onto her face. "See you later, Sandy."

Chapter Thirteen

Tightening his grip on the pickup's steering wheel, Jake made the turn toward the Double Circle. It was dark outside, with a frigid north wind pushing a storm out of Canada predicted to drop six inches of snow before morning. A continuous stream of snowflakes blew sideways in front of the headlights. Hope huddled in the passenger seat, her arms crossed over her chest, elbows hugging her sides, shoulders hunched halfway to her ears.

"That was a great Thanksgiving, wasn't it?" Jake asked.

"Yes."

Hope's reply sounded a touch on the curt side, but Jake figured she was probably cold. Poor little gal didn't have enough body fat to keep a sparrow warm, and she hadn't acclimated to a Wyoming winter yet. He nudged the heater up another notch.

"You know, when we were all living on the Flying M, my family drove me so nuts, all I could think about was getting out of there and having my own place," he said. "But since we've gone our separate ways, it was really fun to get the whole wrecking crew together again."

He paused, but when Hope didn't say anything, he continued. "And could you believe all those announcements? This time next year, we'll have three babies at the table and who knows how many more on the way. The Mamas'll be in heaven."

Hope remained silent. Jake decided he was getting tired of trying to carry on this conversation by himself. "Did you know Marsh and Sandy were planning to elope?"

"No."

Hope sounded even more curt this time. Jake chewed on that for a quarter mile. "Does it bother you?"

"What?"

"That Marsh and Sandy got married."

"No."

"What's wrong then?"

"Nothing."

Jake frowned. He hated it when something was obviously wrong and a woman clammed up. Why did they *do* that? "Did my family embarrass you today?"

"I was afraid they'd embarrassed you," she said.

"Not enough to worry about." Neither of them spoke for another mile, the tension in the truck's cab expanding like a big, dark thunderhead. "Sure you're all right?"

"I'm fine." Now her voice was tinged with impatience, or maybe it was exasperation. Jake was starting to feel both of those things. For God's sake, he was just trying to get a little conversation going, and she was acting— "Why do you ask, Jake?"

"Because it's not like you to be so quiet. I usually have to fight to get a word in edgewise."

"Well, here's your chance to make up for lost time, big guy." Her soft laugh held a surprisingly sharp edge. "Consider my lips zipped and chatter to your heart's content."

"That's not what I meant," he protested. "I only want to know what's going on with you."

"I'm tired."

"Baloney. You're never tired."

There came that sharp-edged laugh again. "A lot you know. Crowds exhaust me, and your family qualifies as a crowd."

She had a point with that one. "Sure that's all it is?"

"Positive."

He still didn't believe her but decided not to push it. Hope rarely was cranky. If he gave her time and space, she'd likely be back to her cheery self by the time they got home.

Home?

The word reverberated in his mind, jarring him with its rightness. But it wasn't right. The Flying M was his home; had always been his home. Nothing had happened to change that.

He'd been staying at the Double Circle for a few weeks, but it was Hope's place, not his. Of course, if they got married... Jeez, Louise, there it was again.

The damned M-word.

Sure, he'd thought about it some earlier that afternoon, but not for long. Being single was tougher during the holidays, and he'd figured he'd get over the qualms of loneliness the way he always did. But he hadn't. Not yet, anyway.

But did he really *want* to marry Hope?

Or did the idea keep popping up today because his family obviously expected him to marry her? Or it might be plain old, stupid peer pressure—he wanted a spouse because the rest of his siblings had them. Or maybe he just liked having sex on a regular basis.

He'd been enjoying that, all right.

He shifted around in his seat, rolled his shoulders to loosen stiff muscles and glanced over at Hope. She sat still as a doe hiding in the bushes, hands folded in her lap, her gaze directed out the side window. He'd bet his last nickel she was pondering something.

Whatever it was—world peace, a letter to the editor of the Cody newspaper or the lyrics to a new song—Jake wished she'd tell him about it. He enjoyed her laughing and teasing, but her reflective moods were equally fascinating. He had to stretch his own mind to keep up with hers. He liked the feeling, and lately he'd found himself reading more and thinking more about the news so he'd have something intelligent to talk about.

The Double Circle's gate loomed on the right. Jake slowed for the turn, and when the big old house came into view, he smiled. There was enough fresh snow to hide the sagging spot in the roof and a few other problems. Put up colored lights and decorations, and it'd look like a Christmas card. And damned if the word *home* didn't pop into his mind again.

An image of kids romping in that yard, playing Fox and Geese, making angels and having snowball fights formed in his mind's eye and a tightness filled his chest.

He parked at the back door, then, acting on sheer instinct, he reached for her arm, holding her in place. "Wait."

"What is it?" she asked.

The words he really wanted wouldn't come out of his mouth, but he had to say something. "I'm...starving."

She looked at him as if he'd lost his mind. Maybe he had. "You ate enough for five people today. You can't be hungry."

"Not for food." He hauled her onto his lap, tipped her chin up with two fingers and brushed his mouth against hers. "For this. Feels like I haven't had a decent kiss in days."

After a moment's hesitation, she seemed to relax and murmured, "Mmm. Me too."

Then she sort of melted into his embrace and returned his kiss with gratifying enthusiasm. The tension between them turned to fog and drifted away. Oh, yeah. This was what he wanted, what he'd been wanting all day.

It wasn't love, but it was more than sex. There was a sense of real...intimacy here, for lack of a better word. He'd missed that and hadn't realized it.

Something thumped hard against the passenger door, rocking the vehicle and startling them into jerking apart. Jake looked at the window and saw Doofus's head rise up into view, then drop out of sight. Rise up, then drop out of sight. Rise up, then drop out of sight, his long ears flying out like wings.

Hope laughed. "The welcoming committee's arrived."

"Yeah and he won't go away until he gets some attention." Hope opened the door and hopped to the ground, lavishing Doofus with pets and coos. Jake wanted her to do that to him. To run her hands over him and smile at him the same way. Oh, brother, now he was jealous of a dog. And not even a very bright dog at that.

He left Hope to tussle with the ecstatic mutt, opened up the house and turned on a light. When he went back outside, Hope was throwing snowballs. Jake would've scolded her for not wearing gloves, but he didn't plan to let her stay out here long enough to do any real damage.

Doofus was in heaven. Every time Hope threw a snowball, he charged after it, jumped to catch it in flight and shook his head in surprise when it exploded in his mouth. Then, tongue lolling, he'd trot back to Hope and dance around her feet, begging for another one to chase.

When he figured they'd all had enough, Jake pointed at the barn and said, "Doofus, bedtime."

The dog hesitated, clearly wanting to go on with his favorite game. Jake repeated the command. Doofus lowered his head and slunk off in the appropriate direction, tail tucked between his hind legs.

"Oh, Jake," Hope murmured, "he wasn't done playing."

"He'll never be done playing." Jake leaned down, put one hand behind her back, the other behind her knees and scooped her into his arms. "He'll chase snowballs until your arm dies."

Hope put one arm around his neck and rested her head in the crook of his shoulder. "But it's cold out."

"That's why he's got fur." Chuckling, Jake carried her into the house and shut the door with his rump. "Besides, he's got more blankets on his bed than we do."

"I still worry about him."

"He's fine, honey. Worry about me instead."

Jake lowered his head and kissed her. Her sigh of surrender hit him hard in the groin. With more haste than finesse, he stripped off their coats and hauled her upstairs to the bedroom. After placing her on the bed, he switched on a bedside lamp, stepped back and gazed down at her.

She raised one hand and held it out to him. Though he knew she was fit and surprisingly strong for a woman, at the moment she looked small and fragile. Her pretty blue eyes held a vulnerability he'd never seen before. And her mouth, her sweet, generous, kissable mouth, trembled slightly.

Oh, boy. His body was clamoring for quick, decisive action, but any fool could see this woman needed tenderness. He didn't know why. He just knew she did.

And he didn't want to let her down.

He turned away, inhaled a deep breath and took a minute to light the trio of fat candles she kept on her dresser. The scent of vanilla filled the room. Returning to the bed, he switched off the lamp in favor of the softer candlelight, sat down beside her and brushed the backs of his knuckles across her smooth cheek.

"Make love to me, Jake," she whispered.

"My pleasure, sweetheart."

And it was his pleasure. He liked good, old, rock 'em-sock 'em, hard-driving sex as much as any man, but sometimes a gentler joining could be just as powerful. If not more so. He got rid of his boots and her shoes, then stretched out on his side, facing her.

He led her into the dance of lovemaking, slowing himself down by pretending he was a teenager enjoying the simple joys of necking with his girlfriend—with no expectation that it would ever go any further. Damn, but he loved kissing her. The soft plumpness of her lips, the slight roughness of her tongue, the taste of her eager response drew him deeper and deeper.

Guided by his own instincts and her responses, he stroked, nibbled and tasted the most sensitive spots on her body, first through her clothes and then skin to skin. Far from passive by nature, she demanded that he take off his clothes, but once he complied, she subsided and allowed him to continue his exploration. In seconds, he was as besotted with her as Doofus.

After her less-than-perfect initiation, she'd taken to sex like an antelope did to running. For which he was utterly grateful. A man couldn't ask for a bigger turn-on than his partner's unbridled enjoyment.

In fact, making love with her made him think of sky-diving or bungee-jumping—dangerous as hell, but exciting and liberating enough to make a man want to repeat the experience. No matter how many times he made love to her, he couldn't seem to get enough. He doubted he ever would.

She was soft and curvy here, sleek and firm there, satin and pure fire everywhere else. Each kiss and caress worked like a drug in his blood. He was addicted to the scent and texture of her hair, the scent and flavors and softness of her skin. To the sounds of her gasps, sighs and moans. To the bawdy things she occasionally shouted when she was in the throes of passion.

He nibbled a path from the side of her neck, around and over her breasts, across her tummy, down to that sweet, sweet spot between her thighs. He slid a finger inside her and found her hot and slick. At the first touch of his tongue, her hips reared up off the bed.

When he took her sensitive little nub into his mouth and sucked on it, she exhorted him to continue. She'd blush purple if she ever really heard herself. Smiling at the thought, he drove her up and over the edge.

While she still had that I'm-floating-on-the-ceiling

look in her eyes, he sheathed himself with a condom and entered her. Her body accommodated him as if they'd been lovers for years instead of weeks. Oh, *jeez.* Feeling her fiercely closing around him nearly undid him, but he didn't want to hurry.

Not because of her, but because *he* didn't want this to end. Being inside her like this made him feel alive and potent and connected. The combination was damn near as compelling and seductive as the promise of physical release.

He raised his gaze to meet hers. Deep in her eyes, he saw that sense of connection reflected back to him, growing more powerful with each rhythmic stroke of his body. She put her hands on his hips and dug her fingernails into his skin.

"Yes. Yes. Yes," she chanted, pulling him into her as if she wanted to completely absorb him.

He struggled to slow down, but when she curled her toes and shrieked a final "Yes!" he lost all semblance of control. Nature took over and he hammered into her as though he'd never have sex again in this or any future lifetime. Stars and planets, hell, entire solar systems exploded inside his head.

Chest heaving, he collapsed, quickly rolling to his side so she wouldn't get crushed. She turned onto her side to face him. They were both trembling, damp from exertion and grinning like a pair of goofballs.

"Marry me, Hope," he said.

The proposal blurted out of Jake's mouth without a hint of prior warning. It was safe to say he'd surprised himself as much, if not more, than he'd obviously surprised Hope. Oh, he'd considered the idea a couple of times during the day, but he hadn't made a clear-cut decision. The impulsiveness of it disturbed him.

Alex, Cal and Marsh were the impulsive ones in the family, not him. Never him. And yet, it felt right. Marrying Hope was exactly what he wanted to do.

The prospect of sharing a bed with her for the rest of his life sounded great; sharing his days with her wouldn't be half bad, either. With Hope around, he'd have fun. He'd never be bored. He'd eat better than the governor. The more he thought about it, the more he liked the idea.

But Hope was still staring at him in wide-eyed, open-mouthed astonishment. Poor little gal, he really had stunned her. It wasn't often anybody could render her speechless.

"Well?" he said. "What do you think?"

"I, um...." She shook her head hard, as if she couldn't trust what her ears had heard. "I don't know what to say."

Grinning at her confusion, he reached over and smoothed her tousled hair out of her eyes. "The answer's real simple, honey. Just say yes."

"It's so...sudden, Jake." She pulled back, dislodging his fingers from her hair. "Give me a second to think."

Uh-oh. Hope wanting to think was not a good idea. What was wrong with this picture?

Shouldn't she be smiling by now? Throwing her arms around him and peppering his face with kisses? Saying *yes,* dammit?

After all, she was the one who'd come after him and started this relationship. She'd given him her virginity. Let him live with her for two months, give or take a few days. Shoot, she'd come right out and said she loved him, and he'd bet his saddle she still did.

Why wasn't she jumping at the chance to become his wife? When a woman was sleeping with a man on a regular basis, she always wanted marriage. A little voice inside his head whispered, *Not always. Not in Holly-wood. Some of those gals don't even get married when they have kids on purpose.*

Jake ordered the little voice to shut the hell up. Hope wasn't like that. It'd taken him a while to learn that lesson, but dammit, he'd learned it.

Knowing Hope, she was just being contrary, as usual. By now he should've expected her reaction to be the most illogical one possible. Not that he was handling the situation a whole lot better. Since he'd acted impulsively and this wasn't a big love match—on his part, anyway—it shouldn't bother him if she wasn't exactly panting to accept his proposal.

But it *did* bother him.

It bothered him a lot, dammit.

Was contrariness catching or what? He didn't think so, but with Hope involved, anything could happen. Aw, nuts. The whole idea was ridiculous. Of course it was. He'd known it and said so all along. But....

Truth was, he knew Hope had already spoiled him for other women. He didn't have to be in love with her to realize that after he'd been with her, he didn't want any-one else and probably never would. They fit so well together in so many ways, the possibility of her refusing him was unacceptable.

Hell, it was unthinkable.

But she'd closed her mouth and her lips were pressed together in a ruler-straight line. The astonishment in her big blue eyes had faded to something he couldn't get a read on. Wariness, most likely. If his proposal made her the least bit happy, she was doing a damn fine job of hiding it.

Hope watched a variety of emotions flicker across

Jake's face and felt her heart sink to the pit of her stomach and beyond. If he'd asked her to marry him yesterday or next week, she would've been delighted. But not now. Not *today*. Not when she could still hear Sandy's flustered attempt to assure her Jake wouldn't marry her to get "his" ranch.

Were the stars and planets out of phase, or did the McBrides simply carry a genetic defect for incredibly bad timing? But maybe she was wrong and Jake finally had realized he loved her. She might be a little overly sensitive about him and his desire to own the Double Circle.

"Why do you want to marry me, Jake?"

He looked surprised, perhaps even a bit affronted by her question. "Why not?"

She wanted to yell at him, beat on him, smother him with a pillow. But she couldn't do any of that without revealing too much. Her heart had been bruised quite enough for one day. She didn't need this.

With grim determination to get at the truth, she produced a smile. "Why not? Pardon me, but you look exactly like the guy who quite recently had a whole list of reasons we shouldn't even date each other."

"I didn't know you very well then." He shrugged one brawny shoulder. "You've grown on me."

"A fungus will do that, too, but you wouldn't want to marry one. I don't think you really want to marry me, either."

"I wouldn't have proposed to you if I didn't."

"What changed your mind?"

"Lots of things."

Hope sat up, propped some pillows behind her back and pulled the sheet up over her breasts, tucking it under her armpits. "Such as?"

"Aw, come on, Hope." He gave her one of those male, don't-make-me-talk-about-feelings scowls. "You know what's been going on between us."

"Humor me," she said. "I want to hear your take on it."

"Oh, all right." Jake sat up, as well, angling his body toward hers. "Well, for one thing, I like living with you. We're more compatible than I ever thought we'd be."

She'd give him that one, but it wasn't what she really needed to hear. "What else changed your mind?"

"We have great sex." He waggled his eyebrows at her, but she simply couldn't force another smile.

Pleating the sheet where it lay across her knees, she nodded, still praying he would give her the one acceptable reason. "What else?"

"My family sure likes you, and you seem to like them. That's a big bonus with a family like mine."

True, but it was hardly a good reason to get married. "What else?"

"We both like kids."

He wasn't going to say it, but she'd come too far to give up without seeing it to the bitter end. "What else?"

"We both like living on a ranch."

Dammit, there it was. George had seen it. Sandy had seen it. Even Blair had seen it and tried to warn her. Hope hadn't wanted to believe it then, but she had to believe it now. "Right. Especially *this* one."

Jake stiffened and a vertical crease appeared between his eyebrows. "What's that supposed to mean?"

Convinced he was being deliberately obtuse, Hope tossed up her hands in exasperation. Time to stop playing games. "You don't want to go back and live at the Flying M and have to hassle with the Papas again. But you can avoid all of that if you simply marry me and take over running the Double Circle. And then you get what you've really wanted all along anyway. How tidy.''

Jake's jaw dropped halfway to his chest. "Where'd you get a screwy idea like that?"

"From you."

"No way." Glaring at her, he jabbed a hand through his hair. "Honey, your imagination's gone completely berserk."

"It makes more sense than any of your other stupid reasons for wanting to marry me."

"They weren't stupid. What the hell were you looking for?"

"Think hard, Jake. You know the answer. If you get it right you win a million dollars and a fur-lined coffee-maker."

"Dammit, Hope, this isn't funny."

"You're absolutely right. It's insulting."

"Insulting!" Even in the candlelight, she could see his face flush. "A marriage proposal is insulting?"

"You might as well be proposing a business deal— some sort of merger—not a marriage."

"I never said that."

"You didn't have to. Just tell me one thing and give me an honest answer." She paused and looked him straight in the eye. "Do you love me, Jake?"

His gaze dropped to his knees like a rock falling off a table. She heard him swallow. And then, as she'd expected, he slowly shook his head.

"It's not that I don't want to. I don't think I *can* love anyone again. Not the way you mean."

Damn Blair for being right. "I see."

He raised his gaze and met hers. His voice sounded husky, as if the words scraped at the inside of his throat on their way out. "I care about you, Hope. I care a lot about you, and I'll do everything I can to make you happy.''

''Not good en—''

He cut her off as if he believed he could change her mind if he talked fast enough. ''Don't think about it so much. Marry me and with time, who knows what'll happen?''

''Not good enough.'' She wrapped her arms around herself to contain the pain ripping into her heart and her soul. Was there a sign on her forehead that said Unlovable Woman or what? ''I grew up with parents who didn't love me the way I needed them to love me. I'm not going to saddle myself with a husband who doesn't love me, either. I deserve better than that.''

''You don't have to have all that head-over-heels junk to have a good marriage.''

''What part of 'not good enough' don't you understand?''

''When you've got everything else going for you, being in love's not that big of a deal.''

''Excuse me?'' Hope grabbed a loose pillow and swung it at his fat head, but he batted it away. ''It's a very big deal and if you can't see that, you're not half the man I thought you were. I feel sorry for you.''

''I don't want your damn pity.''

''Too bad, you've already got it.''

He swung his legs over the side of the bed, turning his back on her. His shoulders and spine looked rigid enough to shatter at a touch and he gripped the edge of the mattress so hard, she expected it to rip apart. His body language practically shouted ''back off,'' but Hope loved him too much to do that. Someone should have made him face this years ago.

''If you believe love isn't a big deal,'' she said, ''I

wonder what your marriage was really like. I'll bet your wife—''

Whipping his head around, he shot her a look hot enough to barbecue a whole steer. "Leave Ellen out of this."

"How can I when you won't?"

"I never mentioned her."

"No. You didn't, but she's here between us every damn minute. And don't you think it's a bit strange you've never talked about her at all with me?"

"No. After a few months, most people—especially women—don't want to hear about a guy's dead wife."

"Your family won't even talk about her if you're around."

"Why should they?" he demanded. "It's damn painful."

"Honestly, Jake, that's an insult to her memory. Are you sure you ever loved her?"

His voice went dangerously soft. "That's enough, Hope."

Believing it was her only chance to shake him up enough to see the truth about his past and his future, Hope plunged ahead. "But you've nearly erased her. If you really loved Ellen, you'd want to share the memories of your happy times with her. You'd want to feel that way again, not hide from it."

"You don't know what the hell you're talking about."

She had an undergraduate psych degree that said otherwise. "I've heard wonderful things about your wife, but you've built her and your marriage into some fantasy that's so perfect, nothing and nobody else could possibly hope to compete. You're hanging on to a woman who's been gone for eight years, Jake. You're stuck in the grief cycle."

He stood and turned around to face her, the tendons in his neck standing out, big fists clenched at his sides. "Stop it."

Though she wasn't afraid of Jake, Hope suspected a smart woman would heed his warning. But she couldn't stop now. She'd already gone too far to take anything back, even if she wanted to. Which she damn well didn't. "If Ellen loved you, she wouldn't want this. She'd want you to finish grieving for her and move on with your life."

"You think it's *easy?*"

His shout echoing in her ears, Hope slid off her side of the bed, yanked the top sheet free and wrapped it around herself. "No, it must be the most difficult, painful thing in the world."

"You've got that much right."

Struggling to rein in her own temper, she deliberately lowered her voice. "But until you do it, you'll never have a decent relationship with anyone else. I don't mind talking about your wife, but I don't want to be her stand-in."

They faced each other across the rumpled bed, breathing hard. At last Jake's fists loosened and his shoulders slumped a bit. When he spoke, he lowered his voice to match hers. "You wouldn't be Ellen's stand-in. You're nothing like her."

"I've gathered as much," Hope said, "but I still want to be loved as much as she was."

"Hell." He closed his eyes and pinched the bridge of his nose between his thumb and forefinger, then looked back at her. "I watched you playing with Kevin today, and I saw how much you love babies. I got to thinking we could make some gorgeous babies together. Wouldn't you like that?"

"I'd love it," she admitted. "But I want my babies to be conceived and born in love. I want them to have the security of parents who love them and each other. You won't give me that."

"I *can't,* Hope."

"Then I can't marry you."

He stared at her for an aching moment, as if he expected her to recant. When she didn't, he swore, bent down and scooped his clothes off the floor. He dressed with brutally efficient motions. He stomped to the doorway, then stopped and looked over his shoulder at her. "This isn't over, Hope."

"That's up to you. My terms are absolutely nonnegotiable."

"We'll see. Let's talk about this again later when we've had time to cool off." Without giving her a chance to respond, he strode into the hallway and was instantly out of sight.

Hope whispered a shaky, "Goodbye, Jake," while his boot heels thumped down the stairs. When she heard the back door open and shut, and his pickup's engine roar to life, she whipped off the sheet, picked up her own clothes and put them on. Damn that big coward. He had no intention of changing his mind.

Well, she had no intention of hanging around and allowing him to go to work on changing hers. She loved him so much, she might weaken and give in. Ultimately that would only hurt both of them, and she'd end up resenting him, if not hating him.

She'd gambled with her heart and lost. It was time to cut her losses and go home. After all, that's where flaky little California floozies belonged. At least in Hollywood she could recognize the phonies when she met them.

Chapter Fourteen

The Thanksgiving snowstorm dropped two feet of snow, and then an arctic cold front with vicious winds moved in behind it. The temperature dropped to twenty below zero and stayed there for five days. Knowing he wasn't ready to see Hope again, Jake helped the Papas feed the stock at the Flying M and sent Dillon to help out at the Double Circle.

There was nothing like battling the elements for a few days to put problems into perspective. Even though the weather improved, Jake stayed away over the next weekend and on through Monday, giving Hope extra time to start missing him. Apparently, however, by the time she missed him enough to call, he'd be older than George. On Tuesday morning Jake decided he'd had enough and headed back to the Double Circle. It was time they talked this all out.

Out of habit, he stopped at the gate and picked up her

mail. A postcard sporting a sun-drenched beach, palm trees, sparkling blue water and with Tahiti written across the top in pink letters sat on top of the stack. Curiosity getting the better of him, Jake flipped the card over and read the message.

Howdy from Tahiti! Heard Jake was living with you. Don't have the wedding before I get home. I'll call you for Christmas.

George

Chuckling, Jake set the mail aside, put the pickup in gear and drove on down the long driveway. He couldn't wait to give Hope the postcard. It'd make her laugh and that'd give him the perfect opening—well, damn. Her car wasn't in its usual spot behind the house. Its tire tracks were almost filled with unmashed snow, which meant the car hadn't been here in a couple of days.

That was odd.

Not that Hope would never leave the ranch. She rarely let a day pass without finding some excuse to go into town. Jake figured she wasn't used to the ranch's isolation just yet, and her trips to Sunshine Gap or Cody reassured her the rest of the world was still out there.

But it was damned odd she hadn't come back since before the last snow stopped falling on Saturday morning. Where was she? Better yet, when would she be back?

His stomach knotting with apprehension, Jake climbed out of the pickup and slogged through the snow drifts toward the back door. Finding the door locked, he knocked, then turned around and scanned the ranch yard while he dug out his key.

Where the heck was Doofus?

Bonnie was probably out feeding, but she wouldn't have taken the pup with her. Doof was still so fond of chasing cows and anything else that moved, he'd be more hindrance than help. Jake unlocked the door and stepped inside, softly calling Hope's name just in case she was here after all.

There might be a logical reason for her car to be missing. It could've broken down on her somewhere and she hadn't had a chance to get it fixed. Or she could've loaned it to someone.

She didn't answer, though, and the house was so preternaturally still, he knew she wasn't going to. The place had that empty feeling a house got when its heart wasn't there anymore. He remembered the feeling too well from the months after Ellen had passed away. It made his stomach ache to feel this way again.

When he walked into the kitchen, the first thing he noticed was a large brown envelope propped against the sugar bowl in the middle of the table. Hope had written his name across it in black marker. A sense of foreboding came over him, but he brushed it aside, went to the table and ripped open the envelope. Pulling out a wad of papers, he quickly read the note on top.

Dear Jake,

I'm afraid seeing you on a frequent basis will be too painful for me, so I'm returning to California. Though I'll be back to visit Blair and Dillon occasionally, you won't have to worry about me showing up in Sunshine Gap without warning.

I once promised you that if I ever decided to give up the Double Circle, I'd sell it to you for fair market value. Unfortunately, I won't be able to keep my promise. I won't sell you the Double Circle, but

I want to give it to you.

It's what you've always wanted, Jake. Please accept it with my best wishes. I hope you'll be very happy here.

I've paid Bonnie for the rest of the year. She says she'd love to stay and work for you, but she'll understand if you want her to leave. Since Doofus has shown so little potential to be a good cow dog, and I couldn't bear to part with him, I've taken him with me. Thanks for everything.

Goodbye and Merry Christmas,

Hope

"Merry Christmas?" Jake muttered. He scanned the page again, trying to make sense of her bizarre message. "What the hell?"

He moved the note to the bottom of the stack and flipped through the remaining documents. A letter of intent from Hope to Jake's brother-in-law, Nolan Larson, a local attorney. A warranty deed for the Double Circle. Legal descriptions of the water and mineral rights that came with the property. A letter from Nolan to Jake explaining the transfer of ownership. Which brought Hope's note back to the top of the stack. His mind reeling, Jake read it again.

I won't sell you the Double Circle, but I want to give it to you?

When the full meaning of her words sank in, Jake's knees nearly buckled. He yanked a chair out from under the table, sat on it and worked his way through the documents a second time. Damn if she hadn't done exactly what she'd said.

She'd *given* him this ranch. He, Jake McBride, *owned* the Double Circle and everything that went with it—the land, the equipment, the buildings, the animals, the tack, the feed—everything. One signature from him and all of it would be his.

It *was* everything he'd ever wanted. Everything since he'd lost Ellen, anyway. At the moment, it was even debt-free. Damn few ranchers got to say that about their operations, even for a day. He'd been saving for so long, he'd be able to go for months without borrowing much in the way of working capital.

And he only had to give up two things in return. His pride was the first. Hope was the second.

He'd always known she'd drive him nuts one of these days. Talk about diabolical. If she wasn't a female version of Satan himself, Hope DuMaine sure as hell worked for him.

Jake slammed the papers down on the table. Even with the proof sitting right there in front of him, he still couldn't believe she'd done this. Didn't want to believe any of it. But those legal documents made it all seem so…final.

Well, it wasn't final. Not by a long shot. Sure, they'd fought, but they hadn't settled anything. He'd told her it wasn't over, that they'd talk again when they'd cooled off. He'd cooled off some, but now he was hot all over again. For God's sake, what *had* she been thinking?

How could she just…*leave* him? How could she take that crazy, idiot Doofus with her and leave him—*her first lover, dammit*—behind? Without so much as a call or a goodbye?

Angry enough to risk a stroke, Jake surged to his feet and looked around the kitchen, clenching and unclenching his fists. He wanted to hit something. Break something. Tear down this old house with his bare hands. Hell, he had to get out of here.

Now.

Without pausing to turn off the lights or lock the door, he stomped out of the house, across the yard and into the barn. He tossed around a few hay bales that didn't need tossing and cleaned out some stalls that didn't need cleaning.

His gut still churning more acid than a battery factory, he moved on, walking past the corral, the storage sheds and the machine shop, the top-of-the-line, double-wide mobile home Hope had bought for her ranch manager after the skunk fiasco at the old bunkhouse.

He climbed a hill and turned in a slow circle, looking back the way he'd come, then out toward the snowy pastures holding the pregnant cows and heifers who'd start producing the new calf crop in the next couple of months. The fences were good and tight. There were trees for shelter from the wind, plenty of hay and fresh water.

It was a good ranch. A fine ranch with potential for a solid future. Plenty of room for kids, friends and family gatherings.

But he didn't want it now. Not without Hope. Without her there to share it with him, it wouldn't mean a damn thing. And that meant...

"Aw, hell," he muttered as realization smacked him upside the head. "I love her."

Hope's doorbell rang at ten o'clock the next Wednesday morning. Doofus went into his usual frenzy of barking. Since she wasn't expecting anyone, Hope ignored him and the doorbell. It was probably just another nosy neighbor who wanted a closer look at Doofus. You didn't see many real mutts in Beverly Hills.

Besides, she was so into writing chapter five of her

new book, *Fifty Ways to Murder a Cowboy,* she didn't care who was at the door or if the book was too gruesome ever to sell. Releasing her anger and frustration at Jake McBride without ending up in prison was all that mattered.

However, she appeared to possess an endless supply of both. She'd been back in L.A. for nine days, and writing nearly nonstop for seven—but the anger and hurt were still there. If it hadn't been for Doofus keeping her company, she'd have gone completely crazy by now. Unfortunately the poor dog was having a rough adjustment to urban living.

At eighty-six pages into the manuscript, she'd already used up forty ways to kill Jake, but she'd barely begun to get that big, stubborn, cowardly, incredibly clueless, downright stupid cowboy out of her system. She might as well go for *A Hundred and One Ways to Murder a Cowboy.*

"Oh, and rude," she grumbled. "Mustn't forget rude."

When a woman gave a man a ranch worth two million dollars, was a simple thank-you note or a phone call too much to expect? Hope didn't think so, but what did she know about cowboy etiquette? If such a thing even existed.

At the same time, she never wanted to hear from him again. She certainly didn't want to hear his voice or see his face. Only a masochist actually wanted such pain. She wasn't that kinky. Dammit, this book could run to ten volumes. How about *A Thousand Ways to Murder a Cowboy?*

The doorbell rang again. And again and again. Whoever was out there meant business and Doofus was going to chomp his way through the door any second. Muttering under her breath, Hope pushed away from her computer, grabbed the dog's collar and yanked open her front door. "What?"

The uniformed delivery man on the other side stepped back as if he feared she might turn the slobbering animal loose on him. Watching Doofus every second, he held up a large white envelope similar to the ones her publisher used to send page proofs. "Express delivery for Ms. Hope DuMaine?"

"That would be me." Hope signed for the package and gave the man a tip, then shut the door, thanked Doofus for his protection and carried the envelope back to her desk. She wasn't expecting anything, but perhaps it was good news. After everything she'd suffered, it must be her turn for good news.

The dog followed. While Hope pulled the tear-strip and took out the papers, Doofus stood beside her, his big head tipped to one side, tongue lolling in a doggy grin, tail wagging. She called it his time-for-a-walk? expression.

"Don't look at me that way," Hope scolded. "You had one not two hours ago. Lie down."

Doofus barked at her. Wagged his tail some more. Drooled on the carpet. Hope rolled her eyes. The pooch obeyed Jake, but Doofus clearly didn't consider her to be alpha-dog material.

Glancing at the papers, she felt her breath catch and her heart stutter. This wasn't from her publisher; the first page wasn't even letterhead. The plain white typing paper contained only one sentence, written in a bold, masculine scrawl.

It wasn't the damn ranch I wanted.

He hadn't bothered to sign it, but a signature was hardly necessary. Of course not. Who else but Jake

McBride would be so blasted arrogant? He *wanted* her, did he? Big deal. If she was impressed with every man who'd ever said he *wanted* her, she'd have been a teen bride. She *wanted* world peace, but to her knowledge, nobody was dismantling the military.

And why had he used the past tense? Was he trying to tell her that any wanting on his part was over and done? Who knew? She might as well try to read a rock's mind as Jake's.

Furious, she flipped through the rest of the documents. Of course, it was all there, everything Nolan Larson had said she needed to transfer ownership of the Double Circle. Oh, that wretched Jake! If he thought he could just throw her gift back in her face, she'd certainly show him.

Marching to her office supplies cupboard, she pulled out a fresh envelope from her express delivery company. Back at her desk, she flipped over Jake's note, scribbled her own note on the back and stuffed the packet into the envelope. After addressing it, she grinned at Doofus.

"Get your leash, boy. We'll take this to the drop box. Then we'll go to the beach for a long, hard run."

It wasn't the damn ranch I wanted either. If you don't want it, I'll donate it to an environmental trust.

Cursing under his breath, Jake crumpled Hope's note in one hand and heaved it at the wastebasket. It wasn't an idle threat, but it was an effective one. The Double Circle was a working ranch. Giving it to a bunch of tree huggers would be a sacrilege, and she knew it.

Everything inside him recoiled at the idea, but he couldn't bring himself to accept such an enormous gift. Especially not from Hope. Damn, but he missed her—her smile, her laughter, her warmth. Why hadn't he realized how much she meant to him until it was too late?

Gut knotted, he looked out the office window at the snowdrifts. He'd go after Hope in a heartbeat, but the snow was so deep, they had to use draft horses to feed the stock. Since Hope didn't own any, he had to help Bonnie over at the Double Circle when they'd finished up at the Flying M. December was barely half gone and it was already shaping up to be the worst winter in fifty years.

He couldn't leave until the weather broke, and he didn't want to do this over the phone. Hope could hang up on him too easily that way. But maybe he could stall her. Plunking his cold, weary behind onto his desk chair, he filled out a personal check, wrote a quick note and shoved the whole packet into a new envelope. If he hurried, he could get this sucker into Sunshine Gap before Cal left for Cody.

Owner financing is a gift. Enclosed find first payment for the Double Circle per our original agreement.

Hope smacked Jake's note down on top of the too-familiar documents. "Hah! Nice try, McBride, but no dice."

Her anger had cooled a bit during the past five days, but it only took one glance at Jake's handwriting to revive it. She dashed off a terse reply, repackaged the papers and called Doofus. When the dog didn't immedi-

ately come, she went looking for him. She found him in
the kitchen, stretched out on his belly in front of the
French doors that led to the patio and pool, his chin
resting on his paws.

"Hey, Doofus." Hope knelt beside him and scratched
behind his ears. "What's up, big guy?"

Doofus raised his head and thumped his tail against
the floor twice before lowering his chin back to his paws.
Concerned, Hope touched his nose and found it cold and
wet. But if Doofus had been human, she'd have said he
looked depressed.

Hope coaxed him into the car and took the package
to the delivery service. As a treat, she drove north out
of the city. When the traffic thinned out, she opened the
sun roof.

Doofus sniffed at the fresh air, then sat up and looked
out the window. Encouraged by his seeming interest,
Hope drove on. The farther she drove into the country-
side, the more animated Doofus became. Somewhere
east of Bakersfield she pulled over and stopped, then got
out and scanned the terrain.

Barbed-wire fences lined the road, enclosing scrubby
pastures with lots of rocks and sparse brown grass. There
were also three black, lumbering cows. Doofus went insane, barking and scratching at the car door. Hope
reached in and got a firm hold on his leash before letting
him out. He nearly tore her arm off trying to get to those
cows.

Hope's heart swelled and she had to sniffle. No wonder Doofus had been acting so depressed. He was home-
sick for cows.

So was she, dammit.

Lord, she hadn't seen a cow in ages. Or a horse. Or

a cowboy. In truth, Doofus wasn't the only one having trouble adjusting to urban life.

She hated L.A.'s smog and traffic. She hated the need for security systems and locking everything before she so much as turned her back. She hated having to keep poor Doofus inside at home for fear he'd disturb the neighbors, and keeping him on a leash outdoors for fear he'd run into the street and get killed.

She missed Wyoming's blue sky, its craggy, towering mountains and far-flung vistas. She missed seeing horses, elk, deer and coyotes. She missed Sunshine Gap and Cody. She missed eating at Cal's Place and laughing with Emma, Marsh and Blair. She missed belonging somewhere and having waitresses and store clerks call her "hon."

Oh, hell, she even missed...Jake.

Not that she'd ever admit it to anyone but Doofus. Her eyes filled with tears, but she forced them back. She should have more pride. Of course, if she had a scrap of pride where he was concerned she wouldn't be wrangling with him over the Double Circle. What a pitiful excuse to hang on to a man.

Her relationship with him was over. Finished. Kaput.

It was time to accept that—really accept it—and get on with her life. And she would. Someday, somehow, she'd find a way to be content, if not happy. Right. Of course she would.

The tears came without warning, spilling down her cheeks in a torrent of misery. Nearly blinded by them, she shoved Doofus into the car, then turned back and wiped her eyes for one last blurry look at the cows.

"Oh, Jake." Her throat constricted, nearly choking her. "Why c-couldn't you just l-l-love me?"

Bracing himself against the inevitable irritation, Jake opened the next packet from Hope. She'd written VOID across his personal check—in bright red ink, no less. He'd expected as much. Her note was more of the same.

I don't want your money, but if it'll make you feel better, give it to charity. The Double Circle is yours.

Jake tossed the whole mess onto his desk and collapsed onto his chair. It was a hell of a thing for a man to realize he was grateful for any contact with a certain woman, even a snotty note like this one. At least she hadn't forgotten him. Not yet, anyway.

But this tag-you're-it note-sending wasn't getting him anywhere he wanted to be. He wanted to be with her, dammit. He couldn't say what he needed to say to her on paper or even on the phone. He needed to see her sweet face, to hear her voice, to hold her in his arms and show her how much he loved her. Then maybe she'd believe him when he said the words.

Unfortunately, he still couldn't leave. The weather kept going from bad to worse. Christmas was only five days off. Calving would likely start soon after that, and then it'd be weeks, if not months, before he could get away.

By then, she'd have given the Double Circle to the tree huggers and replaced him with some slick Hollywood type who could talk to a woman without shoving his damn foot into his mouth clear up to his kneecap.

But Mr. Hollywood couldn't love her the way Jake would. He wouldn't rescue skunk-sprayed dogs with her or teach her to fix fences or vaccinate cows. He might give her babies, but they wouldn't be dark-haired, dark-eyed McBride babies. And Mr. Hollywood couldn't give her a big, nosy family who already loved her to pieces.

Jake laced his fingers together behind his head and leaned back in his chair. Hope needed his family, and whether she knew it or not, she needed him. He had to do something to end this damn impasse for her own good.

With his heart pounding clear up at the base of his throat, he picked up the phone and dialed Hope's number in California.

Chapter Fifteen

Juggling the leash, her purse and the bulging plastic sack of toys she'd just bought for Doofus, Hope pushed open the back door with her hip. "Here we are. You were such a good boy."

Doofus stepped into the kitchen and dutifully waited for Hope to unfasten his leash. Then he trotted across the room, took a slurp from his water dish and flopped down in front of the French doors. Settling his chin on his paws, he heaved a disgruntled-sounding sigh. Hope knew exactly how he felt. She wanted to flop right down beside him and stay there.

Of course, that wasn't a viable option. She had a life and a career to manage. But first, she had to make certain Doofus was on the road to recovery. She'd already taken him to the best canine therapist in Beverly Hills.

According to the treatment plan, she was supposed to give Doofus plenty of fresh air, exercise and social activities. The therapist had specifically recommended a game called flyball, a relay race for dog teams. It was delightfully entertaining to watch, but after this evening's lesson, Hope felt more discouraged than she wanted to admit.

Doofus had tried his best. He really had. But after watching the other dogs race their little legs off for their cheering owners tonight, it was pathetically obvious Doofus's heart wasn't in the game. Or in all the toys she'd bought him. Or anything else she'd tried.

If only her Doof-baby would perk up. She couldn't bear to see him so sad. She probably should send him back to the Double Circle, but she couldn't bear to part with him, either.

She could always buy a ranch here in California so he'd have his own cows to chase and room to run. But she knew her own heart wouldn't be in the project. It'd taken a long time, but she finally could admit she'd bought the Double Circle primarily to be around Jake and his family.

In all honesty, while she loved the privacy and the variety of ranch life, she didn't want the round-the-clock responsibility for the land and the animals. She enjoyed the lifestyle, but, in the end, she was a writer, not a rancher. Having another ranch without Jake to go with it would only remind her of everything she'd lost.

Maybe she could adopt a puppy or a kitten as a playmate for Doofus. That would be cheaper and a lot less trouble than buying a whole ranch. She'd look into that tomorrow.

Relieved to have a new idea, Hope made a cup of tea and carried both it and the mail into her office. Wonder of wonders, the answering machine's red light was blinking, and the counter said she had four new messages.

Wanting to lick her wounds in private, she hadn't bothered to inform anyone in her circle of acquaintances she'd returned to L.A. She couldn't imagine who might be calling her. Please, God, don't let it be a reporter.

She hit the Play button and crossed the room to close the drapes. Halfway there, a deep, achingly familiar voice filled the room, freezing her in her tracks.

"Hello, Hope. It's Jake."

Oh, Lord, Jake's voice sounded gruff, but deep and sexy as ever. Hope pressed one hand to her chest, as if that might start her stalled heart. Doofus trotted into the room, his tail up and his droopy ears on high alert.

"I want to talk to you," Jake said. "It's two o'clock, Mountain Time. I'll be in the office at the Flying M until we go out to feed again at three. Probably won't be back in until five or six, but I'll be here all evening. You know the number."

Darn it, she'd left just before that call had come in. The machine beeped. Doofus barked at it, then ran over and sniffed it when Jake's voice filled the room again.

"Hope? You there? It's Jake again. Call me."

Doofus whined at the next beep, and wagged his tail when Jake resumed talking.

"Hope? Damn, I hate talking to these stupid machines. Pick up if you're there. Oh, all right, call me, will ya?"

Hope grinned at the irritation in his voice. She couldn't help it. It was simply so...*Jake*. The machine beeped again. Doofus whined and looked up at her as if to say, "Where *is* he?"

Feeling the same way, Hope went to the dog and petted his furry head. When Jake came on again, he sounded close to exhaustion and terribly discouraged.

"Aw, hell, Hope, where are you? I can't stand the thought of just giving up on us like this. We had something special going on, and I really want to talk to you about it. I'd come down there, but we're up to our armpits in snow and there's more on the way, so I can't get away right now. Tell you the truth, we could use another good hand. Come on home, honey, and let's talk. Please. I…miss you."

The machine beeped one last time. Doofus whined and butted his head against Hope's thigh. Her knees buckled and she sat down hard, then wound her arms around the dog's neck and indulged herself in a good, long cry.

Christmas Day arrived, but Jake couldn't find a scrap of joy in it. Everywhere he looked there were newlyweds, pregnant women and grinning, supremely satisfied men. He'd even caught the Mamas and the Papas smooching under the damn mistletoe. When your own love life was in the toilet, so much happiness was downright nauseating. Even baby Kevin irritated Jake today.

He'd wanted to spend the day with Hope, but she hadn't returned any of his calls. Man, she must really hate him.

He'd spent a lot of time thinking since she'd left, replayed all the things he'd said to her that last night more than once. He'd been an idiot, all right. And he'd tell her so, if she ever gave him the chance. Jake figured that was about as likely as finding a vegetarian mountain lion.

The family had gathered in the living room for the traditional song fest, but Jake couldn't take another second of togetherness. Not today. He filched a half-empty bottle of bourbon and a shot glass from the liquor cabinet, carried them into his office and shut the door, blocking out most of the damn cheery music.

He settled into his chair, propped his heels up on the corner of the desk and poured himself a shot. He had no intention of drowning his sorrows in bourbon, but he sure could use a couple of belts to take the edge off. He'd just downed his second drink when the door swung open behind him and in barged his cousin Marsh.

Aw, hell. Marsh was the last person Jake wanted to talk to at the moment. This whole stinkin' mess was Marsh's fault. If he hadn't written the screenplay for *Against the Wind*, Blair and the rest of her film crew never would've come to the Flying M. Jake never would've met Hope, and he wouldn't be sitting here now feeling like a gutted trout.

Without waiting for an invitation, Marsh pulled up a chair and poured himself a shot. "Thought I'd find you in here."

"Get out," Jake said. "I'm not in the mood to chat."

"Tough." Marsh tossed back his drink and gasped, then shook his head and grinned. He pushed the glass back to Jake and propped his elbows on the desk. "What did you do to Hope?"

"Not a damn thing." Jake refilled the shot glass and thumped the bottle back down with more force than necessary.

"Right. You guys could hardly keep your hands off each other at Thanksgiving, and the next thing I know, Hope's hightailed it to L.A. and transferred ownership of the Double Circle to you. What brought that on?"

Jake gulped the drink, then shoved the glass back to

the center of the desk. "None of your damn business. Let it go."

"Why did she leave the Double Circle?"

"Damned if I know."

"Come on, you must have *some* idea. Did you have a fight?"

"Sort of."

"About what?" Marsh refilled the glass and pushed it back to Jake.

"Marriage."

"Say, what?" Marsh demanded.

Jake tossed back the bourbon. He was starting to feel a little muzzy, but he'd lost track of how many drinks he'd had, and dammit, he wanted to talk to *some*body. Marsh knew Hope better'n Jake did, so maybe the kid could give him a few pointers on getting her back. "I asked her to marry me."

Marsh's eyes widened. "You *did?*"

"Yeah."

"What'd she say?"

"She said no."

Marsh's eyes bugged out now. "She *did?*"

"Yeah. You got a hearing problem, Marsh?"

"Why?"

"'Cause you keep actin' like you didn't hear me right."

"No, I mean, why did she say no?"

"Beats the hell out of me." Another shot appeared at Jake's elbow. He swallowed it without a second thought. "She said no and then she left. Dang woman just took the dog an' didn't even say g'bye to me."

"Hope's crazy about you, man. You must've said *some*thing that upset her. What was it?"

Jake did his best to remember, but his brain felt about

as tangled up as a plate of his mother's spaghetti. "I think it was more what I didn't say."

"Aw, hell. Tell me you told her you love her."

The disgust in Marsh's voice pretty much echoed how Jake felt about the situation. He shrugged again, then sadly shook his head. "Nope. Really ticked her off, too. Wasn't one of my finer moments, but I never dreamed she'd take off."

"So you're just going to give up on her now?"

"What do you suggest? I called her at least ten times and she won't answer or call me back. I can't figure that woman out."

"All she wants is for somebody to love her. Not because of who she is or who she knows or what she owns. She wants somebody to love her just because she's Hope."

"Well, who the hell is *Hope?*" Jake asked. "One minute she's dressing like a hooker and flirting with me like she means business. And her books aren't exactly prudish. Then I make love to her and find out the hard way she's a virgin. Damn near gave me a heart attack."

"Oh, jeez, Jake." Marsh grimaced, then glanced away. "Thanks for sharing, but—"

"Hey, you know what I'm talking about. She's got me so confused, I hardly know my behind from my elbow."

Jake got up and paced over to the window. "Remember what she was like when she first came here? With the rainbow hair and wild clothes and the long fingernails, and the crazy stuff they were always sayin' about her in the press?"

"Yeah. So what?"

"So, it didn't make me think she'd spent her life in

a convent. How was I supposed to know she was so dang…sweet?''

''If you'd asked me about her,'' Marsh said, ''I'd have told you all that stuff was just a smokescreen.''

''Why would she need a smokescreen?''

''When you grow up in a family like hers, everything you do or say is potential news, especially for the tabloids. If Hope doesn't give reporters something juicy to write about, they make it up. For her, using the wild hair and clothes and the rest is like tossing a vicious dog a meaty bone. Get it?''

''Yeah.'' Jake came back and sat down again. ''It keeps the dog busy so she can walk by and get on with her business.''

''Exactly. She lets 'em think they know a bunch of scandalous stuff, but they don't know squat about the real Hope DuMaine. They never see past the image.''

''I didn't, either. Not for a long time,'' Jake admitted morosely. ''She never did anything I expected her to, and even now I'm not sure I really know who she is.''

''Bull,'' Marsh said. ''You know she's a warm, loving, sensitive woman. You know you're happy when you're with her and miserable without her. Admit it.''

''Hell, yes, I'll admit it.''

''And you love her.''

''Yeah.''

''Then quit being an ass and go after her.''

''It's more complicated than that.''

''It's not complicated at all,'' Marsh said. ''Go after her.''

''I'm not sure I can give her what she really needs.''

''All Hope really needs is just once to be the most important thing in somebody's life. Haul your butt to

L.A. and show her she's more important than a ranch or your damn cows.''

''Of course she's more important. But who's gonna take my place when it comes time to feed all of those damn cows—including hers? You?''

''Hell, no, I still hate cows.'' Marsh's grin was unrepentant. ''But if you dropped dead or got hurt tomorrow, do you think the rest of us would let 'em starve?''

''No way.''

''Right. So if you love Hope, what's *really* stopping you from going after her?'' Marsh picked up the empty bourbon bottle and stared down its neck for a moment before climbing to his feet. ''We've had enough of this. I'll get coffee.''

''Wouldn't hurt.'' When he heard Marsh leave, Jake leaned back in his chair, propped his feet on the desk again and laced his fingers together behind his head. A bittersweet mellowness settled over him, as he flipped through his memories of Hope.

Regret gnawed at him with sharp little teeth every time he spotted another instance where he'd had a chance to tell her he loved her and blown it.

He'd lost Ellen to circumstances beyond anyone's control. And once she was gone, she was gone for good. But it didn't have to be that way with Hope. If he could find the courage to tell her how he really felt about her...

The air backed up in his lungs. Sweat broke out under his arms. His stomach shrank to the size of a walnut and flames of panic flickered at the edges of his mind.

He couldn't do it.

The possibility of having to admit he'd lost Hope for good, that he was alone to face a future without ever knowing such happiness again... Aw, *jeez.* The risk of it felt crushing. Enormous. Impossible.

Jake forced himself to take slow, deep breaths, and his sense of panic gradually eased. Whoa. Where the hell had all of *that* been hiding?

But now that he knew what the real problem was, he figured he could solve it. Hell, there had to be a way.

The door opened and shut behind him. A steaming mug of coffee appeared at his elbow. He took a sip, then cradled the warm cup in his hands. "You're right, Marsh. About all of it. I do love Hope and I'm damn miserable without her. She brought so many good things back into my life…but she's so different from Ellen, I guess I didn't even recognize I loved her."

Jake took another sip. The hot liquid eased the tightness in his throat. "With Ellen, it was warm and sweet and…innocent in lots of ways. Loving her was easy as breathing. But Hope…"

He laughed and shook his head. "Nothing about Hope's ever easy. But damn, Marsh, she's so much fun and she's smart, and she's got grit to burn. She walks into a room and everything lights up for me—it's like goin' from a black-and-white world to full color. Or the difference between eating watered-down potato soup and five-alarm chili. You know?"

His voice cracked. He drank some more coffee. Marsh was turning out to be a surprisingly good listener. "You're right about the smokescreen thing too. Underneath all of that image, Hope's one of the nicest people I've ever met. The only reason I haven't gone after her is because I'm scared to death she won't believe me when I tell her I love her. God, if she told me to get lost…I don't know what I'd do."

He closed his eyes against the pain of imagining how that would feel. It'd probably kill him.

"I have it on excellent authority she would never do that."

Jake's insides froze. He opened his eyes, but couldn't find the nerve to turn around. That hadn't been Marsh's voice. He could've sworn it was Hope behind him, but that couldn't be. He'd had too many shots of bourbon to drive, but he wasn't smashed enough to worry about seeing imaginary folks. He didn't think he was, anyway.

Icy beads of sweat broke out on his forehead. "How...how do you know she wouldn't?"

"Because she loves you, Jake."

Jake carefully set his mug on the desk and lowered his feet to the floor, then slowly turned around. And there she was, standing not three feet from him with big fat tears rolling down her cheeks. When he tried to speak, all he could get out was a hoarse croak. "Am I hallucinating you?"

Her lips twitched at the corners, but she didn't smile. "Nope."

"How'd you get here?"

"Airplanes. Pickup. Snowplow. It wasn't easy with Doofus along."

"But I thought...you didn't call back." Somehow, he managed to get his feet under him and stand up. "Why did you come?"

"You said to come home. So I did."

Home. She'd said *home*. "Does that mean you'll stay?"

"If you want me to." Her lips twitched again and the knots in his gut loosened a little.

"Forever? Will you stay with me forever, Hope?"

"If you want me to."

"Oh, honey, I've never wanted anything more in my life."

He saw a blur of movement, and then she was in his arms, and they were holding each other, kissing each other, laughing and crying at the same time.

"I love you," he said between kisses. "Love you. Love you. Love you." Chuckling, he pulled back and just looked at her, still barely able to believe she was really there. "First I couldn't say it. Now I can't stop sayin' it."

"Please don't. I like hearing it."

"I'm sorry I couldn't say it before. You were right, you know. I never said goodbye to Ellen because I was so afraid I'd never find anyone else to love. And then you came along and I messed it all up. But I didn't mean to hurt you, Hope, and I swear I'll never do it again if I can help it."

She reached up and pressed two fingers to his lips. "Don't, Jake. We both made mistakes. We can talk about it later, but for now, let's just start over and be happy. What do you say, cowboy?"

Jake grinned. "Works for me. Let's go home."

Epilogue

Hope was going to drive him nuts.

Jake figured if he was real lucky, she'd drive him sweetly, seductively and happily nuts for another fifty or sixty years. He ought to get a big reward in heaven for his patience with all the wedding folderol he'd been through. Had it been up to him, he and Hope would've made a quick trip to Idaho or Nevada, tied the knot and gone straight to the honeymoon.

But it hadn't been up to him; hell, he was only the groom. Between the Mamas, Hope and all the other women in the family, it'd taken three months to put this wedding together. If a hard winter and a tough calving season hadn't kept him away from the relentless planning, he'd have run screaming into the night.

Now that the worst was over, though, he'd admit the celebration had gone off without a hitch. Of course, with Hope as the bride, this wedding had been nothing like his first one. Even Ellen would've gotten a kick out of seeing George Pierson applauded as the "official matchmaker" and Doofus trotting down the aisle with a big bow around his neck and the ring bearer's pillow in his mouth.

And then there was Hope's wedding outfit. Oh, she looked beautiful as ever; for all he cared, she could've brought back the blue hair, metallic talons and that little suede halter top she'd worn the day she'd come to the Flying M wanting to reason with him about the Double Circle. But he still grinned every time he saw his bride's wedding finery.

Whatever the designer had been going for, the result was a cross between a fairytale-princess-bride gown and something the queen of the rodeo cowgirls would wear.

Ladylike and sexy at the same time, her Western-cut dress hugged her curves and displayed a fair amount of skin, but it still had lots of lace and silky fringe and a skirt with plenty of swish to it. Instead of a veil, she wore a sassy white cowboy hat with a strip of lace wrapped around the brim and trailing halfway down her back. Her white, old-fashioned button-topped shoes had even more lace and tall, slender heels.

If he could ever convince her it was time to leave, he'd get her alone, peel her out of that sweet little getup and see what kind of slinky undies she had on—

"Here. You look like you could use this."

Jake looked up and found his cousin Dillon standing beside his chair, holding a drink in each hand. Jake accepted one and took a quick gulp. "Thanks."

Grinning, Dillon sat down beside him. "You guys ever gonna go on your honeymoon?"

"I was ready to pack it in an hour ago," Jake said.

"But Hope's having such a good time, I hate to drag her away."

"Blair was the same way at our reception." Dillon set his glass on the table and wrapped both hands around it. "Remember when Marsh brought her and those other Hollywood folks to the ranch that first time? And they were practically begging us to let them film the movie here?"

Jake nodded. "You didn't want any part of it."

"Damn right. I figured we'd get more trouble out of the deal than all the money in the world was worth." Dillon's gaze slowly traveled around the room. "And two years later we've all wound up married, got two new half-grown nephews, a baby nephew and God only knows how many more kids'll show up in time."

"Yeah," Jake agreed, smiling. "Who'd have thought we could make one decision and get a whole new family out of it?"

"Just goes to show ya, sometimes it's good to be wrong."

"Hey, I was all for letting them film the movie here," Jake said. "You're the one who was wrong."

"I was dead wrong about Blair," Dillon agreed. "But you were just as wrong about Hope."

"Yeah. So what?"

"What else do you suppose we've been wrong about?"

"Oh, man, you could've talked all day and not said that." Jake laughed and shook his head. "Makes me wonder how we ever managed to get this far."

"Sheer dumb McBride luck," Dillon said. "Speaking of luck, I think you're about to get some."

Glancing back toward the dance floor, Jake spotted Hope heading straight for him, her fringe swishing with every step. Her cheeks were flushed a pretty pink and her blue eyes sparkled with confidence and so much love for him, he felt humbled by it.

"Hey there, handsome." She stopped beside him, leaned down and held out her hands. "Dance with me one more time?"

"Yes, ma'am." Jake climbed to his feet, took her hands in his and kissed her knuckles. "It'll be my pleasure."

The band struck up a slow, dreamy waltz. Hope snuggled into Jake's arms, fitting there as if she'd been custom made for him. Maybe she had been. He'd been so set in his solitary grief, God must've known he'd need a special woman to yank him out of it. Only Hope had made him really want to live again.

"Thanks, honey," he murmured.

She looked up at him, a puzzled smile on her sweet mouth. "For what?"

"For coming back. For being you. For loving me." He leaned down and stole a kiss. "Take your pick."

"You're welcome. The limo's ready to go any time we are. I think we should make a break for it, ride off into the sunset and live happily ever after. What do you say?"

Laughing, Jake scooped her up into his arms and headed for the doorway. "I like the way you think."

* * * * *

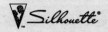

If you enjoyed what you just read,
then we've got an offer you can't resist!

Take 2 bestselling
love stories FREE!
Plus get a FREE surprise gift!

Clip this page and mail it to Silhouette Reader Service™

IN U.S.A.
3010 Walden Ave.
P.O. Box 1867
Buffalo, N.Y. 14240-1867

IN CANADA
P.O. Box 609
Fort Erie, Ontario
L2A 5X3

YES! Please send me 2 free Silhouette Special Edition® novels and my free surprise gift. After receiving them, if I don't wish to receive anymore, I can return the shipping statement marked cancel. If I don't cancel, I will receive 6 brand-new novels every month, before they're available in stores! In the U.S.A., bill me at the bargain price of $3.99 plus 25¢ shipping and handling per book and applicable sales tax, if any*. In Canada, bill me at the bargain price of $4.74 plus 25¢ shipping and handling per book and applicable taxes**. That's the complete price and a savings of at least 10% off the cover prices—what a great deal! I understand that accepting the 2 free books and gift places me under no obligation ever to buy any books. I can always return a shipment and cancel at any time. Even if I never buy another book from Silhouette, the 2 free books and gift are mine to keep forever.

235 SDN DNUR
335 SDN DNUS

Name	(PLEASE PRINT)	
Address	Apt.#	
City	State/Prov.	Zip/Postal Code

* Terms and prices subject to change without notice. Sales tax applicable in N.Y.
** Canadian residents will be charged applicable provincial taxes and GST.
All orders subject to approval. Offer limited to one per household and not valid to current Silhouette Special Edition® subscribers.
® are registered trademarks of Harlequin Books S.A., used under license.

SPED02   ©1998 Harlequin Enterprises Limited

COMING NEXT MONTH

#1531 CONFLICT OF INTEREST—Gina Wilkins
The McClouds of Mississippi
Reclusive writer Gideon McCloud was definitely not baby-sitter material. So, when left to care for his half sister, he persuaded the beautiful Adrienne Corley to help. As his once-empty house filled with love and laughter, his heart began to yearn…for a family—and for Adrienne!

#1532 SHOWDOWN!—Laurie Paige
Seven Devils
Who was Hannah Carrington? Zack Dalton's cop instincts told him there was more to his supposedly long-lost relative than met the eye. Would discovering the gorgeous dancer wasn't who she seemed leave Zack feeling betrayed, or free to pursue the heady feelings she awakened in him?

#1533 THE TROUBLE WITH JOSH—Marilyn Pappano
Handsome rancher Josh Rawlins wanted forever. Blond beauty Candace Thompson couldn't even promise tomorrow. After a near-fatal bout with a serious illness, Candace was not looking for romance. But being with Josh made her feel like anything was possible. Could Josh and Candace find a way to take a chance on love?

#1534 THE MONA LUCY—Peggy Webb
Pretending to be in love with the charming Sandi Wentworth was not what commitment-phobic Matt Coltrane had planned to do. But that was exactly what he *had* to do to keep his ailing mother happy. The sparks that flew whenever Matt and Sandi were together were undeniable, and soon it began to feel less like pretend…and more like the real thing.…

#1535 EXPECTING THE CEO'S BABY—Karen Rose Smith
Widow Jenna Winton was shocked when she was told the lab had mixed her deceased husband's sperm sample with another man's. Then she met CEO Blake Winston, the father of her child, and the sizzling attraction between them was almost more than she could resist!

#1536 HIS PRETEND WIFE—Lisette Belisle
When an accident left loner Jake Slade unconscious with no one to speak for him, Abby Pierce stepped up to the task. Abby would do anything to help Jake—even if it meant pretending to be his wife. When Jake finally woke, he found he'd gained a blushing bride whose tender care was healing both his body…and his heart.

SSECNM0303